Dear Reader:

Everyone has heard of the Joneses, the family with the coveted lifestyle.

Sometimes the Joneses are not what they appear to be. Such is the case with this novel filled with scandal surrounding a family based in the South and their funeral home business.

Royce and Lexi Jones, along with their three children, are held on a pedestal in their community. They are picture-perfect, but eventually, darkness comes to light and showcases a world of shadiness. It's not that they only keep their inner secrets from those on the outside, but from each other as well.

Shelia M. Goss, a prolific, bestselling author of nearly twenty books, makes her debut with Strebor with this dramatic tale that I'm sure you will enjoy.

As always, thanks for supporting the authors of Strebor Books. We always try to bring you groundbreaking, innovative stories that will entertain and enlighten. I can be located at www.facebook.com/AuthorZane or reached via email at Zane@eroticanoir.com.

Blessings,

Zane

Publisher
Strebor Books
www.simonandschuster.com

ZANE PRESENTS

The JONESES

SHELLA M. GOSS

SBI
STREBOR BOOKS
NEW YORK LONDON TORONTO SYDNEY

SBI

Strebor Books
P.O. Box 6505
Largo, MD 20792
http://www.streborbooks.com

ISBN 978-1-59309-522-2
ISBN 978-1-4767-4445-1 (ebook)
LCCN 2013950647

First Strebor Books trade paperback edition February 2014

Cover design: www.mariondesigns.com
Cover photograph: © Keith Saunders/Marion Designs

10 9 8 7 6 5 4 3 2 1

Manufactured in the United States of America

ACKNOWLEDGMENTS

This book is dedicated to the memory of my father, Lloyd Goss, (1947-1996).

I'm living proof that all you need is faith of a mustard seed. To God, I give ALL THE GLORY.

I want to thank my mom, Exie, for her words of encouragement. For always being the voice of reason and pushing me to be the best "me" I can be.

I want to thank Zane. It's an honor to be a part of the Strebor Books family.

I want to thank Dr. Maxine Thompson. Thanks for hanging in there with me.

I want to thank all of my readers for supporting me over the years. Without you, I couldn't still be doing this. Thank you ___________(fill in your name). I appreciate you all.

Shelia M. Goss

CHAPTER 1

Lexi

Everybody wants to be like the Joneses, but do they really know what we go through to maintain our status? I think not. Life as Lexi Jones hasn't always been a bed of roses especially when you're married to Royce Jones. To the outside world, Royce Jones is the perfect pillar of the community. He's taken his father's funeral home business and made it into a multimillion dollar company within the last ten years. He's been on the covers of several national magazines and interviewed for a variety of newspapers across the country.

So why am I sitting here at the country club, humiliated, because my platinum Visa card was declined? I can only imagine what those biddies are going to say if word gets out about this. Thankfully, I always carry cash on me, so I could take care of the bill.

"Mrs. Jones, it probably was just a simple mistake."

I frowned. "I'm sure. I'll call and get it straightened out."

The waitress couldn't even wait for me to get out of earshot. "Girl, what is this world coming to when the Joneses are having financial problems?"

Her friend responded, "That's just one card. I'm pretty sure she has more where that one came from."

I pushed my designer shades over my eyes and looked back at both of the women who had jealousy written all over their faces. I flashed my kilowatt smile, that I'd paid my dentist a mint for, and walked out of the country club.

The valet handed me the keys to my jet black Jaguar. The personalized license plates read *BossLady.*

I drove directly to RJ Jones Funeral Home. The parking lot was empty except for Royce's and his assistant's cars. I remember a time when the parking lot stayed full.

"Hi, Mrs. Jones," Shannon said, when I entered. Shannon was cute, young, and petite. If she wasn't Royce's little cousin, she wouldn't be working in that position.

I didn't tolerate women outside of the family working in close proximity to my husband. I already had to deal with the women in our town who always found a reason to flaunt themselves around him, so I refused to have to concern myself with any of his employees. That was a promise Royce and I made when I agreed to go along with him taking over his father's funeral home: no women workers unless they were related. And they had to be related to him; I didn't trust any of my female relatives. Many would chop off my head to replace me. *Family, got to love them.*

"Shannon, is my husband busy?" I asked. I had no time for formalities.

"He's in his office. You want me to ring him?" she asked.

"No need to." I walked past her and down the hall to Royce's office.

Royce had his chair turned toward the window so all I could see was his short, black, curly, hair. I can recall many days and nights of running my hands through it. Some of my friends' husbands looked their age, but not Royce. My husband was as handsome now as he was the day I met him over thirty-something years ago. He was about to turn fifty and could give any twenty-five-year-old a run for his money in the body department.

"Baby, I know you're there so you might as well say something," Royce said, right before turning the black leather chair around.

I pulled out my Visa card and threw it on the desk in front of him.

"Tell me why my credit card was denied? And I want to know now."

I tapped my foot with my hands planted firmly on my hips.

Royce just stared up at me. "Have a seat, Lexi."

"Not until you tell me what's going on." I responded.

"If you take a seat, I will. I need to show you something." He fumbled on his desk for a folder.

I plopped down in the chair across from his desk. "This better be good."

"I've been meaning to have this talk with you, but it never seems like the right time. Now it seems like I have no choice."

I waved my finger back and forth in the air. "Yada, yada. Enough of that. Get to the point, and stop beating around the bush."

Royce looked me directly in my eyes. "Lexi, the funeral home has lost a lot of money, so I have to consolidate things until we get back on our feet financially."

I blinked a few times, because I knew I didn't hear what I thought I heard. "Come again?" I asked.

Royce reached for my hand on the desk and held it. "Baby, our money is low so we have to curb our spending."

I snatched my hands away. "Royce Lee Jones. Are you telling me that we're broke?"

He stood up, all six feet and one inch of him, and walked around the desk. He got down on bended knee in front of me. "No, baby, we're not broke." His voice trailed off and I swore I heard him add, "Yet."

I couldn't bear to look at him just then. All I could ask myself was, *How could a multimillion dollar company be going broke? All of my hard work, helping him build this funeral home, and he's talking about we're broke.* "I can't believe this. When I was in the office every day, money was flowing in. What happened, Royce? What in the world happened?"

Royce tried to get me to look at him, but I refused to. I leaned back in my chair and crossed my arms.

"Come on, Lexi. I need you to be understanding about this and work with me."

I uncrossed my arms. I stared at Royce directly in his eyes. If looks could kill, he would be in one of the coffins he sold. "I understand things perfectly. There's been mismanagement of funds on your part, and now I have to pay the consequences. Royce, you better handle this situation or else."

Royce stood up. "Or else what?"

Frustrated, without saying another word, I stood up, grabbed my purse, and dashed out.

"Lexi, don't do anything drastic."

I threw my hands up in the air.

"Everything okay?" Shannon asked, as I whisked passed her desk.

"Ask your boss," I said, as I rushed out of the front door of the funeral home.

I got behind the wheel of my car and closed my eyes, taking in a few deep breaths before exhaling.

The knock on my window brought me out of my tranquil moment. I rolled my window down. "What?" I asked with attitude, yet sounding strangely calm.

Royce answered slowly, "For now, all of the credit cards are frozen except for one. And I have that one."

I placed the car in reverse and sped out of the parking lot, not caring if I ran over Royce's foot. I saw him looking at me from my rearview mirror. At that moment, I couldn't stand the sight of him.

CHAPTER 2

Royce

Lord knows, if I didn't love Lexi, I would've left her a long time ago. Her selfish attitude turned many people off. But, I knew where she came from and why she was the way she was. So I overlooked it time after time. Well, except for once. I don't want to relive that moment right now.

I didn't expect Lexi to find out about our financial problems this soon. I realize now I should have listened to my accountant, and told her about it when I first became aware of the problems. It's not like Lexi would have curbed some of her spending, but at least maybe she would be more understanding.

Actually, I thought I had everything under control. I never thought the stock market would crash when it did, sending a lot of my investments south, and causing me to lose millions. Nonetheless, things were slowly coming back around, but not fast enough.

Some people are probably wondering how a funeral home could be struggling if there were always people dying. Well, until recently, my funeral homes served most of the parishes in the north Louisiana area. We were actually doing well until a competitor with a nationwide chain of funeral homes decided to open up a branch nearby, and offer the same services at more discounted prices.

Let's face it. Most people don't have life insurance these days, and burying a loved one can be expensive.

Later that day, a phone call came. It distracted me from my troublesome thoughts—and gave me a few more.

"Royce, I think you should really consider putting some of your property up on the market," Jason Milton, my accountant and best friend from high school, said.

"But the market isn't the best right now."

"Even with it not being the best, you'll still make a profit considering you bought a lot of the properties dirt cheap."

He was correct. But, I didn't want to sell any of my real estate. However, if things didn't start looking up, I would be forced to.

"Jason, please try to find other solutions."

"I'm going to do what I can. Can't promise you anything."

"Just try," I said, as I ended the call with Jason. Shannon was gone home, and here I was alone in my office pouring my sorrows out over a glass of bourbon. Staring at the near empty glass, I wondered how my life had gotten to this point. It was late, and as much as I hated to go home, I was tired of looking at these four walls.

I was locking up, and heading to my car when Charity's candy apple-red convertible eased up right next to my truck.

"Daddy, what's going on? I was at the mall, and my Visa card was declined. Can you say embarrassing?" Charity got all animated with her hands. No hugs, no kisses. My model-thin daughter ranted and raved as she walked up to me.

"Baby Girl, calm down. Your card was declined because I had the card cancelled."

"Daddy, how could you? I depend on that card for my shopping needs."

Charity. I had to laugh as I thought of her name. We sure picked the wrong name for our oldest daughter. She didn't have a charitable bone in her body. Charity had a "me, me, me" attitude. I blame myself for spoiling her.

"The company is going through some changes right now. Once we get a handle on things, you'll get a new Visa and your world will be perfect again," I tried to assure her.

"But, Daddy. I have an event to go to tonight. I had the perfect outfit, but had to leave it at the store."

"I know you have plenty of clothes with the tags still on them in your closet."

Charity pouted. "Yes, but still. I wanted something new."

"I suggest you go shopping in your closet. Or better yet, get a job so you can finance your own shopping sprees."

"Daddy, I can't believe you said that."

"Look. I've already had to deal with your mom and her attitude today, and I refuse to deal with yours. Now if there's nothing else, I'm going home. It's late, so I suggest you do the same."

I refused to entertain Charity and her tantrum. Without another word, I jumped in my truck. I watched Charity from the window of the driver seat, as she huffed and puffed before getting in her sports car. She turned her music up as loud as it could possibly go and sped away.

I let my window down and detoured to the liquor store before heading home. I had a feeling I was going to be in for a long night, and the only solace I planned to get was at the bottom of a liquor bottle.

CHAPTER 3

Charity

I can't believe my dad just dismissed me like that. Doesn't he realize it's embarrassing to be at your favorite store and have the clerk smirk in your face when she tells you your credit card is declined? To make matters worse, the clerk was the same chick who tried to steal my senior prom date seven years ago.

"Whose car is this?" I asked out loud while pulling in beside Hope's car. Hope was my baby sister by two years.

The black truck wasn't familiar. I was barely through the doors of our townhouse when I heard loud, erotic sounds coming from upstairs. I rushed up the stairs only to see Hope with her behind in the air, as some dude was pounding inside of her.

Hope didn't even have the decency to close her door. I closed it for her. They stopped.

Hope hurried from the room. She looked frazzled. "I'm sorry. Thought you were gone for the day."

"Who is that?" I asked.

"Some dude I met last week at the club."

"Hope, are you serious? Why do you keep bringing home these strays? You're going to catch something if you don't stop what you're doing."

"All of us aren't prissy like you."

"All of us aren't sluts like you," I responded. I dared Hope to come after me because after the day I'd had, I was ready to rumble.

Hope backed down and went back to her guest, closing the

door behind her. I went into my bedroom. A few minutes later, I heard the front door shut.

I sat at my desk going through my bank account when I sensed Hope standing in my doorway.

"He's gone. Satisfied?"

"He was your guest, not mine."

Hope took the liberty of sitting on my bed without asking. "So what has your panties in a bunch?"

I turned my chair around and faced her. "Maybe I shouldn't tell you and let you find out on your own, but since I'm a good sister, I'll save you the embarrassment."

Hope looked at me with a confused look on her face. "Spill it."

"Daddy cancelled all of our credit cards. So, I hope you have some money saved in your bank account."

"What? Are you serious? I was supposed to go to New York next week with some friends. I haven't even bought my plane ticket yet."

"Well, lil' Sis, I guess The Big Apple will have to wait."

"I'm calling Dad. I don't believe you."

Hope has always been a spoiled little brat. I called the toll-free number on the back of my credit card and put it on speaker. I pressed the key to announce the credit card balance. The voice read, "No funds are available for purchase."

"Are we broke?" Hope asked, sounding worried.

"I'm not. I have some money in my account."

"All of us aren't you. I only have a few thousand dollars. That's not enough for me to live on."

"I'm going to tell you like Daddy told me. I suggest you get yourself a job."

"A j-o...," Hope started to say. "I can't even say it."

"Yes, I know. Hard to believe that we have to look for work, isn't it?" I smiled.

"Charity, how could you laugh at a time like this? This is no laughing matter."

"I have to laugh to keep from crying."

"So what are you going to do?"

"I have two degrees, so I guess it's about time I put one of them to use."

"I guess."

"I'm going to go by the art gallery in Shreveport and see if I can get a job there. Something part-time, of course."

"Of course," Hope responded.

While Hope dealt with the realization that we would have to get jobs, I updated my resume and printed out a few copies.

This had been a long day, but I had an event to get ready for. I pushed my problems aside and got ready to attend what could very well be my last charitable event. If things kept going this way, I would be in need of charity myself.

Two hours later, I was standing behind a podium, facing approximately one hundred and fifty people who were there to support my sorority chapter's annual fundraiser. I gave a heartfelt speech before taking my seat.

Lisa, my sorority sister and best friend since high school, whispered, "Girl, you nailed it."

I smiled. "Thanks."

"Also, I think you have an admirer. I haven't seen him around before, so I'll have to ask around and see who he is."

My eyes landed on the man who had captured Lisa's attention. He looked like he'd stepped out of the pages of a *GQ* magazine. He was dressed in a gray, tailored, pinstriped suit. His clean-shaven head seemed to glisten as the light hit it. He stood up, stretching to at least six-one. He had the same stance as my dad. He was a tall glass of chocolate that no doubt had every single woman in that room thirsty.

"He's headed this way," Lisa whispered.

I could see that. My hands started sweating the closer he got to our table. I picked up the napkin and wiped my hands dry.

"Ladies, how are you?" he asked.

"We're just fine." Lisa responded for the both of us.

"I'm Tyler Williams," the mystery man said, extending his hand out to me.

I shook it as Lisa continued. "She's Charity and single, and I'm Lisa."

I wanted to hit Lisa, but instead I gave her the evil eye.

"Charity, your speech was very motivating."

"Thank you," I responded.

Tyler removed a business card from his wallet and handed it to me. "Maybe we can get together for lunch or something. My numbers are on here."

I placed the card in my handbag. "Maybe."

Lisa said, "She'll definitely call you."

"I'm counting on it." Tyler winked his eye and left our table.

"Lisa, you act like I'm desperate the way you kept pushing me off on that man."

"When was the last time you got laid?"

I didn't respond.

"Exactly. You can thank me later."

Before I could respond to that comment, Lisa had grabbed her drink and moved on to socializing with other people.

I looked up to see Tyler looking in my direction. He smiled and winked. My eyes followed his every move until he walked out of the hotel ballroom.

Lisa walked up behind me and whispered, "Like I said, you can thank me later."

I couldn't do anything but smile.

CHAPTER 4

Hope

I can't believe Charity thinks I'm going to get a job. As long as there are able-bodied men out there, I'm going to find me a sponsor. I can't do a regular nine-to-five job. I tried it once, and it's clear that taking direction from someone else was not in the cards for me.

That's why I'm at the Horseshoe Casino right now, wearing my short, tight red come-screw-me dress with my red stilettos. My hair was fierce, if I do say so myself. Many women have paid hundreds of dollars to have the long, curly mane that's natural for me. Of course, I still pay my beautician nice money weekly to make sure it's always looking just right.

I've turned down several passes from men because after inspecting their shoes, I knew they would not be able to fulfill my needs. One thing Charity and I could agree on, I needed to be more selective about who I give my goodies to. It's way past time that I stepped up my game. *No more strays,* as Charity puts it, for me.

Thanks to my older brother, Lovie, I could play poker with the best of them. I didn't want to chance losing the little money I had, but sometimes you have to take chances. I found a poker table near where the real high-rollers were, and placed a few bets. I'd increased my winnings to a level that would gain me entrance into the back room. I should have taken my huge winnings and left. The average person would have, but I'm not your average person.

I was a woman on a mission, and my mission hadn't been completed yet. Flashing my kilowatt smile, I gained entrance to the back and sat at the table. I scanned the faces of my competition and placed my bet.

Each one of the players, except for one, threw in their hands. I wasn't one to back down. I placed some chips in the center. The older gentleman licked his lips, smiled, and matched my bet. When all was said and done, I walked away from the table thousands of dollars richer. Mission was partially completed as I pushed away from the table.

"Do you need some help?" one of the men I'd been admiring asked. He smelled as good as he looked.

"Sure, thanks," I said, as he held my chair while I held my earnings and clutch in my hands.

"I can make sure you get to your car if you like," the same man stated.

"Who's going to protect me from you?" I flirted.

He laughed. "I guess I should have introduced myself first." He reached into his pocket and handed me a business card.

I glanced over it. It read, *Tyler Williams, CEO of Williams Construction.* "I'm sorry, but you're still a stranger to me."

"Let me treat you to a late dinner so we can change that," Tyler stated.

"I'll think about it." I walked away. Correction, I *switched* away leaving him standing there watching me go cash in my chips.

The cashier asked, "How would you like this?"

"Since that's a lot of cash, please deposit it directly into my account."

I filled out the necessary forms and waited patiently while the transfer occurred. Satisfied that I was now $100,000 richer, I turned around to walk back to my new friend. I looked and looked, but he couldn't be found.

Disappointed, I decided to leave and go to another casino. "Hope Jones, is that you?"

I turned to face the familiar voice. "Brett?"

"Brett Simmons in the flesh, baby." Brett pulled me into a long bear hug.

"Whoa. We haven't seen each other since what…graduation night?"

Brett was no longer the skinny nerd that I befriended to help me with my school work. Gone were the Coke-bottle glasses. His broad chest and defined chin made him very attractive now.

Brett was all smiles. He responded, "I know. It's been a while. Looking good, too." He admired me from head to toe.

"I try to keep myself up," I responded.

"Brett, there you are," a petite woman with short, platinum blonde hair said as she walked up to Brett, and wrapped her arm around his waist.

The woman rolled her eyes at me. I was used to women hating on me. She needed to check her man though, not me. Besides, if I wanted Brett, I could have him. I was his first. Since she wanted to give me the evil eye, I would give her something to really be upset about. I reached into my purse and handed Brett a card with my number on it.

"Brett, call me so we can catch up."

Brett stuttered, "It was nice seeing you again, Hope."

"You too." I rolled my eyes and continued to walk toward the elevator.

"There you are. You disappeared on me," Tyler said, as he rushed up near me.

I didn't slow my pace. "I'm leaving now."

"Can I get a rain check?" he asked.

I pushed the down button for the elevator.

I avoided looking at him. "I'll think about it." I looked down at his feet. His shoes were not run over. They were well-kept. My eyes scanned him from his feet all the way up to the tip of his bald head. I thought about it.

I faked a yawn. "I'm a little sleepy tonight, but if you're available tomorrow night you can take me to dinner then."

The elevator door opened. "I'm at a disadvantage. You know my name, but I don't know anything about you," he said.

"I'm Hope. No last name right now. When I call you, you'll have my number."

"I guess I'll have to wait until then."

"Good night, Tyler."

"Good night, Hope," his raspy voice responded, just as the elevator door closed.

My night wasn't a complete failure after all.

CHAPTER 5

Lovie

I enjoyed my job at the club, Bottoms Up. It really wasn't a job to me because I got to be around beautiful women all night and hang out with my boys. I also drank as much as I wanted, even though I rarely drank while on the job. Life could get no better than this.

My cell phone had been blowing up all night with text messages from my sisters, the drama queens. I would call them later during the week. I wasn't in the mood to deal with their homemade drama. They were always going at it, and it took me being the mediator to get them back on track. Being the older brother wasn't always easy.

Cindy Bell, my latest girlfriend of one month, would be the one to make me forget everything tonight. We were both naked by the time we made it in to the bedroom of my condo.

"Lovie, I love you," Cindy said, as she rode me like a stallion.

I ignored her declaration of love, and continued to enjoy the ride. I did my best to maintain my cool, but Cindy knew how to push me over the edge. I screamed out in ecstasy, and dumped my sperm in the Magnum condom before rolling over and going to sleep.

During my slumber, I felt my body shake.

"Lovie. Some woman claiming to be your mama is on the phone," Cindy said, waking me from my deep sleep.

I snatched my phone from Cindy. "You shouldn't be answering my phone anyway."

"Your phone kept ringing. I thought it was an emergency."

"Whatever. I think it's time that you go." I sat straight up in bed.

Cindy fussed, but she got her stuff and left out of my room. I heard my front door slam. "Mom, you there?" I asked.

"Yes, and I heard all of that drama. I've told you, you're a Jones and you need to be careful. These hoes will do anything to trap you. I hope you at least used a condom."

"Mom, we're not going to have this conversation."

"Lovie Lee Jones, you're twenty-six-years old, but not too old for me to put my foot up your behind if you try to sass me."

"Mom, I'm just saying. What I do in my personal life is just that—personal."

"As long as I'm footing the bill for that condo you're in, I have a lot to say."

"That's just it. I don't need you to do that. I got my own money coming in. I've been meaning to tell you that for a while now."

"So now you don't need your mama? After all I've done for you," my mom ranted and ranted. I pulled the phone from my ear, but could still hear her.

"Mom, calm down. I appreciate everything you and Dad have done for me. I really do. But, I'm a man now. I just want to make it on my own. Know what I mean? I'll talk to you later." I hung up the phone without waiting for her response.

My mom was trying to stress me out and it wasn't even nine o'clock in the morning. I got up and turned on my fifty-inch television and PlayStation. I sat on the edge of the bed. Before I could get five minutes into my game, I heard a knock on the door.

I looked through the peephole, and there on the other side of my door was my mom. It wouldn't do me any good to ignore her. "Coming. I need to put some clothes on."

"Boy, I birthed you. Open up this door. Now!" she yelled.

I unlocked the door, rushed back to my room, and threw on a pair of gym shorts and a T-shirt.

When I returned to the living room, my mom sat on my sofa with her legs crossed and a frown on her face.

"Lovie, I want to know how you're making enough money to pay your expenses."

I sat on the opposite end of the couch. "Duh. I do work. Don't you remember?"

"That job you got as the manager of that club isn't enough to pay my dry cleaning bill."

"It's legit, so you should be happy." Of course, I wasn't going to let her know that it was a front for the other business I had going on. I was good at numbers. My customers weren't your average businessmen. I handled the books for men who got their money by dealing, hustling, and yes, even killing and stealing. At least I was putting my accounting degree to good use.

"Son, you should be working for your dad. He really needs you."

"He's been doing fine all of these years. I'm sure me working for him wouldn't make or break him."

She reached for my hand. "I hate to be the bearer of bad news, but Son, we are going broke. Your dad has mismanaged the funeral home's funds and is about to put us in the poorhouse."

"What's going on?" I asked. I was really concerned. There was no way my mom could go back to living the type of life she grew up living.

"Business at the funeral home isn't as lucrative as it once was, but what really put us in this fix is your dad. Royce made several bad investments with the funeral home's money."

I looked at her in disbelief. Not my penny-pinching Dad. He liked nice things, but he was as thrifty as it comes. It's my mom who liked to splurge.

This was serious. Real serious.

CHAPTER 6

Lexi

I had to think of a way to get Lovie to see why I needed him. I needed him working at the funeral home in some capacity. I couldn't lose everything. I couldn't go back to being poor. I refused to, and I wouldn't.

My baby boy looked at me with confusion in his eyes. "Mom, what can we do to save the business?"

"I've been up most of the night trying to figure it out. First thing we need to do is fire Jason and hire someone else. That's where you come in. You're a CPA. You should have been doing your father's books anyway, and maybe we wouldn't be in this fix."

"Mom, you know me and Dad don't always see eye to eye, so working together wasn't an option for either one of us."

"It's time to squash all of that. Your dad needs you. *I* need you."

Lovie rubbed his forehead. "Does Dad know you're over here?"

"No, but if you show up at his office, he's not going to turn you away."

"I don't think it's a good idea. You know he can be stubborn. If he calls me and asks me, then yes, I'll come help him out. But if he doesn't, count me out."

Lovie got up and went to the kitchen. I followed him. "You two are trying to drive me crazy."

Lovie looked from behind the refrigerator door. "Are you staying for breakfast? I still make a mean omelet."

"No, dear. I'm going to the spa. I need to relax my mind."

"See, if you're still able to go to the spa, things aren't as rough as they seem."

"I hate smart-alecks," I responded.

"But you'll always love me. I'm your only son." Lovie walked up to me and pulled me into a hug.

He was right. He was the oldest, and we had a special bond. He would always be my baby no matter how old he got.

"You know how to soften me up," I responded.

"Have Dad make that call and I'll be there, but until then, just let me know if there's anything else I can do to help."

"Well, there's something else you can do, but I'll wait to discuss it with you later. I'm hoping we won't have to resort to it."

Lovie escorted me to the front door. "What? You got me curious."

"We'll talk later. Love you." I gave Lovie a quick peck on the cheek and left.

Thirty minutes later, I was lying across a massage table with nothing but a towel covering me. I closed my eyes as tension left my body with each touch from the masseuse. For the next forty-five minutes, I pretended to be trouble free.

After the massage, I got dressed and went to the room designated for manicures and pedicures. I felt like a million bucks afterward. I reached for my credit card out of habit but recalled there was no money available. So, I retrieved cash from my wallet.

I heard some laughter from behind me. I paid my bill, turned around, and came face-to-face with Julie Washington and Mattie Adams. The cackling hens were the two women who tried to make my life in Shreveport a living hell.

"Lexi, darling, we're surprised to see you here." Julie's voice sounded like fingernails scraping a chalkboard. She'd been the product of one too many facelifts. There wasn't a doctor alive who could fix her face now.

Mattie, looking like Julie's twin, added, "Yes, word on the streets is your credit is no good around these parts."

Without flinching, I looked directly in Mattie's eyes. "Jealousy is an ugly color on you. So why are you all up in my business?"

Julie grabbed Mattie's arm. "Come on, Mattie. Don't even entertain her with a response."

Julie and Mattie rushed passed me and in to the spa.

"Y'all better go because I'm from the West Side. I still know how to throw down with the best of them." I stood with my arms crossed.

"She still has no class," I heard Mattie say as they walked.

The clerk at the front desk looked away, but not without me catching a grin on her face.

"I'm sure the rest of your day will be boring compared to the scene you just witnessed," I stated, before leaving.

Women like Julie and Mattie got under my skin. No matter how hard I tried to fit into their world, they were always trying to look down on me. Royce said I shouldn't care, and he's right, I shouldn't.

Speaking of Royce, he and I need to have a little talk. He purposely didn't talk to me last night and left before I got up this morning. He can run, but he can't hide.

CHAPTER 7

Royce

Avoiding Lexi hadn't been easy, and it seemed that it was all for naught. I heard her coming long before she made it to my office. I looked up toward the door awaiting her entrance.

Lexi stormed in my office enraged. "Royce, you can run, but you can't hide. You caused this problem and you're going to fix it. Now tell me how you plan on doing it, so I can deal with other things." Lexi plopped down in front of my desk.

"Hello to you, too, my beautiful wife."

"Save the pleasantries for your customers." Lexi held her hand in the air and then looked around. "Snap! There are no customers."

"Calm down. If there were some, you would run them off with that mouth of yours."

"Calm? How can I be calm when according to you, we're going broke?"

"Look. We still have money, but just not as much. So yes, I need for you and the kids to be more responsible and stop spending money like it's water."

"I refuse to go back to the life I knew before we got together, Royce Jones. You promised me the good life, and I'm holding you to that promise."

I threw my hands up in the air. It's clear where Charity and Hope got their drama queen antics from. From the Queen of Drama herself, my wife, Lexi.

"Wipe that silly smile off your face," Lexi snapped.

"Baby, I need for you to bring your tone down a notch or two. I'm not your kids, and you will show me some respect. Or, you can leave."

I listened to Lexi complain, before calming herself down. "Royce, sorry, but ever since I got embarrassed at the country club, this has been eating away at me."

I rose up from my seat and walked behind Lexi. I massaged her shoulders. "Baby, I know it has. I promise to make things right. Things are going slower than I had anticipated, but I will make it right."

Lexi placed one hand on top of mine while moving her neck from side to side. "I know who can help, too. Lovie is a CPA. Have him come in, look at the books, and see what else needs to be done."

"Lovie is not living up to his full potential. He may be a CPA, but how has he utilized his license? He's managing a nightclub. He could be working for a firm or even have his own."

Lexi stood and glared into my eyes. "But Royce, it was always my dream that you two would work together."

"At one time, I thought it would be possible. But we are too much alike. Our relationship is fine now, but if we work together, believe me, it would be strained."

"Please. At least get rid of the accountant you have now."

"Jason's a trusted friend. He's the only one I trust to look over my financial affairs."

"Well, I don't trust him and neither should you."

"Don't be taking out your frustrations on an innocent man." I hugged Lexi.

Her body tensed up before she hugged me back. "In your eyes, Jason can never do any wrong."

I let go of Lexi. I shut the door and locked it. I was frustrated in more ways than one. Lexi held a drink. I removed it from her hand

and placed it on the desk. I didn't want to talk about Lovie, Jason, or the business. I needed a stress reliever.

Before Lexi could respond to me taking away her drink, my lips were on top of hers. The moans seeping out of her were enough to make me turn it up a notch. My tongue dipped in and out of her mouth. I picked her up and carried her to the brown leather couch in the corner of my office.

"Royce, maybe we should—"

Before Lexi could finish her sentence I had her moaning. I didn't want others to hear us. I placed my mouth over hers to quiet her as my hand roamed over her body. We tore each other's clothes off. With a glazed-over look in her eyes, I entered Lexi and we both escaped into our own private world. Our eyes locked as we climaxed together.

The door jiggled. Lexi and I looked at each other and giggled.

"Who is it?" I yelled out.

"Mr. Jones, you have a customer," Shannon yelled from the other side of the locked door.

"I'll be there in a minute." I responded, as I eased off Lexi.

I went to the bathroom attached to my office. I looked under the sink for a towel and began washing up. Lexi took the towel from me and washed my lower body. My manhood stood at attention again. I looked down at it and back up at Lexi. "I guess he's not finished."

"I see. Well, I'll take care of him some more when you get home."

We dressed and I walked Lexi to the door.

"Think about what I said about Lovie. He can be an asset to the company."

"I'll think about it." I kissed her on the cheek.

She left, and I went to console a grieving family.

CHAPTER 8

Charity

Although I haven't had a paying job since I interned in college, I've been working. I work with several charities and I host events. In fact if this job interview at the art gallery doesn't go well, I'm thinking about using my party planning skills and starting my own event planning business.

It took me fifteen minutes to decide what to wear to the interview. I opted for the blue power suit. I picked up the pearls that were given to me on my eighteenth birthday and held them up to my neck.

Hope burst through my bedroom door without knocking.

"Have you talked to Mom?" Hope asked.

"Yes, and I'm not looking forward to this family dinner she insists we have." I looked at Hope. "Can you fasten this clasp?"

My hair was pulled up in a bun with a few curly strands falling down on each side. I turned around as Hope made sure the clasp was secure.

"Thanks." I sat on the edge of my bed and put on my heels.

"Where are you off to?" Hope stood in the doorway and asked.

"I have a job interview. Speaking of jobs, how's your search going?"

Hope looked away. "It's going."

"Something tells me you haven't been looking."

"I tried working once, remember? That didn't work out. I need something where I can be my own boss."

"See, that's your problem. You want everything handed to you. Hope, it doesn't work like that."

Hope laughed. "Of course you would say that. Mom and Dad have given you everything."

I had to laugh at that statement. "Child, please. We both have been spoiled by Mom and Dad. But the difference between you and me is I don't mind a little hard work."

"Have you told Mom your plans yet? I'm sure she would love to hear how her favorite daughter is doing."

I rolled my eyes. "I haven't shared my plans with anyone but you. You're good at something. Just figure out what it is and find a job that you feel will utilize those skills."

Hope placed her finger on her chin. "I think I've found my area of expertise. I'll let you know if it works out."

"You're good with makeup. Maybe you can get a job at the M·A·C counter," I suggested.

"You can be so cruel."

"I'm just saying. That's one area you're skilled in."

"You're such a hater." Hope stormed out.

"Whatever," I said under my breath.

Hope was accustomed to using her good looks to get whatever she wanted, but this time it wasn't going to work. She needed to find a job so she could help pay some of these bills. If she wasn't my sister, she would have to look for another place. I'm only letting her stay here because my mom begged me. I'm tired of dealing with her immature ways.

I glanced at the time. Talking to Hope put me behind schedule. I didn't want to be late for my interview. I grabbed my purse and rushed out of the house.

The art gallery was located in an upscale area of Shreveport.

The houses surrounding the museum were older, but the owners were wealthy. I'd attended several private events at the gallery, and looked forward to speaking with the manager, Lenora Brady, one on one.

"Ms. Jones, glad you made it," Lenora said, as she led me into her office.

After the pleasantries, she got straight to the questions.

"What makes you think you're qualified to work here?" She glanced down at my short resume.

I wasn't one to be intimidated. "My love for art stems back as early as five years old. My parents were sure to nurture that love over the years."

I watched her write as I talked. She didn't say anything, so I continued, "I interned in Paris for one semester. I've been instrumental in acquiring exquisite, yet rare, pieces for some of your patrons. I would be happy to provide their names as references, if needed."

"I recall meeting you at some of our private events. I'm impressed by your knowledge; however, what concerns me is the fact that I don't see any steady solid work history."

"I assure you, although I haven't held a regular job, I'm far from a slouch. I've been active with several charities. I believe they are listed on my resume."

Lenora scanned my resume again. "I see. Well, we have one more person to interview. I'll have my assistant call you if you get the job."

Lenora extended her hand out to me. I shook it. I smiled as I walked out of her office. Her handshake was loose. I didn't have a good feeling about how things went, but I would try to remain optimistic.

When I got back in my car, I saw I'd received a text from Lisa. I dialed her number as I pulled out of the parking lot.

"So, how did it go?" Lisa asked.

"It went okay. Not sure if she liked me, but I guess I'll know something soon enough."

"You don't sound too enthused."

"Something about it just didn't seem right."

"There are other places you can apply, so don't worry," Lisa responded.

My phone clicked and I saw an unfamiliar number on the display. "Lisa, I'll call you back."

"May I speak to Charity Jones?" the male voice asked.

"This is she."

"I'm Lenora's assistant. I'm sorry I was out when you had your interview."

"No problem. I wasn't expecting to hear back so fast, but I'm glad you called."

He paused. "Regrettably, Lenora's decided to go with another candidate, but she wanted to encourage you to reapply for another position."

I hung up on him. The heifer lied to me. She told me she was going to interview another potential candidate. I just left there, so there was no way in hell she could have interviewed someone that fast.

I dialed Lisa's number back. "Girl, I just got a call telling me they gave the position to someone else. I wasn't even out of the parking lot good before getting a phone call."

"Calm down."

"Calm down? I was depending on that job. Now I got to scramble and find something else," I shouted. I was so frustrated, I did not pay attention to the speed limit.

My day went from bad to worse when I heard the sirens and saw the flashing lights of a Shreveport police car behind me.

I hit the steering wheel. "Damn. Damn. Damn. Lisa, got to go. This ticket is the last thing I need."

I pulled over on the side of the road. I reached in the glove compartment and pulled out my registration and insurance information.

I glanced in my rearview mirror and watched the tall, dark, and handsome police officer walk up to my car. He tapped on my window. I rolled it down. I batted my eyes and tried to show a lot of cleavage, but he ignored me.

"Miss, I need to see your license and registration."

I frowned as I watched him write my ticket.

CHAPTER 9

Hope

"Brett, it was as good as I remembered," I lied, as he lay in the hotel bed watching me get dressed.

"When can we do this again?" Brett smiled, but I didn't.

Sleeping with him after all of these years was a huge mistake. I'd given Brett a sob story claiming I needed money. He fell for it and brought me the cash I'd asked him for. The money clouded my judgment, and a simple thank-you hug led me to sleep with him.

I faced him. "Your fiancée might not appreciate me being with her man."

Brett scooted to the edge of the bed. "She can be replaced."

"Uh, I don't think so." I continued to put on my clothes. "What we did was great, but I'm not in love with you."

"But—"

I walked up to Brett and placed my finger over his lips. "Let's just savor this moment for what it was. Two friends catching up and enjoying each other's company one last time."

"Where is it?" Brett snapped.

"Where's what?"

Brett tried to pull my purse from my hand.

I held on to my purse with a tight grip. "What the hell are you doing?"

"The money I just gave you. You set me up. You're just a high-priced whore."

I moved back. "You weren't saying that when you were all up in this."

"Biatch, I will—"

I removed a small silver pistol from my purse. "You'll do what? Try it."

Brett backed all the way down. "You played me."

"No, Brett, you played yourself. I didn't promise you a lifetime. I only slept with you. Get over it. I suggest that you learn how to keep your pecker in your pants and save it for your fiancée."

"I can't believe you did this to me," Brett said over and over.

As I looked for my shoes, I said, "Think about this experience the next time you think about creeping on your woman. Tell her she can thank me for you being faithful to her from this day forward."

"Hope, you're still as vindictive as you were in high school."

"And Brett, you still can't fuck. So since that's established, I think we can agree that neither of us has any problem going our separate ways and letting this be a distant memory."

I could feel Brett's eyes cutting into my back as I left him staring at my backside while he sat on the edge of the bed.

I needed to run home to take a quick shower, so I could go deal with my family. I would be late, but that's nothing new. I'm always late.

All eyes were on me when I breezed in to my parents' living room. My father was sitting in his big chair. My mom sat next to him on the arm of the chair. Lovie and Charity were each sitting on the sofa, faking like they were the perfect children that they were not.

"You're late," my mom said, as she stood up.

I glanced at my watch. "I'm only thirty minutes late."

"Tardiness is inexcusable," she snapped.

My eyes pled with my dad to come to my rescue, but as usual he didn't. When it came to my mom, he had no backbone.

My mom stood in the doorway. "What are y'all waiting for? Let's go before I have to warm everything up in the microwave, thanks to Hope."

I made faces behind her back.

"Hope, you can stop that. Act your age."

I looked at Charity and Lovie. They both shrugged their shoulders. Sometimes I thought it was true. Mothers do have eyes in the back of their heads.

We obeyed the queen of the house and followed her to the dining room. All of my favorite dishes were sitting on the table. I couldn't eat like this on a regular basis because I had to keep my figure in tip-top shape. But every now and then, I loved to splurge. My mom definitely could cook a good Southern meal.

The conversation was light as we all dove into our plates of brown, crispy fried chicken, homemade macaroni and cheese, and homemade rolls that melted in your mouth the moment you took a bite.

I took my last bite and closed my eyes. I opened them when I smelled the aroma of the peach cobbler my mom now placed in front of each one of us. I was full and about to burst, but peach cobbler was my favorite. I took a bite.

My mom didn't eat. She said, "I called you all over here today because we are in a family crisis." She looked at my dad. "Dear, would you like to explain things to them or should I?"

My dad took big gulps of his drink. "I wanted to talk to you kids to let you know what's going on." He looked at each one of us.

My mom rolled her eyes. "Get to the point. Look, we're going broke."

He ignored her comments. "Lexi, sometimes you blow things out of proportion. RJ Jones Funeral Home is going through a little rough patch, but we're not going out of business."

Charity chimed in. "Any time I get embarrassed at the store because my credit card doesn't work, it means we have a serious problem."

"Exactly." My mom shook her head in agreement. "See, Charity understands why we should all be concerned."

Lovie asked, "So how did this happen? Where did the money go?"

My dad looked down at the table. "Bad investments. I got a little greedy and invested more money than I should. I thought doubling or tripling our money would be good but instead, I lost a lot of it."

Lovie shook his head back and forth. "You should have come to me."

"I have an accountant, remember? Jason." my dad responded.

"He's not a good one if you've lost most of our money," I added.

"First of all, it's *my* money. It's a company that my father built. If any of you were concerned, you would be working with me instead of always being so busy spending the money as soon as I make it."

Ouch. Well, he did have a point. I had no interest in working at the funeral home. Being around all of those dead bodies always freaked me out.

CHAPTER 10

Lovie

I sat there and listened to my father go on and on about his bad investment choices. I was stunned. I couldn't believe he'd gambled away the family business' money.

"Dad, I told Mom I was going to stay out of this. But if I don't intervene, you're going to lose everything. Big Daddy is probably turning over in his grave knowing that you've run his business into the ground."

"Lovie, I got this under control. You just worry about getting yourself a real job."

I clenched my fists under the table. "I have a job. In fact, my clients are very happy because they *always* make money with the investments I make for them."

My mom asked, "What clients?"

I ignored her question. "Dad, you need to put your pride aside and allow me to look over the books so we can figure out a way to get you out of this mess."

Charity tried to be a voice of reason. "Yes, Dad. Lovie is a CPA. I mean, it wouldn't hurt, would it?"

My mom rubbed his arm. "Come on, baby. If not for you, for the family. Think about what your dad would do."

My dad looked in Hope's direction. "Hope, you're awfully quiet. You have anything you want to add?"

Hope shrugged her shoulders. "Whatever everyone else decides is okay with me. Lovie is good with numbers."

My dad sighed. "It looks like I've been outvoted. I hope I don't live to regret this decision. Lovie, will you come work with me so we can get this business back on track?"

I smiled. "Dad, I would be honored to. Let me let the guys at the club know they'll need to find a new manager."

My mom poured herself a glass of wine. She passed the bottle around. "My two favorite men working together. This is a good day for the Joneses."

We each poured ourselves a glass. My mom held her glass up in the air. "To the Joneses."

We all joined in. "The Joneses."

My phone chirped alerting me to an incoming text. I glanced at the text. One of my customers needed me. "Mom, Dad. I hate to leave, but I have something I need to attend to."

"Fine. I'll see you first thing in the morning, right?" my dad asked.

"Sure. I'll be there by ten."

"Make it nine."

"Nine-thirty."

"Just get there before noon," my dad finally gave up and said.

My mom walked me out. "See, that wasn't so bad. Now, you'll be in position to implement my other plan."

I stopped walking. "What plan?"

"Go ahead and handle your business. We got time to talk about my other plan later," she assured me.

I left, but I was curious to know what else my mom was up to. I pushed those thoughts out of my mind as I rushed to Bottoms Up to meet one of my clients.

I found Slim sitting in the back with his normal entourage of people. Slim was far from slim. He reminded me of the deceased rapper, Big Pun. Slim looked up as I approached his table. "Hey, y'all move out of the way and let my man get in here. In fact, y'all need to bounce. Me and him got some business to discuss."

The crowd of women and men moved so fast you would have thought the police were in close proximity. "What it do?" I said, as I shook Slim's hand before taking a seat.

"Man, the Feds are on me and I need to make sure some of my money is cleaned. You did take care of that for me, didn't you?"

"That's what this is about? I got you. I don't know about your other dealings, but the money I've been handling has been all legit. You don't have to worry about that."

"You sure? Because I'm going to need access to those funds to pay my lawyer."

"I'm a Jones, and all I got is my word. If I don't have my word, I don't have anything," I said. That's something my grandfather instilled in me before he died.

"My man. Now I can sleep a little easier." Slim held up his hand to get a waiter's attention. "Bring us over a bottle of your best champagne."

I held my hand out to signify no. "No, man. I'm on the job. I don't drink while working. Have to keep an eye out on the money, so you know I can't be drunk and do that."

"I feel you. That's why I like you. You got your head on straight."

I stood up. "I'm going to be working with my dad for the next few months, so you might not see me here often. You got my number, so if you need me, reach out and touch."

"It's all good, fam." Slim shook my hand.

Before I could get to the back office, Slim's table was filled with thirsty women. They all hoped they would be picked to go home with Slim and get access to his funds.

I liked making money, but I liked sleeping well at night too. A job like Slim's came with no peace. You were either worried about the cops or about the next guy who could easily come in and knock you off. Slim could have his money and street celebrity status. I had my peace of mind *and* his money. My services didn't come cheap.

CHAPTER 11

Lexi

This was one of those days where I wanted to stay in the bed, but I wasn't the type of woman to wallow in self-pity. I didn't get this far by just allowing things to happen. I was a take-charge type of person, and I wasn't about to change now.

I'm glad Royce agreed to let Lovie work with him. My plans to get up early and cook were spoiled. The stress from the last few days affected me, and I overslept.

I didn't have a regular nine-to-five job, but being Mrs. Jones was a full-time job. There were plenty of things for me to do on a daily basis to keep me busy. With the way things were going at RJ Jones Funeral Home, I needed to work overtime.

The cream-colored pant suit accented my curves. I fastened the clamp on the matching cream pumps and headed out the door. I almost tripped over the paper.

Royce must have been running late himself. He normally read the paper over coffee. I threw the paper in the passenger seat and drove to my destination. The women, who I considered more like frenemies than friends, were already seated around the table at the bistro for our monthly get together.

All of our husbands were prominent businessmen. There was Ruby Williams. Her husband owned several chicken shacks. Ruby and I are the same age, but she looked twenty years older. Time wasn't a friend of hers. If she laid off the booze some, maybe she could regain some of her youth. Then again, I doubt it.

The one wearing the bright orange skirt suit was Jackie Gray. Her husband owned a few car dealerships within the Ark-La-Tex. She's the youngest, and might I add the dumbest, of the group. Everyone, but her, knew about her husband's extramarital affairs. He was the biggest whore this side of the Mississippi River. There's not a woman outside of the nursing home he hadn't tried to sleep with. She's wife number three. Or is it four? So, she shouldn't be so clueless. When God was handing out brains, she got skipped.

Last, but not least, was the Queen B. I don't need to spell out what the "B" stood for. Her husband got his money from owning land. When the oil companies came in and leased his land, they became instant millionaires. The way Mrs. Sylvia Morrison acted, you would think she came from old money. Her nose was always up in the air. She held it up there so much, I'm surprised a few bugs hadn't found their home there.

When they saw me approach the table, they got up and we hugged and air kissed.

"For a moment, we thought you weren't going to make it," Jackie said.

I leaned back a little and looked at her. "Why wouldn't I be here? I have no reason *not* to show up."

Ruby and Sylvia exchanged glances. Sylvia cleared her throat. "Have you read the day's paper?"

Ruby said, "If it's happening to her, she doesn't need to read the paper."

I looked from one to the other. "What are you talking about?"

Jackie placed her hand on top of mine. "Don't worry about today's meal. I got you."

I jerked my hand away. "Okay, somebody needs to tell me what's going on."

Sylvia pulled out an excerpt from the newspaper and handed it to me. I scanned the page. It didn't take me long to see my name in big, bold letters staring back at me from a gossip column in the Lifestyle section.

The article read: *Rumor has it that life for Lexi Jones might not be all that it's cracked up to be. A source tells me that Mrs. Jones tried to pay with her credit card at said location and it was denied. Is there trouble in the Jones household? Will she become the ex-Mrs. Jones? Hmm. To stay in the know, check back next week.*

I couldn't believe what I was reading. I knew exactly who leaked this to Ms. Gossip. I looked at the three sets of eyes staring back at me. The women were all quiet, waiting on my response.

"Here, take this trash," I said to Sylvia. I threw it in her hand.

"Why didn't you tell us you and Royce were having problems?" Ruby asked.

"Because we're not. You would think that you, of all people, wouldn't believe everything you read in Ms. Gossip's column."

"Jackie said she heard that your credit card declined too," Sylvia jumped in and said.

I looked at Jackie.

Jackie rolled her eyes at Sylvia. "Lexi, dear, I just happen to come to the country club shortly after you left on that day and heard the attendants talking."

"Talk." I placed my hand on top of my heart. "Folks are jealous. Of course they are going to talk."

Ruby added, "If you are breaking up, just know that we are here for you. Nothing has to change. We can still have our monthly meetings."

"Read my lips." I dragged my words as I spoke. "Royce and I are not breaking up. In fact, my marriage is stronger now than it's ever been. So you all can tell whoever is concerned that all is well at the Jones house."

I looked each one of them in the eyes. They each averted their eyes looking everywhere but at me.

Jackie said, "Nevertheless, lunch is on me today."

I held my hand up. The waiter stopped at the table. "Can you bring me an apple martini?" No matter how much I protested, these women were going to believe what they wanted to believe. I normally didn't drink this early, but today was an exception.

CHAPTER 12

Royce

I'm still not convinced it was a good idea to have Lovie come work at the funeral home. He walked in my office as if he didn't have a care in the world.

I glanced at the clock and then at him. "I thought I asked you to be here at nine o' clock? I had a twelve o'clock appointment, but they're running late."

"Well, I'm right on time then, aren't I?" Lovie responded. He walked up to the chair in front of my desk.

"Don't sit. I got you set up in your own office."

"I'm going to need access to your computer."

"There's a computer already set up in the office. I'm going to give you access to whatever you need."

"Fine with me. By the way, since you're my dad, I'll give you the family discount."

I burst out laughing. "You got to be kidding."

"This is business. Not personal. Time is money. You taught me that."

I threw my hand up in the air. "Fine. Bill me whatever you need to bil me."

I got up from behind my desk and led him to his office. "I can't believe you're charging me. Shoot, I should make you pay me back for all the money I've given you over the years."

"I'll take all of that under consideration when I bill you," Lovie said.

I laughed. "You're definitely my son."

I unlocked the office door and flipped on the light.

"Nice. Jones men know how to live it up," Lovie said as we entered the room that mirrored my office, but smaller.

I picked up the notepad off his desk and handed it to him. "This is your login information. I've also included all of my login and passwords to the financial information."

"Great. Looks like everything's covered."

"So, you get settled and find me when you need me."

"Sure thing. Dad, have you told Jason about my new role?"

"No, in fact I was going to tell him today."

"Don't. I think under the circumstances, until I can find out what's going on, it's best that we keep this information in the family."

"But he's like family," I responded.

"Dad, if we're going to work together, you have to trust me. If not, then I'll leave now."

Lovie and I were the same height so we were eye to eye. "Fine. We'll do it your way, but if it doesn't work out, I'm pulling Jason in on this."

"Give me some time. I'm going to figure out where things went wrong and how we can start making a profit going further," Lovie assured me.

"My two favorite men." Lexi entered the room and gave me a quick hug and peck on the lips.

"I wasn't expecting to see you here," I said.

"I had to come see how Lovie's first day was going." Lexi walked over to Lovie and hugged him.

"Mom, you can't be doing that at the office."

"You'll always be my son and I can hug you whenever I want to."

"Dad, will you tell her that we have to keep this professional?"

I shook my head. "That's your mom. You know I can't tell her anything."

We all laughed.

My phone vibrated. I read the text. "I'm going to leave you two alone. My customer's waiting for me in my office."

I rushed back to my office and greeted the bereaved couple that was seated in front of my desk. "I want to thank you for entrusting RJ's with the burial of your loved one. We promise to make this as easy as we can on the family."

The grieving daughter spoke and handed me a check and the completed application. "Here's everything your assistant said we needed."

"Have you decided on what day yet?"

Her husband responded, "Saturday at one."

I checked the calendar to make sure there wasn't a scheduling conflict. "Saturday at one is fine. Don't worry about a thing." I glanced over the form. "If we need anything else, someone will give you a call."

The grieving daughter extended her hand out to mine. "Thank you. My mom spoke highly of you, so I wanted to honor her last wishes."

"Mrs. Berry was a pillar of the community. She will be missed," I responded.

I went over a few more preliminary items with the couple, then walked them out.

"I watched you with that couple. You're one of the most compassionate men I know," Shannon said.

"Shannon, when people come in here, they are already going through something. Remember, it is our job to be a light during a dismal time of their lives."

"Spoken like a true mortician," Shannon said.

"No, I'm speaking as a man who's been on the other side of the desk. Losing my mom at an early age and then my father, I know firsthand how grief feels."

"I admire how you deal with people. Sometimes my patience isn't what it should be." Shannon sat back behind her desk.

"You'll get there," I assured her.

I spent the next few hours getting bodies ready for family viewings.

CHAPTER 13

Charity

I'm still upset about not getting the job at the art gallery. But, my mom didn't raise a quitter. I wasn't going to put myself through the torture of interviewing with anyone else. I'm going to do something I should have done in the first place.

I logged on to the Internet and started researching ways to start my own business.

Hope burst in my room. "Sis, can I borrow your car?"

"You and this bad habit of not knocking are getting old. Respect my space."

"I respect your space. You're always in here by yourself. When you start having male company, I'll knock."

"Whatever." I continued surfing online without looking at Hope. "What's wrong with your car?"

"I'm low on gas and I don't feel like going by the gas station."

I looked up from my computer screen. "You got your nerve. You better dig into your pretty little pocket and buy your own gas."

Hope frowned. "You're such a mean older sister."

I threw the "talk to the hand" sign in the air. "Call me what you want, but you are not using my car."

"Fine. I'll leave you to doing whatever it is you're doing."

"I'm starting my own business. If you're nice, I'll let you be my assistant."

Hope rolled her neck. "I don't think so."

She left my room without shutting my door. I opened my mouth to say something to her, but decided to ignore her and went back to my research.

After spending another hour on the computer, I'd found everything I needed to get started. Mahogany Event Planning was about to be in business.

I hit the print button, but a red flashing box filled my screen. "Ugh. I hate when that happens." I was out of ink and I needed to print out the form so I could mail it in to register my business name.

I slipped on some shoes and rushed out to the office supply store. I wanted to get the form printed and in the mail no later than tomorrow.

"Excuse me," I said, when my basket accidentally bumped into a familiar face.

"So, we meet again." Tyler rubbed his leg.

"Sorry. I should have been looking where I was going."

"I'll forgive you, if you'll have dinner with me."

I couldn't think of an excuse. I did feel bad for hitting his leg with my cart. "Sure. Meet me at Copeland's. In fact, let's go now since I'm out."

He looked at his watch. "Now? It's only four o'clock."

"Now or never." I shrugged my shoulders.

"The lady wins. I'll meet you over there."

"Sure thing. I'll be on my way as soon as I pay for my stuff."

Twenty minutes later, I pulled up in the Copeland's parking lot. Tyler stood outside waiting for me.

"I thought you stood me up." He greeted me with a hug.

"No. I would have called you if I changed my mind," I assured him.

It'd been awhile since I'd gone out on a date. Things with my last boyfriend didn't end well, and honestly it was hard for me to trust men after that experience. Tyler came across as a smooth operator, so I knew I would have to keep my guard up with him.

"You're one of the most beautiful women I've ever had the pleasure of meeting," Tyler said.

"Thank you." I didn't know what else to say. Normally guys went crazy over Hope and her looks.

"I hope this won't be the last time we talk." Tyler looked at me like I was Miss America.

"It doesn't have to be." I tilted my head and batted my eyes.

"You have me at a disadvantage. You have my number, but I don't have yours. My phone's been glued to my hip waiting for your call."

I laughed out loud. "I'm sure you get plenty of calls."

He winked his eye. "But none were from you. You're who I want."

"Tyler, let's cut to the chase. You're a handsome man. I can tell from how you dress that you're doing quite well for yourself. Finding a woman isn't a problem for you."

"You're correct." He looked around the room. "I could have any woman in here, but Charity, I have eyes only for you. You are who I want."

The desire in his eyes made me squirm in my seat. I don't know if it's because it had been awhile since I had sex, or if he was just that doggone sexy. But at that moment in time, I wanted him. No, my body needed him.

❦

I threw caution to the wind and found myself tangled up in between some sheets at Tyler's place. I didn't come to my senses until he had my legs shaking for the umpteenth time.

"I hate to leave, but I need to get home." I didn't have to leave, but my body couldn't take any more.

Tyler stared at me with his big, brown, puppy dog eyes. "Don't tell me you have a man waiting for you at home." He placed his hand over his heart.

"No, there's nobody else. I have business to take care of, and I sort of let things get out of control."

Tyler kissed me on my naked shoulder. "I'm glad you did. I hope I can convince you to see me again. I don't want this to end."

"You're still glowing from the sex. Give it a day or two, and you'll forget all about me." I held on to the sheet to cover my body. I located my underwear and slipped them on.

Tyler gently brushed his fingers over my back, causing my body to shiver. "Promise me you'll call me when you get home."

"I promise. But, I won't be mad if you don't answer." I stood up and put my clothes on.

Tyler put on a pair of jogging pants and walked me out to my car, bare chested. He snuck in a kiss while holding my door open. I melted as I slid behind the wheel. My car seemed to be on auto-pilot as I drifted down the street toward home.

CHAPTER 14

Hope

I'd been calling this dude for the last few hours. I'd never been stood up before. I waited at the Horseshoe Casino lounge and Tyler never showed up. I'd expected to see Charity in her room, but she was nowhere to be found. It's a sad day when she's out having fun and I'm stuck at home bored.

"I got love on my mind," Charity sang as she passed by my bedroom.

"Hold up. Stop the presses. What is going on with you?" I rushed out of my room to confront her.

"Nothing. Just had the best evening of my life."

"Do tell," I asked.

"Let me take a shower and I might tell you. Then again, I might just keep it to myself." Charity went straight to the bathroom.

She was glowing and singing so she must have gotten some. What's wrong with this picture? A few minutes later, I heard the shower come on and her singing loud and off key.

My phone rang. I rushed back to my room and answered. "It's about time you called me back."

Tyler's raspy voice responded, "I can't always answer the phone. I was in a meeting."

"Oh. Why didn't you send me a text message? I waited at the Horseshoe for two hours."

"Business before pleasure," Tyler responded.

"Are you available now?" I asked. My sister couldn't be the only one jolly. I needed me a chocolate fix and Tyler was just the man to fulfill it.

"It depends on what you have in mind," Tyler responded.

"Invite me over and you'll find out."

"So it's like that?"

"That and then some, if you catch my drift." I licked my lips.

"The door will be unlocked. Just come on in."

Tyler gave me his address and directions. I put a few items in my purse then knocked on the bathroom door.

Charity opened the door. "What?"

"Just wanted to tell you that I was going out. You can turn the alarm on. I won't be back until tomorrow."

"Who is he this time?" she asked. She tightened up her robe and walked out of the bathroom.

"When you tell me who you're sleeping with, I'll tell you who I'm sleeping with."

"There's nothing to tell." Charity walked past me toward her room.

"Well, I'm out until the morning. Good night."

Tyler lived in an apartment complex not far from where I lived. I knocked and then turned the knob as instructed. I was greeted by the flickering of candles and rose petals. I followed the rose petals to the bedroom. There was Tyler, nude and lying across the king-sized bed. He looked like he could be the centerfold for a women's magazine. My eyes scanned him from head to toe. I removed my clothes while walking toward the bed.

He licked his big, juicy, brown lips. "I see you found me without any problems."

"You gave good directions." I reached behind my back to remove my bra.

Tyler took his hand and stopped me. "Let me."

Tyler pulled my lips on top of his. His hands removed my bra while our lips ravished each other. He gently pushed me down on the bed. His soft lips on my neck sent a chill down my spine. His kisses traveled down my body. He was awakening parts of me I never knew existed.

He gently tugged on my panties and pulled them off. He dipped his tongue into my cookie jar and made me scream out in pure ecstasy. He had my body singing its own songs. I was used to being in control, but Tyler was clearly in control of my body. A part of me tried to fight it. But, the more I fought it, the more intense the feeling got. Once I relinquished control, the floodgates of my desire filled his mouth and he lapped up every single drop.

With a satisfying smile and glistening face, Tyler reached over to his nightstand and picked up a condom. I tore the paper off and slid it on to his stiff, long manhood. Our eyes locked and he entered me with the precision of a skilled marksman. His tool was a perfect fit. Most young men couldn't go as long as Tyler. Tyler dipped in and out and 'round and 'round. He had me making all sorts of sounds. The bed rocked with the sway of our movements. Three condoms later, I laid on his chest in full bliss. A smile swept across my face as I closed my eyes and drifted off to sleep. For the first time ever, I was in love.

CHAPTER 15

Lovie

My eyes were glued to the computer screen. It'd been two weeks since I had access to the company files. Thus far, I'd come across a few questionable transactions, but nothing that warranted me talking to my dad about. I would need to dig a little deeper.

"Knock. Knock," my mom said, outside of my office door before walking in.

"Hi, Mom," I said, briefly looking up from the computer.

She stood behind me. "How's it going? Find anything yet?"

"Not yet. But if it's something there, I'll find it."

She went and shut the door. She eased into the seat in front of my desk. "Your dad's in with a customer, so we shouldn't be interrupted."

"What's on your mind?" I asked.

She slid to the edge of her seat. "I've been doing some checking myself. I now know why you're not too concerned about not getting a monthly allowance anymore."

I brushed the bottom of my chin. "I have nothing to hide. Everything I've done is legit. I told you I have clients."

"Baby boy, I wasn't always the fine, refined woman you see now. I grew up on the streets. I know the game. There's a thin line between what's legal and what's not, and you've been on that thin line for some time now from what I understand."

"You said all of that to say?" I asked.

"Boy, don't be getting smart with me. I can still beat your ass."

"Whoa. Mom, it's not that serious. What's on your mind? Spill it."

"Since some of your buddies are already in the business of eliminating people when they feel like it, I want you to make sure these families know about our services. We'll price match and offer discounts to avoid them going to one of our competitors."

I laughed. "Mom, I'm an accountant, not an advertiser."

"You'll be what I need you to be. I'm having brochures made. You just need to make sure they get out into the community. Give some of your associates some, or pay some kids in the neighborhoods a few bucks and get them distributed."

"Have you checked with Dad about this?"

"RJ's is as much mine as it is his. I don't need to check with him about anything."

"I don't think he's going to be too happy about these discounts you want to offer."

"Also, a reporter wants to interview the family for a feature on the evening news. I will let you know the date and time. I will need all of you present. We have to show the city that the Joneses are a united front."

I laughed. "Mom, you act we're the Ewings from Dallas or something."

"We are the Joneses of Shreveport and we have an image to uphold."

It wasn't that serious. My mom was too busy trying to fit in. I really didn't want to be a part of her plans. "I'll have the brochures passed out, but that's it. I'm not talking to my boys about doing anything else. I might be many things, but a criminal is not one of them."

"Son, you are the company you keep. You might not want to admit it to yourself, but if you're doing business for any one of your low-life friends, then you're just as guilty as they are in the crimes they commit."

My phone rang. "That's one of my low-life friends now. Mom, I'll talk to you later."

She stood up and pointed at me. "I'm counting on you."

I didn't respond to her. I gave the caller my undivided attention. "Slim, what's going on?"

"I got my girl calling you on the three way. They got me, Man."

I swiveled my chair around. "What you need?"

"Make sure my attorney gets paid. I need for you to give my girl a bank card for the account.'"

That was a code word for the bank account he had set up specifically for her to take care of his kids just in case something happened to him. It didn't house the majority of his money, but it was enough for her to live off on comfortably.

"I'm on it."

"LJ, don't give anybody any information. I don't care who they are," Slim said in a stern voice.

"My lips are sealed," I responded. I knew the rules of the street. I also knew Slim wasn't one to cross.

I had just hung up the phone when Shannon burst through my door. "Cuz, when are you going to hook me up with your boy, Slim?"

"Shannon, Slim's on vacation, so that'll have to wait. Besides, he has a girl."

"She's just his baby mama."

"I don't know why you want a thug like Slim when there are plenty of other guys who would love to go out with you."

"I heard Slim knows how to take care of his woman."

"Shannon, Slim's a player. He will chew you up, spit you out, and won't think second about it. But again, he's on vacation. Right now, freedom is on his mind not who he wants to hook up with next."

"Well, what about your boy, Big Willie?"

"Oh, hell no. Girl, you better chill out. Big Willie is known to beat his women. That's what you want? You want to get your ass beat?"

Shannon held her head down. "Those are just rumors. You can't believe everything you hear."

"I've seen him do it. I had to stop him from killing one girl. One more blow and she would have been one of our clients."

"So you don't have anybody you can introduce me to?"

"Actually, I do. His name is Stephen Carter and he just opened up a practice on Jewella. You need some counseling, and I'm sure he'll give me the friend discount."

I laughed. Shannon didn't. She left me alone.

CHAPTER 16

Lexi

The family, minus Hope, was in Royce's office. We were waiting on the reporter and her cameraman to set up in another part of the funeral home.

"Where is your sister? I told her not to be late." I brushed the stray hair I saw in Charity's head back with my hand.

Charity looked at her cell phone and responded, "I just got a text from her. She's on the way."

"Why is she texting and driving? I've told her about that," Royce said.

"That's your daughter." I sighed.

Shannon knocked and then walked in. "Maxine said they'll be ready to start filming in a few minutes."

"Come on, y'all." I looked at Shannon. "When Hope gets here, escort her back. I hope she's dressed appropriately. I don't have time to inspect her."

Shannon went back to the front desk, and we all walked to the room where Royce sometimes met with families to discuss funeral plans. Maxine and her cameraman were all set up.

Maxine looked at Royce and me. "We would like it if you two sat here." She pointed to the other chairs. "And if we could have your children sitting behind you. Wait, we're missing one, aren't we?"

"She'll be here any minute."

As if on cue, Hope burst through the door. "Sorry, I'm late."

Maxine greeted her with a smile. I rolled my eyes behind Maxine's back. Hope avoided eye contact with me. At least she was dressed in something decent. I wanted us all to wear shades of purple. Purple looked good on camera.

I looked at my family. Royce wore a pinstriped suit with a purple dress shirt and contrasting tie to match. My purple silk blouse matched his shirt; I made sure of it. Lovie left off his jacket and wore a light purple suit that complemented his Hershey-chocolate complexion well. Hope and Charity looked more like twins with the purple sleeveless dresses they wore. Hope's dress was shorter but decent.

Maxine said, "We're not live, so we may have to do several takes and that's okay. Don't be nervous. I want you to look at me when you respond. Any questions?"

We looked at each other. No one had any questions.

"Let's roll. On three," Maxine said.

The cameraman held out three fingers and counted down.

"This is Maxine Griffin, and tonight I have the pleasure of interviewing the owners of RJ Jones Funeral Home. They have been a pillar of the community for over fifty years. Royce, can you tell us a little bit about you and your family and how you've stayed in business so long?"

Royce made me proud. In a clear, baritone voice, he looked directly at Maxine. "Maxine, it's by the grace of God and the people we serve that we're here today. We treat our customers like people and not just numbers."

Maxine interjected, "Losing someone can be devastating."

"Exactly, and I feel it's very important that we offer our customers compassion during the difficult time of burying their loved ones."

"Mrs. Jones, can you tell me what your role is here at RJ Jones Funeral Home?"

"I don't have an official role, but I'm here just as much as any of his employees. I'm here to step in anywhere he needs me."

Royce stated, "Lexi has been very supportive over the years. If one of my employees is sick, she steps in. And, I can't count the times she's been there for grieving families."

I squeezed Royce's hand.

Maxine looked in Lovie's direction. "Are any of your kids working here with you?"

Royce responded, "Yes. I'm proud to announce that my son, Lovie, is working with me. He's been doing his own thing, but now he's working in the family business."

"Lovie, how has it been working with your father?"

With my plastered on smile, my eyes remained on Maxine as we all waited for Lovie's response.

"I'm doing my best to learn as much as I can. This is my legacy. I hope to carry on the family business when and if my dad retires."

Maxine looked at me. "Introduce these two beautiful young ladies."

"Maxine, these are my two daughters. Hope is the baby of the family. Charity has her own business, Mahogany Event Planning."

Royce added, "Hopefully, one day, Hope and Charity will be more active in the family business, but for now they are both doing their own thing."

Maxine asked a few more questions before turning to the camera and saying, "I would like to thank the Joneses for taking time to speak with me tonight. What a lovely family. Who wouldn't want to be like the Joneses? This is Maxine Griffin reporting from RJ Jones Funeral Home. Tune in tomorrow, I'll be reporting live from Mansfield."

The cameraman said, "That's a wrap."

Maxine turned to us. "Thank you. This should air tonight. I'll never forget how easy you made my mom's homegoing service, so I wanted to make sure I highlighted you during my hometown segment."

I shook her hand. "We appreciate it too."

Once Maxine and the cameraman were gone, I turned and faced my family with a sincere smile on my face. "Good job, everybody."

CHAPTER 17

Royce

Lexi insisted we watch our interview together. After pleasing my wife, I slipped out of the house to go hang out with Jason at our favorite bar. Growing up, people thought Jason and I were brothers because when you saw one, you usually saw the other.

"What made you decide to do the interview? I know you like keeping a low profile," Jason asked.

"A happy wife leads to a happy life," I said to Jason, as we talked about the interview that aired earlier.

"You did look good on there, man. Maybe that'll bring in more business." Jason nursed his drink.

"I hope so. I need to get Lexi out of my ear. If I can get her back in the stores, she'll quiet down."

Jason laughed. "I hear you. Well, why am I just finding out that Lovie's working with you?"

"I wanted to make sure he would stay around. You know kids are fickle."

"So, what is he doing? Don't tell me he's doing embalming."

"I'm teaching him the business. So, when I decide to retire or Lord forbid something happens to me, he'll be able to take over."

"Oh, okay. For a minute, I thought my job was in jeopardy."

"Oh, never that." I sipped my glass of bourbon slowly.

"Business is slow for me, too, so I'm trying to hold on to all my current clients."

"As long as I'm in business, you got my business," I assured him.

"Here's to many more years." Jason held his glass up.

I held my glass up and tapped his. I took a big gulp and motioned for the bartender to fill up my glass. I looked at my watch. "It's getting late. I better get home to my wife. She's in a good mood, and I want to take advantage of it."

I stood up but staggered a little.

Jason jumped up and assisted me standing up. "Maybe I should drive you home."

"I'm all right. Just needed to catch my balance."

"No, man. I'll drive you," Jason insisted.

I didn't feel drunk, but I didn't feel like arguing with Jason. So, I let him drive me home.

He pulled up in the driveway. "I got it from here," I said.

"I'm going to walk you in," he responded.

I fumbled with my key, opened the door, and staggered in. "Honey, I'm home."

I ran right into Lexi. Lexi fanned in front of her. "I could smell you before you said anything."

I sniffed. "Maybe I did drink more than I should have."

"Hi, Lexi," Jason said from behind me.

Lexi responded, "Thanks for driving him home."

"No problem. You know I always got his back."

"So you say," I thought I heard Lexi say but wasn't sure.

I felt the room spinning. I held my head.

"Do you need any help?" Jason asked.

Lexi responded for me. "I got it from here. Just make sure you lock the door on your way out."

I heard the front door close as Lexi led me up the stairs and to the bathroom.

"Baby, you need to control your drinking." Lexi assisted me in taking off my clothes. "It's becoming a problem if Jason has to drive you home."

"Just a one-time thing. We were celebrating. I feel confident after our interview that business is going to pick up. I can just feel it."

Lexi turned on the shower. "I'm surprised you can feel anything. Come on, let's finish getting you out of those clothes."

I did as instructed. I stepped in the shower. The hot water felt good hitting my body. "It's no fun being in here alone."

"The things I do for love." Lexi removed her clothes and hopped in the shower with me.

I closed my eyes as she took the towel and washed my back. I loved this woman with every pore in my body. We'd been through several rough patches in our marriage, but we'd overcome them. I would do anything to protect my marriage. Nothing and no one would come in between us.

Two hours later, we cuddled up in bed together. I may have been a little drunk, but I could still take care of my business. Lexi was lying in my arms sleeping hard and snoring loud.

I gently brushed my hand to move the hair from her eyes. She shifted but remained sleep. I kissed her. "I love you, baby."

I squeezed her tight and drifted off into my own dream world.

CHAPTER 18

Charity

If business kept picking up like this, I would have to give my mom a commission check. My phone had been ringing off the hook ever since she mentioned the name of my business during our interview. Good thing I had the foresight to put up a website and Facebook page. I checked the calendar on my iPad. I was booked for the next few months.

My first event was coming up soon. I needed to figure out which companies I wanted to partner with. I was not only looking for the best price, but for companies who prided themselves on providing good services. My reputation would be on the line. I could not fail. The success of my business depended on word of mouth.

I knocked on Hope's door. "Come in," she responded.

She was lying across her bed, looking up at the ceiling.

"So, do you have your half of the mortgage and the bills for the month?" I asked.

She got up off the bed, went to her purse, and counted out several hundred dollars. "Satisfied?"

"Where did you get this?" I placed the money in my bra.

"You should be happy that I have it to give you. That way you won't have to complain to dear ol' Mom about how you're taking care of your baby sister."

Hope plopped down on her bed.

"I'm just concerned about you. You're rarely at home these days, and contrary to what you may think I do care about you. I love you. You're my sister."

"We would get along a whole lot better if you didn't always try to control me. I have one mother. I don't need two."

"I take my role as the oldest very seriously. I'm only trying to teach you responsibility."

Hope laughed. "Please. You're just as spoiled as I am. When was the last time you had a real job?"

I remained silent. I refused to let Hope spoil my good mood.

Hope continued with her rant. "Exactly, so get off your soapbox, Sis."

I sighed. "The difference between you and me is that I don't mind working. No, up until now, I never had a real job but I've been working. My event planning business is off to a good start. Why not help me with it? You can be my assistant. I'll agree to pay you by the job and who knows? It may get to the point where I can pay you a salary. What do you say?"

Hope picked up her television remote and clicked the television on. "I'll think about it."

"What's there to think about? You need a job. I will need help with some of my stuff."

Hope rolled her eyes. "I said I'll think about it."

I softened the tone of my voice. "I know I tease you about being nothing but a pretty face. You're more than that. I got to go. I got a date tonight, so I'll be looking for your answer tomorrow."

I left Hope alone with her thoughts. I showered and met Tyler at his place. Tyler liked to pull disappearing acts, so instead of looking at him as being a viable love interest, I categorized him for what he was, a booty call. When I needed some sexual healing, he was my man.

I found myself laughing out loud every time he tried to convince me that he was so in love with me. His words went in one ear and out the other. Eventually, I would be ready to get into a relationship, but as for now, Tyler was my in-between time man. The go-to guy to scratch the itch. The one who could fulfill my sexual desires. Nothing more, nothing less.

Tyler greeted me with a long, sensual kiss. "How are you, sweetheart?"

"Just fine." I opened up my coat and let it fall to the floor revealing my glistening, naked body. I used a half bottle of body oil to make sure I would be soft and shiny.

Tyler scooped me up in his arms and carried me to his bed. "You came for business."

"I sure did. Now get on your knees, so I can feed you."

Tyler got on his knees as instructed. "I'm your genie. I'll make all of your wishes come true."

I opened up my legs and he ate me like he was at a buffet. I had no problem providing the main course. My body shivered in pleasure as I reached climax after climax.

With wet lips, he looked up at me. "Anything else, Madam?"

"Yes. I need you inside of me. Now."

He didn't hesitate to oblige me. Within minutes, he was dipping his latex-covered chocolate stick inside of me. I wrapped my legs around his waist as he dove deeper and deeper. I matched his movements with each stroke, bringing us both pleasure over and over again.

When it was all over, I took a quick shower, put on my long coat, and kissed Tyler on the cheek. "Thanks, we must do this again sometime."

"I wish you would stay."

"No, I don't think so. I'll call you later this week." I winked at him.

Tyler had this magnetic pull. Good chocolate could be addictive.

CHAPTER 19

Hope

Once again, Tyler ignored my calls. I don't know how much more of this I could take. He claimed he loved me and I was his girl, so his actions needed to line up with his words. I refused to be ignored.

I grabbed my keys and drove straight to his house. I beat on his door. "Open up, Tyler. I know you're in there. I saw your car."

Tyler, with a towel wrapped around his waist, opened up the door and pulled me inside. "Are you crazy? Knocking on my door like a madwoman."

"I've been trying to reach you. I know you got my messages. That phone stays glued to your hip."

"Some of us work. I just got home and out of the shower. Can a brother take a shower?"

"You could have called me when you got out of your meeting."

"If you must know, it was a conference call. Now sit in the living room and chill out. Let me go get dressed."

I wrapped my arm around his neck. "No need to get dressed. Since I'm here, we can do a little something something."

Tyler moved my hand from around his neck. "Not tonight. I'm tired. It's been a long day."

"But...," I pouted.

"Give me a few minutes. There's some wine in the fridge."

Tyler left me alone. I wasn't in the mood to drink anything, and

I wasn't hungry. I looked through his DVD collection and placed one in the DVD player.

It didn't take long for Tyler to dress. He took the remote from me and turned everything on. "Which one you got in there?"

"It's a scary movie," I responded.

For the next hour and a half, I felt content cuddling with my man on his couch watching a movie. I felt my body shake.

"What?" I said, as I stretched, unaware that I had dozed off.

"It's getting late. It's time for you to go," Tyler said.

"Why don't I just stay over? I'll leave in the morning." I snuggled up closer to him.

"No can do. I have an early meeting." He pushed me away.

"But, I'm still a little sleepy," I said.

"I can drive you home, but you're going home."

"Fine, but I can drive myself." I could barely breathe. I had to get out of there. I couldn't believe he was kicking me out of his apartment.

I jumped off the couch, grabbed my things, and stormed out of his apartment. I sped off and let out a scream as I drove home.

I was minutes away from home when my cell phone rang.

"Was just calling to make sure you made it home safely," Tyler said from the other end.

"I'm surprised you care, since you kicked me out."

"Hope, you have to learn that you can't always have your way."

"Good night, Tyler. I'm too tired to talk."

I hung up. He called me back, but I ignored his calls. I turned the volume up on the radio to drown out the sound of the phone.

I eased inside the house soon afterward. Charity's snores could be heard in the hallway. I went directly to my room and fell on top of the bed, wondering where I went wrong. I made the mistake of falling in love with Tyler before I could get him to fall in love with me. I wasn't used to being in this position. I didn't like feeling rejected. Is this how guys felt when I brushed them off? If so, it wasn't a good feeling at all.

I leaned back on my bed and plotted ways to get Tyler to fall in love with me. I knew the sex was good, so it had to be something else. I recalled my mom saying that a way to a man's heart was through his stomach. A light bulb went off in my head. Tyler had never tasted my cooking. I had to show him I had skills in other areas outside the bedroom.

The next day when Tyler got off, I was waiting for him with a basket full of home-cooked food.

"I should be mad at you," Tyler said, as he bit into my homemade rolls.

"Are you?" I asked with a mischievous grin on my face.

"It's hard to be upset when a sexy woman has provided you a home-cooked meal."

"If I had a key to your apartment, there would be more meals like this waiting for you."

Tyler laughed. "Maybe you can show me your breakfast skills."

"I sure can. So, that means I can stay tonight?"

Tyler moved his chair and patted his leg. I jumped out of my seat and sat down. "Ain't nobody leaving this camp tonight."

Tyler kissed me. The kiss started off slow but intensified. We ended up ruffling up his sheets. Our lovemaking session lasted for hours. I was exhausted, but he still had stamina.

He got out of the bed to take a shower. His cell phone rang several times. I tried to ignore it, but whoever it was wouldn't stop calling. I glanced at the phone and saw the name *Baby* on the display.

"What in the world?" I hurried up and hit the button to answer. "Hello?"

"Sorry, I must have the wrong number." An unfamiliar female voice was on the other end.

"No, you got the right number," I yelled.

"Who is this?" the caller asked.

"You called my man's number, so you tell me." I was livid.

"I don't have time to play games. Put Tyler on the phone."

"Tyler's busy. Coming, baby," I yelled out.

"Don't have me come over there and whoop your ass." The woman screamed in my ear.

"I dare you."

"Expect an ass whooping." The caller hung up.

I stormed in the bathroom and ran smack into Tyler.

"Slow down," he said.

I hit him on his chest. I shoved the phone in his face. "Who is Baby?"

Tyler grabbed the phone. "Why are you answering my phone?"

"Stop trying to avoid the question."

Tyler moved and dried himself off. "It's none of your business."

"Well, Ms. None of Your Business is on her way over here."

Tyler grabbed my clothes and threw them at me. "You need to go. Now!"

"I'm not going anywhere until you tell me who this woman is blowing up your phone."

"Hope, I'm warning you. You need to stay in your place and mind your own business. Now, I'm telling you nicely, get your stuff and get out of here."

My eyes watered. I kept telling myself, *I'm not going to cry*, over and over. Enraged, I got dressed. I sat in my car outside Tyler's apartment and waited. I needed to see the identity of this mystery woman. Tyler was my man, and I was not about to let her or anyone else mess up what we had going on.

I waited and waited, but nobody stopped by. I drifted off to sleep.

CHAPTER 20

Lovie

"Hello?" I answered the phone in a sleepy voice. It was after midnight.

"This Dre. I just saw Hope. She's sleeping in her car."

"Are you sure she's sleeping?"

"Yeah, man. She told me she was waiting outside for her boyfriend, but she was asleep when I first noticed her."

"Where did you see her at?"

While Dre talked, I put on my clothes.

"At the Bridgewood Apartments. Over here by the lake."

"I'm about to head that way now. Thanks for calling me to let me know."

"You want me to wait here until you get here?"

"No man, I got it."

It took me fifteen minutes to get to her location. I tapped on the window. Hope jumped.

She rolled down her window. "Lovie, what are you doing here?"

I leaned down. "I should be asking you that question. You're too pretty to be stalking some dude."

"I'm not stalking anyone. I was too sleepy to drive home, so I took a nap."

"Yeah, right. Who is he and do I need to go beat him up for hurting my baby sister?"

She laughed. "No. Everything's okay now. You don't have to worry about me."

"Start your car up. I'll follow you home."

"I don't need you tailing me."

"This is not up for discussion."

Hope stopped protesting, and I followed her home. Once she was inside, she flicked her bedroom light. Now that I knew she was inside safe and secure, I pulled out of the driveway.

Since I was out and wide awake, I decided to stop by my old place of employment, Bottoms Up, to see how things were going. I spoke to everyone as I made my way through the club toward the office.

Clarence sat behind his desk with one hand under the desk on his gun.

"Man, it's just me," I said, as I walked in.

"LJ, you know you need to announce yourself before entering. I was about to reach for my piece."

"How are things going?" I sat down in the chair across from him.

"Business is good. Several people have asked about you. Told them to reach out and touch you if they were that concerned."

"I've heard from a few people. But, you know in this game, it's out of sight, out of mind."

"You heard what happened to Slim?" Clarence asked.

"He might have to do some time, but he'll be all right." I picked up a candy bar on his desk and opened it.

"That leaves a market wide open, so you know what that means."

"Stay vested up because there's about to be some bloodshed." I thought about what my mom and I had discussed. I guess this is as good of a time as any. "You know I'm working with my pops now."

Clarence leaned back in his chair. "How is that working for you?"

"Boring, but easy money. At least I ain't got to watch my back. Dead people can't shoot back."

Clarence nodded his head up and down in agreement. "So what you need?"

"I want to drop off some company flyers. We're offering discounts on services."

"Man, you don't even have to ask. Leave some at the front. Shoot, I'll have an ad put on my website."

"I wouldn't ask, but I promised my mom I would help with the advertising."

"It's your family business, so do what you need to do."

"Glad you understand. I'm new to this."

"You always dress sharp, so it was just a matter of time before you gravitated toward your family business."

"Oh, you always got to joke with me about how I dress. Some guys dress in jeans or jogging suits; my style of dress has always been like this."

"You dress preppy, but you just as 'hood as I am."

"Don't let the suit fool you."

Clarence gave me a fist bump.

Someone knocked on the door. "Come in," Clarence said.

A waitress I hadn't seen before entered. "Mr. C, there's some people out here fighting."

We both looked through the two-way glass. Clarence jumped up, and put his gun in his waist. "Man, let me go handle this. I'll chat with you later."

I followed Clarence out of the room. He handled his business. I left so I could get a few hours of sleep before going in to the office. I also wanted to avoid any type of confrontation if Clarence couldn't get it under control.

CHAPTER 21

Lexi

Shannon called in sick, so Royce asked me to do her job until she felt well enough to return to work. I played the games *Words with Friends* and *Family Feud* in between answering the phones. I accessed the calendar and saw that we were booked for the entire week. For a funeral home business, that was good news. Business seemed to be going better.

Lovie rushed through the door. He stopped at the desk. "Mom, what are you doing here?"

"Shannon's not feeling well, so your dad needed me."

"Is he here yet?"

"He had an early funeral to attend to. What do you need?"

"I need to talk to him." Lovie seemed frustrated.

"Maybe I can help."

Lovie paused as if he was thinking. "I don't know. Maybe I should wait."

"If this is about the business, I have a right to know, too."

Lovie grabbed a chair and sat down next to me behind the desk. He repositioned items on Shannon's desk and placed his laptop on it. "Mom, I think Uncle Jason has been embezzling our money."

My mouth flew open. "That can't be. Royce told me he, not Jason, made some bad investments and that's why our funds are low." It made me question Royce's loyalty. *Would Royce cover up for Jason?*

"On the surface, it appears that way. But after going back over the books and checking the market for the dates listed on the printouts Jason provided, Dad didn't lose any money. In fact, he made at least a twenty-five percent increase on top of the money he originally invested."

I hit the desk with my fist. "Wait until I see that Jason. I'm going to kill him and then bury him in a pine box full of lead."

"Mom, calm down."

"Calm? How can I be calm? Your father trusted that man. How could he steal from us?"

Lovie looked at me. "We can alert the police about this, but if we do I doubt we'll get our money back. He's hidden the money in an offshore account."

"Jail is too good for him anyway. After I make him sign over his life insurance to me, I'm going to kill him." I thought of a thousand ways to kill Jason, but each one resulted in me getting caught.

"Mom, the last thing I need is for you to get yourself locked up. Let me and Dad handle this."

"I hate to say this, but I don't think Royce is going to believe you. I remember years ago I tried to tell Royce about something Jason did and he nearly bit my head off. I think this is something that you and I need to handle."

Lovie pointed at the computer screen. "This is the proof right here. He can't deny it."

"Son, trust me on this. I know your father better than you do. The only way he's going to believe it is if he hears Jason confessing with his own mouth."

"Oh, that can be arranged. Trust me," Lovie said.

I placed my hand on top of his. "I do not want you getting any of your thuggish friends involved in this. I can't lose you to the system in the process."

"Mom, I'm not a little boy who you have to cradle. I know how to handle things without getting caught."

"I want our money back, and I want Jason to pay and get out of our lives."

With confidence, Lovie said, "I will figure out a way to make it happen."

Lovie gathered his stuff and went to his office. It was hard for me to concentrate. Little did Lovie know, Jason's betrayal went far deeper than stealing money.

CHAPTER 22

Royce

This day hadn't gone well at all. I did my best to provide comfort to the families, but sometimes facilitating funerals back to back could be overwhelming; especially when having to bury a child.

Seeing Lexi sitting behind the receptionist desk reminded me of old times. My dad thought giving teens in the neighborhood jobs would keep them out of trouble. He'd seen something in Lexi that others didn't. He gave her a part-time job as a receptionist.

I smiled at the memory because for me, it was love at first sight.

Lexi greeted me with a hug and kiss. "You okay?" she asked.

"Let me wash up and we'll talk." I grabbed some extra clothes from one of the closets in my office and went into my personal bathroom.

After showering and changing, I walked back to the front of the building. "So, how have things been here at the office?" I leaned on the desk.

"The phones have been ringing steady. I counseled the couple you told me about. They will be using us to preside over their aunt's funeral."

"I appreciate you doing this for me today."

"Royce, you can count on me to always have your back."

"That's why I love you so much. You're one of the few people I can depend on."

Lexi tapped on the desk. "Before I forget, Shannon called. She's doing better, so she'll be in tomorrow."

"Too bad. I wanted to be able to see your pretty face all day."

Lexi blushed.

"Dad, we need to talk," Lovie walked up behind me and said.

"Lovie, he just got here. Whatever it is, can wait." Lexi shifted so Lovie could see her face.

"It won't take long," Lovie responded.

I turned and faced Lovie. "What is it, Son?"

Lovie looked at Lexi and remained tight lipped. I wondered what that was all about.

"What is it?" I repeated.

"I just wanted to let you know that I like being here. I'm glad you allowed me to work with you. I promise I won't let you down."

I patted Lovie on the back. "I'm glad you're here, too. You've proven to me you are a hard worker." I smiled. "You stopped dragging in after noon and started coming in on time."

"I admit that it was hard at first. It was an adjustment for me, but you got to remember I was used to working nights."

"True, that's why I didn't complain too much. But since you're standing here, I wanted to find out from you how the research was coming along."

Lexi started coughing out of control. "Mom, you all right?" Lovie asked.

"I'm fine. Somebody get me some water," she said, in between coughs.

I rushed to the water cooler and poured her some water. Lexi took a huge gulp. She placed her hand over her chest. "Thank you, baby. I'm all right now."

"You sure? I hope you're not coming down with what Shannon has. Lovie, go get some Lysol, so we can disinfect this desk."

Lovie did as I instructed. By the time all three of us sprayed and wiped off Shannon's desk, there shouldn't have been any germs left.

"Isn't this pretty? The Joneses working together."

We all looked up at the sound of Jason's voice. I reached out to greet him, but forgot I had gloves on.

"Jason, did we have a meeting?" I asked. I glanced at my watch. It was after three.

"No, I was just in the area and since I'm here, I wanted to go over your latest earnings."

"Cool. Lovie, come on. We can do it in my office."

Jason said, "This is something that we should discuss alone."

"Lovie's going to be taking over, so he might as well start being in on these meetings."

Jason seemed reluctant. He could run his business like he wanted, and I would run mine the way I deemed fit. Lovie would be in the meeting.

A few minutes later, we were all seated at the conference table. I glanced at the printed spreadsheet. I scratched my head. "Jason, explain this to me."

Jason looked between Lovie and me. "It's simple. I'm having to pull your money from your other account to pay for some of the losses resulting from the market failure."

Lovie said, "I'm looking at these numbers and they aren't adding up."

Jason said in a stern voice, "Son, I've been doing this for years. You just got your certification, so I think you better look at those numbers again."

"Uncle Jason, I mean no disrespect when I say this." Lovie placed the papers down in front of him and looked Jason directly in the eyes. "I think you and my dad need to separate your business relationship from your personal relationship. It is my recommendation that we terminate your services. There's no need to use you when I'm here."

Jason looked at me. "Royce, are you agreeing to this? We've been working together since I graduated from college."

I scratched my head. I wished Lovie had discussed this with me before firing Jason. I wasn't in total agreement with the decision. "Jason, I'll call you later."

Jason pushed away from the table. "I'm serious, man. This is some bull."

I stood up and walked Jason to the door. "You know how these youngsters are. They come in and think they can run everything." I patted him on the back. "We're cool. There won't be any changes."

"You need to let that boy know who is in charge. You or him."

"You're right."

Jason patted me on the shoulder. "Good. I'm glad we could work that out."

I watched Jason walk to his car. I turned and saw two sets of eyes on me.

"What?" I asked.

"Dad, I feel you're making a huge mistake."

"If I am, I take full responsibility. But remember, I, Royce Lee Jones, am the man in charge."

"But, Dad—" Lovie stuttered.

"Lexi, talk to your son. I got to get ready for another funeral."

I left them standing in the foyer as I prepared for the six o'clock funeral across town.

CHAPTER 23

Charity

Hope and I were in the living room with the television blasting. She seemed to be engrossed in her own little world on the opposite end of the couch. I flipped through the latest issue of a party planning magazine to get ideas for an upcoming event.

The doorbell rang. "Will you get that?" I asked.

"I'm not your personal servant," Hope responded.

"You're the closest."

Hope rolled her eyes, but got up to answer the door. She walked back in the room with Lovie on her heels.

"Good, you're both here," Lovie said, as he took a seat in the chair.

"If this is about me sleeping in the car, I promise you, it won't happen again," Hope blurted out.

"I'm missing something. When did this happen?" I stared at Hope.

"I'm sure Lovie came over to blast me about it."

"I came over here about something else." Lovie looked annoyed with Hope. "But since you brought it up, let's address it."

Hope looked back and forth between me and Lovie. "I got mad at this guy. I was too tired to drive home, so I took a quick nap. There's nothing more to tell."

"But in your car?" Lovie asked.

"I told you I was tired."

I ignored Hope and looked at Lovie. "Maybe you can get Hope

to tell you more about this mystery man. Every time I ask her something about him, she gives me a smart-aleck response."

"Oh, so here you go with the double teaming. Just in case you both don't realize this, I'm over twenty-one. In this country, that means I'm grown." She moved her neck. "And as a grown woman, I don't have to answer to either one of you." Hope crossed her arms and leaned back on the sofa.

Lovie leaned forward and looked directly at Hope. "The moment I got a phone call from my friend about you sleeping in the car is the moment your business became mine. Now, spill it."

Hope rolled her eyes. "This dude and I got into it. I think he's cheating on me, so I was waiting outside to see if this other woman was going to drop by."

Lovie didn't have to respond, I did. "Hope, if you got to do all of that, you don't need the man. You're beautiful. You're smart. You don't need that type of drama."

"I can't turn my feelings off and on like a faucet," she blurted out.

Lovie shook his head from side to side. "Don't tell me you're in love with this joker."

Hope's head fell down. "I didn't plan this."

"Who is he? Do we know him?" I asked.

"No. He's nobody you know. Until I find out for sure if he's cheating, I think it's best I keep his identity to myself."

"I'll let you handle it for now," Lovie responded. "Besides, there's something far more pressing I need to discuss with you two."

Lovie had my full attention. "You rarely stop by, so it must be important."

Lovie looked back and forth between Hope and me. "As you know, I've been working with Dad."

"If we didn't know, we would have to be under a rock. Mom talks about it all of the time," Charity said.

Lovie continued, "I found out some things that lead me to believe Uncle Jason has been embezzling money."

I almost fell out my seat. "Are you serious?"

"I wouldn't make these accusations if I didn't think they were true. I found it hard to believe myself."

I rubbed my temple. "How could he? What is Dad going to do?"

"Dad and I sort of got into it earlier. I fired Jason, but Dad didn't agree. So, I don't know what's going to happen."

Hope said, "You can't go around accusing a man without proof."

"I got all the proof I need. I'm not going to let that man steal any more of our money. Dad doesn't know this, but Uncle Jason is no longer authorized to make any type of transactions on RJ Jones Funeral Home's behalf."

"When he finds out, he's going to be pissed." I couldn't help but think about how this would affect Lovie and Dad's relationship. Things were going so well between the two of them.

"I'm not worried about it. Mom will handle Dad," Lovie responded.

I frowned. "I'm not going to be able to look at him the same anymore. He's like Dad's brother. This is the ultimate form of betrayal."

"That's why Dad's not looking at this situation objectively. He doesn't want to believe the man he's called a brother for over forty years is stealing from him."

Hope picked up her phone. "I'm going to call Dad now. He has to come around."

Lovie removed the phone from Hope's hand. "No. Let me handle this my way. I just wanted you two to know what was going on."

"He's the cause of all of our financial problems. I will never forget the embarrassment I felt when my credit card wouldn't go through that day at the store."

"Because of him, I've been stuck here in Shreveport. I can't remember the last time I took a trip with my friends. I can never forgive him for that." Hope pouted.

Lovie held up his hand. "I hate to break up your pity party, but it's past time for both of you to stand on your own two feet. What he has done was mess with our family legacy. Dad and Big Daddy worked hard to build RJ's and I will not let anyone tear down what took them decades to build."

"What do you plan on doing?" I asked, as I crossed my legs under me.

"Whatever it is, count me in on it," Hope added.

"The less details you know, the better. But know this, I'm on top of things. Dad's problems will soon be over. If things work out the way I want them to, all of his money will be returned." Lovie looked at me and then at Hope.

"And Uncle Jason will regret the day he decided to steal from the Joneses."

His words sent a chill down my spine.

CHAPTER 24

Hope

I was lying across my bed thinking about the bombshell Lovie dropped on us. My mind felt like it was going to explode. Uncle Jason had been a part of our lives forever. Maybe Lovie was mistaken. Uncle Jason couldn't be the crook he was making him out to be.

Charity walked in and sat in the chair near my bed. "So what do you think?"

I sat up in bed. "I don't know what to believe. Maybe Dad's right. Maybe Lovie is overreacting."

"Maybe Lovie is right and Uncle Jason is a thief."

"I hope he's wrong."

Charity shifted in her seat. "I didn't come in here to talk about him anyway. I came to address the issue with the man you claim you love."

"I do love him," I blurted out.

"Let's talk. I'm here."

I didn't know where to begin. "Everything has happened so fast."

Charity moved her chair closer. "Tell me about him. What is he like? Tell me the good stuff first and then we can address this cheating thing."

"He's older than me. He's almost thirty. He owns his own business. He adores me." I tilted my head. "I adore him and he's everything I want in a man." It felt good to finally be able to talk to someone about Tyler.

"On the surface he sounds fine, but earlier you mentioned you thought he was cheating. If he loves you, he wouldn't cheat on you," Charity responded.

"I think you're just bitter because of what Scotty did to you." I shifted on the bed.

"Let's not go there."

"You can't stand for someone else to be happy and in love."

Charity's hands flew up in the air. "If this guy was all of that, why haven't I met him? Why are you sleeping in cars? Ask yourself that."

"To answer your questions, I don't have a problem with you two meeting." I picked up my cell phone and sent Tyler a quick text message about dinner. "In fact, let's make it happen this week. We can meet for dinner."

"Fine. Give me a time and location and I'll be there," Charity responded in a sharp, harsh tone.

I placed one hand on my hip. "And another thing. I fell asleep. Don't you think it's best that I sleep in a parked car instead of trying to drive?"

"Whatever, Hope. I know what you said when Lovie was here. Heed these words. If you think he's cheating, nine times out of ten, he is. If he loves you, he wouldn't be cheating on you. Simple as that."

I stared at Charity without blinking once. "You and I both know love is not that simple."

"In my world, it is. Good night, Sis." Charity got up and left.

I dialed Tyler's number, but my calls were sent straight to voice mail. I located my keys and left the house without telling Charity. I got to Tyler's place in record speed.

I knocked on Tyler's door and waited and waited for him to answer. After what seemed like forever, he finally opened up. He looked as if he had been sleep, wearing nothing but his pajama bottoms. He rubbed his eyes. "Hope, what are you doing here?"

I walked past him and he shut the door.

"I've been trying to call you," I snapped.

"After we got through texting, I laid down and went to sleep."

"But my calls were sent directly to voicemail."

"My phone's on the charger. I turned it off before laying down."

"I don't believe you." I stood with my arms folded.

Tyler grabbed my arm and dragged me to his bedroom. The sheets on his bed were tousled. He picked up the phone and showed it to me. It was hooked up to his charger.

Embarrassed for my unnecessary outburst, I said, "I thought you were ignoring me again."

Tyler sat me down on the bed. "Hope, if we're going to be together, we have to have some level of trust."

"But—"

"But nothing. As I explained to you on the text message, Baby is my sister. That's her nickname and I make no apologies."

"She's the one who was acting like she was your woman."

"Baby is crazy like that. You had no business answering my phone. How would you like it if I answered your phone?"

"It wouldn't bother me. I have nothing to hide."

"You sure about that?" Tyler stared directly into my eyes.

I didn't blink. "Positive. Since we've been together, I have not been seeing other men."

Tyler wrapped his arm around my shoulders. "And I haven't been seeing other women. I'm just as committed to you as you are to me."

"That's good to know. For a minute, I thought you were playing games with me."

"You young girls have a lot to learn."

I ran my hand up and down my chest. "I'm all woman."

He looked me up and down. "That you are."

"This has been such a stressful day," I admitted.

Tyler planted kisses on the nape of my neck. "I can think of plenty of ways to relax you."

The only thing on my mind was pleasing Tyler. We undressed each other. He'd become my everything in such a short period of time. I wanted him. Correction, I needed him. I didn't want to go back to a life without him.

"Hope, I love you." He eased himself inside of me and we made love on top of his sheets.

I lay on his chest and drifted off to sleep. We slept that way until the next morning. I hated to leave him, but he had work to do and I had to figure out how to deal with Uncle Jason's betrayal.

CHAPTER 25

Lovie

Sleep didn't find me last night. I tossed and turned throughout the night. I slid on my shades. I exited my car and used my key to enter my parents' home.

"Lovie, is that you?" my mom yelled out.

"Yes. It's me," I responded.

"I'm in the kitchen."

The aroma of the food filled my nostrils as I entered the kitchen.

"Your dad's already left for work, so it's just the two of us," she said. "Take those shades off. This is not the club."

I did as instructed. Removing the shades exposed my puffy eyes.

"Did you pull an all-nighter? I told you to stay out of the clubs."

"No, Mom. This situation has me stressed." I took a seat at the kitchen table.

She placed a plate full of food in front of me. She sat at the opposite end of the table.

"I wanted to talk to you, but not at the funeral home. I didn't want to take a chance of our conversation being overheard." She poured two glasses of orange juice and handed me one.

I took a bite of my food first before talking. "Sorry about storming out yesterday, but the whole situation with Uncle Jason had me pissed."

"Your dad was still upset with you about giving Jason his walking papers. I tried to talk to Royce about it last night, but he didn't want to talk. He was in a better mood this morning, so hopefully he'll listen to reason now."

I drank some juice. "Uncle Jason's no longer authorized to make any more transactions on our behalf. I had his privileges revoked on all of our accounts."

"Royce is not going to like it when he finds out."

"I would rather deal with his rants than to see Jason steal any more money from us."

"I agree," she said. "I see business has increased, but it does no good to increase revenue if the money is being taken out as quick as we make it."

"Exactly. That's why I'm going to stop Jason. He's going to regret the day he decided to steal from us." The veins in my forehead were popping.

My mom placed her hands on top of mine. "Calm down. I plan to stop by Jason's office today. Let me talk to him. Let me see what's going on before you do anything."

I squinted my eyes. "For some reason, it seems like you're trying to take up for him, too. I thought you were with me? I thought you wanted him to pay too?"

"I do, but baby, Jason is someone that's been close to this family. We have to handle this situation delicately."

"My friends know exactly what to do to handle a thief."

"That's what I was afraid of. Do not, and I repeat do not, get any of your friends involved in our situation. You and I will handle this together," she assured me.

"I told Hope and Charity about Jason." I got up and put more meat and bread on my plate.

"See, this is what I was afraid of. You're going about this all wrong."

"They deserve to know that the man we call Uncle is a traitor."

"Maybe so, but I wish you would have waited."

"So, what do you suggest we do now?" I sat back down and went back to eating.

"We need to get Jason to confess."

"Men like Jason don't confess unless they feel like their life is threatened," I said.

"I got this. You just go smooth things out with Royce. Convince him that you two are the only two people who should be authorized to sign checks."

Less than an hour later, I was sitting in my father's office. I checked my Facebook page while waiting for him to end his phone call.

"Lovie, I don't have much time. I have a funeral to facilitate at eleven," he said, as soon as he hung up.

"I know you don't agree with me about Uncle Jason. But I think it's best that we be the only two authorized to sign checks."

"Son, I don't have time to handle that part. Business is picking up and I might have to hire some more workers."

"Fine, then let me take care of it. If it wasn't for you, I wouldn't be a CPA. Just look at it as your investment paying off. Well this time, anyway."

"Fine. I'll temporarily take him off the accounts. Don't make me regret this decision."

"You got a funeral to attend to. I'll take care of everything." I kept the fact that I'd already removed Jason from the accounts to myself.

We went our separate ways. I pulled out my cell phone. I got my mom's voicemail. "I got Dad to agree to take Jason off the accounts." I paused, but before hanging up I added, "Mom, whatever you plan on doing, please be careful."

The hairs on the back of my neck stood up as I ended the call.

CHAPTER 26

Lexi

"Ma'am, you can't go in there." Jason's receptionist stood up. She tried to block me from entering his office.

"He's been avoiding my calls all morning, and I will not be ignored." I pushed her out of the way and entered Jason's office.

"Lexi, what are you doing here?" Jason asked, looking up from his desk.

The young lady ran in behind me. "Mr. Milton, I tried to stop her, but she pushed me."

Jason looked at her and then at me. "That's okay. I'll see Mrs. Jones. Close the door on your way out."

"Should I call Security?" she asked.

Jason laughed. "Everything is fine here. Hold all of my calls."

I turned and faced her. "Yes. Hold all of his calls because we have some serious business to discuss."

I didn't wait on Jason to offer me a seat. I sat down in the chair directly across from his desk. I glanced around the room and admired the items that our money bought. Of course, when a person was spending someone else's money, they would buy top-of-the-line items. His walls were covered with expensive-looking paintings.

"Lexi, what brings you to my office?"

I crossed my leg, exposing some of my thigh. "Jason, you know exactly why I'm here."

"Just like Royce to send a woman to do a man's job. He's always been a little soft."

I clenched the arms of the chair. "Royce is more man than you will ever be."

"And you would know." I wanted to slap the sly grin off his face.

"I will regret that night for the rest of my life."

Jason licked his lips. "I still remember how good you tasted. Sweeter than honey."

I hit his desk with my fist. "Look. I didn't come over to reminisce about my biggest mistake. I came here to find out from you how long you thought you would be able to get away with stealing our money."

"Clearly, you've been drinking. Nobody's stole anything from anyone." Jason leaned back in his chair.

I eased to the edge of my seat. "I don't know how or how long it will take, but Jason, you will pay for what you did. I want our money back and with interest."

Jason leaned forward on his desk. "Dear, I'm not Royce."

"Clearly, you're not. Royce is a man of integrity."

"I know some things, but I'll keep them to myself."

"What do you mean?"

Jason rubbed his hands together. "You need to tell our son to back off."

"Excuse me?" I knew I must be hearing things.

"You heard me. Tell *our* son, to back off or your little secret will be exposed."

All of a sudden the room seemed smaller. The oxygen seemed to evaporate out of the air. I felt a panic attack coming on. It took everything within me to control my breathing. "You don't know what you're talking about."

Jason removed his wallet and pulled out two pictures. He placed them in front of me. "This is me when I was a baby." He pointed at the other picture. "This is Lovie. Now tell me Lovie isn't my son."

I opened up my mouth to speak, but nothing would come out at first. "Lovie is Royce's son."

"Are you sure about that? You know there's this thing called DNA."

"Jason, I'm warning you. You've already stole money from us, but you will not rob me of anything else. You got that?"

"And Lexi, I'm warning you. Either Lovie stays out of my business, or everyone will know that he's our love child."

"There's no love between us. I only put up with you because Royce loves you like a brother."

"His mistake, not mine."

"You've always been jealous of him, and he's been too blind to see it. I knew you were no good when you made a pass at me."

"I knew you were no good when you gave in to my advances."

I lost control and slapped Jason.

He grabbed my wrist. "That'll be the last time you put your hands on me."

I attempted to twist my arm away but was unsuccessful. "Let me go," I said, between clenched teeth.

"I know you're a little upset because your secret is not really a secret, but you better get a handle on your anger." He released my arm.

I rubbed my wrist with my other hand. "I came here to speak with you to see if we could come to some type of agreement. I see now that coming here was a huge mistake."

"Lexi, you have no room to negotiate with me. Sure, expose me. But, lose the man you claim to love in the process."

I stood up. "I can't wait for Royce to find out the type of man you really are. You're a snake, and it's about time someone chopped your head off."

"Many have tried, but I'm not going anywhere. Deal with it."

His receptionist burst through the door. "Is everything okay? I could hear you two arguing outside."

I looked at Jason and then at her. "Things are fine. I think our conversation here is over."

"Remember what I said. Let's keep this between us."

I threw my hands up in the air and hightailed it out of his office. I was fuming mad when I reached my car. Something needed to be done about Jason and fast.

CHAPTER 27

Royce

Today had been another busy day. Once I worked the last funeral, I decided to head to my favorite bar instead of going home. I sent Lexi a text message to let her know. Her response let me know she wasn't too happy about it, but oh well. She would be fine.

I needed to unwind and forget all of life's drama.

I scanned the room from my bar stool. The normal crowd filled the place. Men and women were talking and drinking. I turned my attention back to the drink sitting in front of me. It was my usual, a glass of bourbon with no ice, no soda, straight.

"Do you mind buying a thirsty lady a drink?" a woman in a short, tight red dress asked.

I shook my head. "I'm sure someone will be happy to, but I'm not the one."

"Aww, you come in here in your fancy suit. Think you all that."

Jason walked up to me. "There you go."

"Man, you rescued me just in time." I got up and walked with Jason to a table.

The woman was still talking as we walked away.

As soon as we sat down, Jason asked, "Have you talked to your wife today?"

"No. Haven't really had time. I had back-to-back funerals. After the last one, I headed straight here."

"She showed up at my office today causing a ruckus with my secretary. You need to handle her or else I will."

I'd been drinking, but I wasn't drunk enough to have any man disrespect my wife. "I'm sure she had a reason for coming to your office."

"She was quick to tell me that my services were no longer needed. What I want to know is why am I hearing it from her? You should've been man enough to come tell me yourself."

"I'm beginning to think what everyone else said is true. We should have never mixed business with our personal relationship."

"But I've been your accountant for the last fifteen years. All I'm saying is, you should have come and talked to me man to man."

"I didn't realize I needed to consult with you on how I chose to handle my business."

"We have a contract. So, you can't just take me off your account."

"Truth is, our contract expired several years ago. Neither one of us bothered to renew it." I looked at Jason as if daring him to disagree. "So Jason, please, let's just table this for now and enjoy the rest of our night."

"Maybe you can push it under the rug, but I feel like I'm getting the shaft."

I knew Jason would be upset, but I never thought he would pitch a tantrum. I looked at him. "I've had a long day. I'm not in the mood for no drama. If I wanted to deal with drama, I would've gone home to my wife."

Jason slammed his glass on the table and left.

Lovie walked up to the table. "Looks like Uncle Jason is a little upset."

"He wasn't too happy about being let go."

"If he's innocent, then he'll be cleared."

"It's a complete mess. I hope you hurry up and finish your investigation, so things can get back to normal around here. I'm sick and tired of all of this. Money is important, but it's not worth me losing my friends and loved ones over."

Lovie got the waiters attention and then took a seat. "Get him another bourbon and bring me a glass of Cîroc."

Lovie looked at me and said, "Let me deal with Uncle Jason. Concentrate on the other part of the business. I got this."

"It's hard. I'm not used to giving up control."

"You trusted Jason with everything. I'm just asking you to trust me to figure out a way to recoup your money."

I took a drink. "Have you talked to your mom today?"

"Not since this morning."

"According to Jason, she caused a scene at his office."

"You know Mom. She can be a little over dramatic at times."

"Don't I know it. Her and your sisters."

We both laughed.

I looked up just in time to see Jason look in my direction, turn, and storm out of the bar.

CHAPTER 28

Charity

With my family drama, I needed a reprieve. So, after stopping by Tyler's last night, I decided to spend the night for the first time.

Tyler walked in with a tray of food. "Breakfast in bed for my queen."

He sat the tray over my lap. He sat beside me and fed me grapes. "Charity, what do I have to do to convince you that I'm sincere?"

After swallowing the grapes, I responded, "Right now, I'm trying to build my business. I don't have time for a relationship. Besides, most men would be happy with our arrangement."

"I'm not most men."

I gently brushed his face with the palm of my hand. "If you decide to see someone else, please let me know. I don't want to be the side chick. I would rather preserve our relationship and just be friends if it comes to that."

"If I decide to commit to anyone else, you'll be the first to know."

I twisted my head with a "yeah, right" expression on my face.

He added, "Well, the third person to know."

"Exactly. Don't be like some men, who try to have their cake, icing, and pie."

Tyler licked his lips. "All this talk of sweets got me hungry."

Tyler removed the tray of food and placed it on the floor beside him. He eased his head under the covers, and I became his morning dessert. No complaints from me because I was enjoying every minute of it. He had all the muscles in my body responding to the sensation of his tongue.

Two hours later, I was in the shower at my own place. I couldn't help but smile as I thought about my morning escapade with Tyler. He was becoming an addiction. More addictive than a box of chocolates. I might not want to be in a relationship with him, but I sure didn't want to give up our sexual encounters. I hoped it would be a very long time before he got into a serious relationship. Needless to say, my two-year drought was over and I didn't want it to end anytime soon.

I dried off and put my clothes on. I heard something that sounded like Hope crying. I eased her door open and saw her laid across her bed in tears. I rushed to the bed. "What's wrong?"

"Nothing. Every man I trust end up lying to me."

I patted Hope on the back. "It'll be okay. What did your man do this time?" I still didn't like the fact that I hadn't met him.

Hope looked up at me with puffy, red eyes. "I called him all night and he never returned my calls. I promised myself I wouldn't run over to his place, but maybe I should have. That way I would know for sure if he's cheating on me."

"Hope, I've told you if he was really in love with you he wouldn't be putting you through all of these changes. You should reconsider this relationship, and think about getting out while you still can."

Hope sat up in bed. "I've tried. It's something about him that won't let me stop loving him. Now I see what all the guys go through who confess their love for me."

I laughed.

Hope didn't see anything funny.

I grabbed her by the shoulder and made her look at me. "Are

you serious? Girl, you're a Jones. We may fall down, but we dust ourselves off and we get back into life. Don't let this man take any more from you than he already has."

"For the first time, I experienced a real orgasm," Hope confessed.

"That explains it. You're not in love. You just love how he makes your body feel."

"No, it's more than that. We have this connection. It's hard to explain." She looked down.

"Hope, look at me."

Hope looked up. I continued. "Trust me, he is not the only man capable of making your toes curl and your body tremble. You might find better."

"But, I want him."

"Just from what you've shared about him, he is clearly not the one for you."

"Would you be saying that if Scotty hadn't broken off your engagement?"

Ouch. She wanted to hit below the belt. Little did she know I'd come to terms with the demise of my relationship with Scotty a long time ago. I was naive like her then. "My friend Lisa tried to warn me about Scotty, but like you I ignored her. I wish I hadn't because it would have saved me heartache and grief."

"But he is nothing like your Scotty. When we're together, he makes me feel like I'm the only woman in the world."

"You've been warned. I hope you're using protection. The last thing you need is to get pregnant by this dude."

"We are, but he did want us to start sleeping together without one," she confessed.

"If you don't listen to anything else I've told you, please listen to this. Do not, and I repeat, do not sleep with him without protection. There's disease. You could get pregnant. Trust me on this. Please."

"Fine. I will always use protection."

I sighed. "Good. I hope I'm wrong about everything else. I still want to meet him, so make it happen and soon."

I got up and left Hope alone to deal with her feelings. I'd spent too much time on personal things. It was almost noon and I needed to get focused on planning my next event.

CHAPTER 29

Hope

Tyler seemed to think because I was younger than him, he could continue to string me along. He needed to know there were plenty of men who wished they were in his position. I refused to spend another night alone crying over him.

Tyler finally returned my call. We argued right away. He snapped at me. "Hope, you need to grow up. Better yet, get a job like the rest of us, and you'll understand why I'm not always available to you when you call."

"T, that's bull and you know it. You have access to text and email. It doesn't take but a second to respond."

"I'm not going to be rude in front of a customer and text you back."

I threw my hand up in the air. "Whatever. Call me when you can fit me into your busy schedule."

I clicked the end button on my phone. Tyler called back, and I sent each call to voice mail. Two could play that game. Like Charity reminded me, *I'm a Jones and Mama didn't raise no fool.*

I sent a quick text to someone, and got dressed in a violet pant suit with purple alligator-printed heels. I grabbed my matching designer clutch and drove to the other side of town.

"Ms. Jones, here's your key," the clerk at the front desk of the Horseshoe Casino said.

The hotel suite's bar was filled with food and drinks. I hadn't eaten anything all day, so I chose a sandwich and sat at the table while waiting on my guest to arrive.

An hour later, I heard a knock at the door. By this time, I'd become relaxed. I'd removed my shoes and was watching one of my favorite soap operas. I placed the television on mute and went to the door. I looked through the peephole before opening.

Jason walked in and attempted to hug me, but I moved. "What's wrong with you?" he asked.

"You're late," I responded.

"I was actually surprised to hear from you. It's been a few months."

Jason attempted to kiss me. His lips were met with the back of my hand as I blocked him. I sat down on the couch. He sat next to me. I scooted toward the other end.

"What's with the attitude? You called me." Jason popped his knuckles.

"This was a mistake. Our whole relationship has been a mistake," I blurted out.

"You've been listening to your brother, haven't you?" Jason said.

"No, this has been wrong from day one. I shouldn't have ever allowed our relationship to get to this point. If my parents ever find out, they are going to be so disappointed in me." Tears formed in the crevices of my eyes.

Jason placed his hand on my knee. "Haven't I always been good to you? Whatever you wanted, I made sure you had. Who has been keeping money in your pockets? Wasn't I the one you called when your dear ol' Dad cut off your credit cards?"

"Yes, Jason, you've been good to me. But, come on. What we've been doing is wrong."

"You were an adult when our love affair started, so don't get it twisted."

"Barely. I was eighteen when you took advantage of me."

Jason laughed. "Dear, you came on to me first. I'd tried to ignore your advances, but I'm a man. You caught me at a weak moment."

He was delusional. His recollection of things was way different than mine. I recalled the time we had our first sexual encounter. He'd financed a trip to Dallas for me and some friends. He conveniently was in the Dallas area at the same time. While my friends were busy doing their thing, he invited me up to his room. The next thing I knew, he'd given me a few drinks, and we were having sex.

Instead of being ashamed of what we had done, our relationship had continued off and on since. We were good at hiding our attraction to one another. At first, I was with him because of the admiration I'd always had for him, and I was able to live a childhood fantasy. The relationship then became more of a business transaction for me. Whenever we slept together, he was more generous to me with gifts and cash.

A part of me was ashamed of what I'd done. I came close to confessing our relationship the other night to Lovie and Charity, but was too embarrassed to bring it up.

"Jason, let's keep it real. If my dad ever found out you've been sleeping with me, he would kill you. And don't let my mom get a whiff of it. You would definitely be good as dead."

Jason gripped my knee. "That's something you don't want to do. You forgot about the videos we made. If you tell, I will make sure they are uploaded on the Internet." He chuckled. "With a body like yours, your videos would be an overnight hit."

I hit his hand off my knee. "You're sick. I regret the day I ever let you touch me."

Jason shifted his body and leaned over me. "Don't be that way."

"No. I don't want to do this with you anymore."

Jason kissed me. I bit his lip. He raised his hand to hit me, but stopped. "Ooh, Hope, you're pissing me off."

I pushed myself up from under him and stood up. "I think you should leave."

"I'm the one paying for this room. I'm not going anywhere."

"Fine, then I'll leave." I picked up my shoes and my handbag.

He blocked the doorway. I could feel his hot breath in my face. "Remember what I said. Keep this our little secret, or else."

I couldn't leave the room fast enough.

CHAPTER 30

Lovie

Slim was one of the luckiest men I knew. After only being in jail for a short period of time, he was back out on the streets. He wanted to meet with me so I could give him an update on how his finances were looking.

We met at the club like we normally do. This time, it was during the day and without his normal entourage.

"I'm glad I was smart enough to use you. The government seized the rest of my money, but thanks to you I'm still a rich man," Slim said.

"That's what friends are for," I responded.

"You were always the smartest in our class."

"Thanks to you, I didn't have to worry about anyone trying to beat me up."

We continued our trip down memory lane for a few minutes before returning to the present.

Slim took a puff of his cigar and blew out smoke. "Word on the street is that your Uncle Jason has been stealing money from some of his clients. One of them came to me. Out of respect for you, I wanted to talk to you about it."

I looked Slim straight in the eyes. "Between you and me, ain't no love lost between the two of us. That's his business, not mine."

"Word. Well, fam, you know we look after each other. Just wanted to clear it with you."

Under normal circumstances, I would have tried to convince Slim to let it go. Not this time. His situation didn't have anything to do with me. I glanced at my watch. "Man, I'm supposed to meet my mom, so I'd better go. If I'm late, I'll have to hear her mouth."

"Understood." We gave each other a fist bump.

Thirty minutes later, I was sitting on the couch at my parents' house. My mom paced back and forth in front of the fireplace.

"Mom, you're going to wear a hole in the carpet if you don't stop. Come sit down, and tell me why you needed to see me." I patted the couch next to me.

She stopped pacing. Her forehead wrinkled with stress. She blurted out, "It's Jason. He's going to be a big problem."

"What do you mean?"

"I need you to promise me something." She walked and sat next to me.

"I can't do that until you tell me what it is."

"I need for you to promise me that what I am about to tell you will remain between the two of us. That means, don't repeat this to your sisters." She paused. "And, definitely don't share this with Royce."

There wasn't anything I wouldn't do for my mom, so I responded, "Sure, Mom. I promise. Now what is it?"

"Your Uncle Jason wants me to convince you to back off. He basically threatened to tell your father something if I didn't."

"In other words, he's trying to blackmail you."

"Exactly. I love Royce, and I won't let anything come between us. I do mean anything."

"Looks like I need to pay dear old Uncle Jason a house call."

"No. You need to stay away from him. I'm going to deal with him."

"Mom, that's what you told me earlier. Now he's threatening

you. What does he have over you that could destroy your relationship with Dad?"

Her eyes shifted away. Her head drooped down. "I'm ashamed to say."

"Please tell me it's not what I think it is." I bit my bottom lip.

"It only happened once, but I regret it happened at all."

I didn't know how to take this information. I couldn't believe my mom cheated on my dad. If my dad found out, it would kill him. I looked away. "How could you? Dad's given you everything."

"Son, it was during a time your father and I were having problems. He was taking weekend trips. It would be days before I knew where he was. Jason, of course, was always around to offer a shoulder to cry on. One night, he made a pass at me. In my vulnerable state, I allowed things to get out of control."

"But, that's no excuse."

"You're right. There's no excuse for me allowing it to happen. You don't know how many times I've beat myself up about it."

"Sleeping with your man's woman is a serious violation." The veins in my forehead tensed up.

"I tried to tell your dad that Jason couldn't be trusted, but he wouldn't listen to me. So over the years, I've pushed the incident to the back of my mind and dealt with Jason because he's your dad's best friend."

"I have one question. Did he lay his hands on you when you confronted him at his office the other day?"

"No, dear." I could tell she was lying. She continued to say, "But he did threaten to expose what happened between us to your father."

"Not on my watch he won't." I got up and stormed toward the door.

My mom grabbed my arm, but I jerked it away. "Please, don't. Just leave it alone," she begged.

"He's not going to get away with blackmailing you."

"Lovie!" she shouted out as I rushed to my car.

It was still early, so Jason would still be at his office. I sat and waited in the parking lot until he came out of the building. I eased my car behind his and followed him home without him noticing me. I ignored my mom's phone calls and text messages.

I waited for him to go inside before parking my car behind his. I got out and rang his doorbell.

He opened the door. "Lovie, what are you doing here?"

"We need to talk."

He opened the screen door. As soon as I got inside, I pulled back my arm and smacked him in the mouth with my fist. He wobbled and fell back. "That's for threatening my mom." I hit him again in the face. "That's for stealing from my family."

Blood dripped from his bottom lip onto the front of his suit. I let go of his collar, and he hit the floor. As I left out the front door, Jason yelled, "You and that ratchet mom of yours are going to pay for this."

I shook my fist. It hurt a little bit, but the satisfaction of punching him eased the pain. The only thing that saved him from me putting a bullet between his beady eyes was the vision of my mom having to visit me behind bars.

CHAPTER 31

Lexi

Lovie wouldn't answer his phone. I was beginning to worry. I decided to cook dinner to keep my mind occupied. Royce strolled in after eight o'clock. I ended up having to microwave his food.

He sat in his favorite chair in the den. He looked up at me with appreciative eyes as I handed him his plate. "Lexi, I appreciate you. I really do."

"I know you do," I responded.

"I'm serious. You take care of the house. You try to keep our family together. You make sure I have what I need."

"I'm just doing what any good wife and mother would do." I took a seat in the nearby chair.

"This issue with Jason and the money has me stressing out. I'm sorry I haven't been myself lately."

"Don't worry about Jason. He'll get over it," I tried to assure him.

"He feels I'm cheating him out of work."

I laughed. "The gall of him. He's been cheating us out of money. I say turn him into the police and let them deal with him."

"It's not that simple. Lovie doesn't have concrete proof yet. I want to make sure before I go around accusing anyone." I rolled my eyes as I listened to Royce continue his praises. "Jason's been a good friend to me over the years, and I would hate to ruin his reputation because of speculation."

I shifted in my seat so I could see Royce's face. "That's just it. Jason is not the friend you think he is. He's always been jealous of you, but for some reason you have this blind loyalty. You're loyal to him, but Jason's never been loyal to you."

"I'm a pretty good judge of character. I would know if Jason wasn't the friend you claimed he's not. I don't know why you don't like him. He's done nothing but be nice to you and the kids."

I shook my head in disbelief. Frustrated and confused about which direction to go in, I changed the subject. "I know this sounds morbid, but I'm glad business has picked up."

"That's the thing about being in the funeral home business. Someone has to die in order to make money."

"It's part of life, so we might as well benefit from it."

"Lexi Marie Jones, you can be so cold."

"I'm just saying. We are born. We live. We die. It's just a part of life."

"You sound like my daddy."

"He was a wise man." I picked up a magazine and flipped idly through it.

"That he was."

My cell phone rang. I glanced at it and saw Jason's number on the display. I hit the ignore button. Jason called back.

Royce said, "Whoever that is really wants to talk to you. Maybe you should answer."

"It's nobody important. They can wait."

Royce's cell phone rang. He looked at it. "Speaking of the devil. Guess who this is?"

I had a good suspicion I knew exactly who it was. I closed my eyes and said a silent prayer. I prayed Jason would keep his big mouth shut.

Royce hung up the phone. "Jason's on his way over."

I tried not to panic. "I thought tonight it would just be me and you. You know, so we could do what married couples do?"

"After he leaves, it'll be on. So I hope you took your vitamins today." Royce winked his right eye.

I took the empty plate from Royce and went to wash dishes. By the time I was finished, I heard Royce letting Jason into the house. Their voices got lower and lower so that meant Royce was leading Jason into the living room.

I dried my hands off and walked toward the living room. Instead of going inside, I stood outside the door.

"Jason, I'm glad you reached out. I was hoping this ordeal wouldn't interfere with our friendship."

"No, man. I just had a lot on my mind. I overreacted. Forgive me," Jason responded.

"We cool as far as I'm concerned."

"Good, because I would hate to lose your friendship over something as small as this."

"I trust you. How long have we known each other?" Royce asked.

"Practically all of our lives."

"Exactly. That's why a little misunderstanding is nothing. Blood brothers for life remember."

I peeked inside. Jason nodded his head. "For life."

I wanted to knock the smug look off Jason's face. I walked in. "Oh, Jason, you're here." Jason looked like someone had beat me to the punch. His lip was bruised and swollen. "What happened to your lip?"

"As I was telling Royce when I got here, I got into a little altercation with someone, but I'm alright."

"Maybe you should get that looked at."

Royce cleared his throat. "Dear, do you mind getting something out of the medicine cabinet and doctoring on him?"

I blinked my eyes several times. "Actually, I do. I'm not a nurse. I'm sure he has insurance. There are several hospitals between his house and ours."

"Lexi, you don't have to be so cruel."

Jason said, "Man, that's okay. I'm fine. Let Lexi go do her thing and we can get back to talking."

He wasn't going to get rid of me that easy. This was my house, and I wasn't going anywhere. I picked up a magazine off the coffee table and took a seat in one of the chairs. I leaned back, crossed my legs, and opened up the magazine as if I was really interested in what was going on in the world of entertainment.

My cell phone vibrated. It was a text message from Lovie. Now I knew the identity of the person who gave Jason that fat, lower lip. I laughed out loud. I should have been mad at Lovie for disobeying me, but I wasn't.

CHAPTER 32

Royce

I looked at Lexi. She didn't look too pleased with Jason's intrusion into our private time. Jason didn't appear to be leaving any time soon. I needed to get him out.

I yawned. "Jason, I hate to end this night, but I have a full day ahead of me. I want to retire early."

Jason looked at me and then at Lexi. "I guess I've overstayed my welcome."

Lexi, without looking up from her magazine, responded, "I guess so."

"Let me walk you out," I said.

I walked Jason to the door. Before leaving, Jason turned and asked, "Is everything okay with Lexi? She seemed cold and distant."

"She's probably PMS-ing. I just go with the flow, man."

"Well, I just wanted to make sure everything was okay between the two of you."

Lexi walked up behind me and placed her arm around my waist. "Things are great. Good night, Jason."

Jason looked at Lexi. "Oh. I didn't see you there."

"We'll talk later," I assured him.

"We sure will. There's something else I need to talk to you about." He was talking to me, but he kept looking at Lexi.

Jason left. I shut the door and faced Lexi. "Jason is right about one thing. You've been a little distant ever since he came over tonight."

"I don't trust him, and I do not want him in my house anymore."

"This is my house, too, and I have a say-so about who comes and goes just like you do."

"Fine. You can sleep in the guest room tonight because all of a sudden, I'm no longer in the mood."

Lexi stormed off, leaving me looking bewildered and confused. I was frustrated and horny. This was going to be a long night.

❦

I tossed and turned the entire night. I dragged myself out of bed the next morning. I smelled the aroma of breakfast cooking, which usually meant Lexi was in a good mood.

"Hi, baby," I said, as I walked up to her at the stove and gave her a quick peck on the lips. She didn't hit me, so that was a good sign.

"Sorry that I overreacted last night," she responded. "How did you sleep?"

I rubbed my lower back. "My back will probably be hurting all day."

"I'm sorry." She stuck out her lips and pouted. "I am trying to make it up to you."

I poured a cup of coffee and sat at the table. Lexi placed a big plate of food in front of me. "Homemade biscuits. You are forgiven."

The biscuits melted in my mouth. She fixed a smaller portion for herself and sat next to me.

"So, what's on your agenda today?" she asked in between bites.

"Back-to-back funerals, again. I need to hire at least three or four more people."

"I'm on it. I'll see who I can find and set up some interviews," Lexi responded.

That's what I liked about Lexi. I just told her what needed to be done, and she took care of it for me. We had our little system going. She wasn't at the funeral home every day, but she still contributed to the business. I didn't have an official Human Resources department. There was no need to since Lexi was good at handling my staffing needs.

I finished eating and instead of going to the funeral home, I met some of my staff at a church on the other side of town. After the funerals, I was feeling a little depressed. Some days at work were better than others, and this was one of those days where words eluded me.

"Royce, do you want me to lock up? I'm about to leave for today," Shannon walked to my door and said.

"No, I got it. Be careful out there."

"I will. Mama said call her. She wants you and Lexi to come by for dinner one weekend."

"Okay," I responded.

As soon as Shannon left, I got my cell phone and synched the office calendar with my phone's calendar.

"So this is where 'The Man' spends his days?" a familiar voice said, startling me.

I looked up. "Tyler, is that you?"

Tyler stood in the doorway but didn't make any move to come inside. His unfriendly stance took me by surprise. "I'm surprised you know who I am."

"Come on in." I pointed to the chair. "Have a seat. I'm glad to see you."

Tyler looked around my office before taking a seat. "Nice." He picked up the frame that enclosed a recent family photo. "So this is your other family?"

I took the frame from his hand and placed it closer to me. "Yes. How's your mom doing?"

"Like you really care. But since you asked, she died." He stared at me with cold black eyes. "She died six months ago."

My heart ached with pain. "Why didn't you call me? I would have been there. What happened?"

"You happened. The day you left us, pieces of my mom died, and she was never the same."

"I don't understand. Whenever I spoke with her, she seemed okay."

Tyler slammed his fist down on my desk. "That's just it. You couldn't leave her alone. She may have been okay if you would have stopped contacting her. She hoped after each phone call that you would come visit her, but you never did. Broken promises are what broke her heart."

"Tyler, you don't understand. I cared about your mom, but what we were doing was wrong. I already had a wife and family. And regardless of how it looked, I loved my wife, and still do. Your mom knew the deal going in. She knew I would never leave my wife and family behind for her."

"That's the thing, my mom never asked you to. You just took it upon yourself to cut her out of your life. When your phone calls stopped, she started drinking. She became a shell of herself. Do you know how helpless I felt to watch her kill herself with alcohol because of you?"

"The last time I talked to her, she told me she was going to get married. That's when I decided it was best to cut off all forms of communication."

Tyler laughed. "Married? I doubt if she even talked to another man after you."

"I swear. I didn't know. I believed her. I was only trying to do the right thing."

"The right thing would have been to leave her alone. You were married, so you shouldn't have ever started something with her. And to make things worse, you were around so much, I began to think you were my dad."

"Son, I'm sorry."

"Yes, keep calling me Son. Who knows, I might become your son for real."

"What do you mean?"

"Let's just say, I have a dilemma." He paused. "I don't know which one of your beautiful daughters I want to be my wife. Maybe Hope. She's trainable. She pretends to know the ways of the world, but she's no match for me."

I didn't know what kind of game Tyler was trying to play, but he was going to leave my girls out of it. "What do you want? Is it money? I can write you a check."

Tyler stood up. "I want you to pay. I'm going to destroy your life like you destroyed mine." He tossed a business card on my desk and walked out.

CHAPTER 33

Charity

"Dad, what are you doing here?" I asked, surprised to see him at my door.

He gave me a hug and kiss on the cheek. "I can't stop by to check on my girls?"

"Of course, but we normally meet up at home or stop by the funeral home."

"I wanted to catch up with you." He followed me into the house.

"Well, Hope's not here."

"Do you know where she is?"

"No, she didn't tell me. We only tell each other when we're not coming home for the night."

I put my hand up to my ears. "I don't know if I want to hear this."

"Don't ask a question you don't want to know the answer to," I said, as I looped my arm through his, and we walked to the living room.

I picked up a folder with some information about my business and handed it to him. "I'm glad you're here. Some people may need help planning a repast, and I plan to offer all types of services. So, I was wondering if you could include some of my information in your packets?"

He glanced at the material. "Of course. That sounds like a good idea."

"I know most families have friends, family, or church members cooking, but then you get clients who don't, so I want to be a resource for them."

"I'm so proud of you. You are really taking this seriously."

"I just hate it took you losing money for me to come to this decision," I confessed.

"I have a feeling this situation will be over with soon."

I picked up the television remote. "I was just about to watch a movie. You want some popcorn? I think I have a bag or two in the kitchen."

"I'm not going to keep you long," he responded. He blurted out, "Have you been seeing anyone special?"

I shrugged my shoulders. "No."

"You can tell your dad. You're a beautiful young lady, and I want you to find a nice, young man to settle down with."

"Maybe one day, but that's not on my agenda right now."

"Dear, don't let what Scotty did to you make you bitter toward all men."

"I haven't. My priorities are just a little different right now."

He seemed relieved. "That's good to know. Well, I'm going to go and let you get to your movie. When Hope gets in, tell her I need to speak with her."

He got up and I walked him to the door. That was odd. I wondered what the visit was really about. I rushed back to the couch so I could watch the movie. I hit the rewind button to watch it from the beginning.

The phone rang.

"You said you wanted to meet my new man. I'll be at the Horseshoe, so stop through," Hope said from the other end.

"I really wanted to watch this movie."

"Suit yourself. You can't say I didn't try."

We ended our call. The movie didn't hold my attention since I really was curious to meet Hope's new man.

"Forget the movie." I hit the stop button.

Thirty minutes later, I was valet parking my car and walking inside of the casino. I sent Hope a text. She responded with her location. For a weekday, the casino was packed. I rarely came through and didn't see a lot of people.

Hope met me in the doorway. "I see you changed your mind." She grabbed my hand.

"I had to meet the man that has my sister's heart."

"I'm glad you came."

I followed Hope through the casino. She stopped and looked around. "Where is he?"

"Don't tell me you lost him?"

"We were sitting right here. I told him I would be right back."

"What does he look like?" I asked.

"He's a little bit over six feet. He's bald. He's wearing a pair of khaki slacks and a blue Polo shirt."

"I'll wait right here while you go look for him." I took a seat at one of the slot machines.

My phone vibrated. It was a text from Tyler.

Tyler: Where are you?

Me: I'm at the Horseshoe. What's up?

Tyler: Missing U.

Me: LOL. Sure U R.

Tyler: I'm still out of town. Can I see U when I get back?

Me: Maybe.

Tyler: Think about it. I love U.

Me: LOL. Goodbye Tyler.

Tyler: One day you will believe me.

I didn't bother to respond to his last text. Tyler was something else. If he didn't know how to lay the pipe, I would have stopped dealing with him a long time ago. I wasn't mad at him for trying though.

Hope walked up to me looking upset. "He left. I can't believe he left me here."

"What? See, I don't like him already."

"He just sent me a text telling me he had an emergency at work and had to leave."

"He could have waited to tell you that in person."

"Exactly. I'm so pissed at him right now."

"Where's your car?" I asked.

"I used the valet."

"Since we're both here, might as well enjoy ourselves."

I placed a dollar in the slot machine and watched the images line up. "Whew. I just won a hundred dollars." I cashed out. "Okay, I'm ready to go now."

Hope shook her head and laughed. She followed me to the cage to collect my winnings.

CHAPTER 34

Hope

Charity mentioned that my dad wanted to talk to me. Instead of calling him, I decided to pay him a surprise visit at the office the next day.

"Hey, Shannon. Is my dad here?" I asked when I walked in.

"He's inside with a family now, but he should be out shortly," she responded, not once getting off her cell phone.

"Is Lovie here?"

She pointed toward the back. "He's in. Go on back."

"What's up, Big Bro?" I said, as I walked into his office.

He got up from behind his desk and greeted me with a hug. "You look like you lost your best friend," Lovie said.

I sat down. "Got a lot on my mind."

"If that dude is giving you the blues like this, you don't need him."

"That's the same thing Charity said."

"Then why are you putting yourself through all of these changes?"

"I love him," I confessed.

"Baby girl, take it from me. I'm a man. When I really care about a woman, I treat her with the upmost respect. I've had some girlfriends who I treated any kind of way. You want to know why?"

"Why?"

"They allowed me to. I could run over them. Like the one I'm with now, she barely sees me but she don't give me no flack about it. She's there when I need some loving. Do I care? No, because I don't have to put in any work. I'll keep her until I meet someone else better."

"But that's not fair to her. She probably cares about you. You shouldn't string her along when you know you really don't want to be with her."

"Exactly. So you see, the guy you're with, he don't respect you. You seem to be the only one committed in your relationship."

Lovie gave me something to think about. I left his office reconsidering the relationship with Tyler. My dad's office door was now open. He wasn't inside. I took a seat and waited for him to return.

"There you are. Shannon told me you were here," he said as he walked in, leaned down, and hugged me.

"Charity told me you stopped by last night."

"Yes, and from what I understand you were out. Who's this young man you've been seeing?" he asked, as he removed his jacket and hung it up on the coat rack.

"Dad, I didn't come here to talk about my personal business."

"Well, that's why I wanted to see you. You girls don't hang out with your old man no more. You definitely don't tell me what's going on in your lives. If it's not about me giving you money, I don't hear from you."

Ouch. That stung. "Dad, I'm not that bad, am I?"

He looked at me without saying a word. "You can remedy that. Why don't you bring your boyfriend over for dinner tonight?"

"I'll have to check with him."

"Call him or text him. Just let me know. Your mom's going to kill me. You know she don't like last-minute things. But I really want to meet the man who has been getting a lot of my little girl's time."

"Oh, I didn't know you had a guest," Jason said.

My dad responded, "Come on in, man. Have a seat."

I turned, looked at Jason, and rolled my eyes.

"My favorite niece. How've you been?" Jason said, as he took a seat next to me.

"Fine."

Shannon walked in. "Royce, someone's up front to see you."

"My office is like Grand Central Station today. Y'all wait right here, and I'll be right back." He got up, grabbed his jacket, and put it on before leaving us alone.

Jason leaned over. "Miss me? Or better yet, do you miss my money yet?"

He placed his hand on my knee. I knocked it off. "I wouldn't do that if I was you."

"You can make things up to me. Meet me at our spot in about two hours."

"It will be a cold day in hell before I let you touch me ever again." I looked him in the eyes and didn't flinch.

Jason laughed. "Hope, I don't know who this man is you've been seeing, but dear, don't get the big head. Once mine, always mine." He winked his eye.

"I know I didn't hear what I thought I heard," Lovie said.

He caught Jason and I both off-guard. I looked up with a shocked expression on my face.

Jason stood up. "It depends on what you heard."

"Sounds like you were threatening my sister."

"No, man. LJ, what have I done to you? You seem hell bent on accusing me of something. First it was the money, and now your sister."

Lovie looked at me. "I'm not talking to you. Hope, is he threatening you?"

"No." I lied.

I felt the room closing in on me. I left Lovie and Jason in my dad's office by themselves.

I ran into my dad near the front door. "Dad, I'll get back with you on dinner."

"Pudding, you don't have to go," my dad insisted.

"I promised Charity I would pick something up for her." I told another lie.

Being close to Jason made me ill. I couldn't get out of there fast enough. I headed straight to Tyler's office. The receptionist at the front desk said, "We don't have a Williams Construction in this building."

"Are you sure? Because this is where he told me he worked."

"Ma'am, I've been working in this building for fifteen years and I know everybody here."

I left the lobby, and went and sat in my car. If Tyler lied about his place of employment, what else was he lying to me about?

CHAPTER 35

Lovie

I sat in my dad's seat, while staring at Jason. I refused to leave him alone in his office.

Jason rubbed his face. "I should sue you for hitting me."

I responded, "Go right ahead, and then we can tell my dad why I knocked you the hell out in the first place."

"Son, you need to stay out of your parents' business."

"You forget. This is my business, too, and I will die before I let you or anyone else come in and destroy what my parents have built, and that includes their marriage."

Jason clapped. "I could tell you some things about your parents that would have you eating those words."

All of the tension I was feeling settled right in the middle of my chest. "Jason, I'm not my dad. I see you for the snake you are."

"If you only knew the whole story, you might change your mind."

"I know enough. In fact, follow me to my office."

I stood up and walked out of the room with Jason on my heels. I went to my office and pulled out several documents out of a huge brown folder. His eyes bucked when he read over the documents.

"Where did you get this?" Jason stuttered.

I leaned back in my chair and smiled. "You did a good job covering things up, but not good enough."

"What you have here are trumped-up documents."

"We can handle this one of two ways. I can give it to the authorities, and let them decide whether they're authentic, which you know may lead them to check into some of your other clients' accounts."

Jason shifted in his seat. "What's the other option?"

"I'm glad you asked." I picked up a sheet of paper with the amount of money I calculated he owed and handed it to him. "Or you can transfer the amount of money you owe my dad to his account within the next twenty-four hours. I don't have to give you the account number. You should know it by memory."

He looked down at the sheet of paper. "Twenty-four hours. That's a lot of money."

"Not my problem. Steal from one of your other clients if you must, but in twenty-four hours when I check the balance on the account, it better have a deposit."

"I'll see what I can do." Jason stood up.

"Tick-tock. The clock is ticking."

I watched Jason walk out. I picked up the phone and dialed Hope's number. "What was that all about in Dad's office earlier?" I asked as soon as she answered.

"Lovie, I told you nothing. Now drop it," she snapped.

"I can tell when you're lying, but I'll drop it for now."

I hung up the phone. If I find out for sure that Jason had been messing with my sister, he's as good as dead.

My mom's incoming call interrupted my thoughts. "Is Jason still there?" she asked.

"No. He just left."

"Good. I came by there earlier, but saw his car and kept driving."

"After tomorrow, I hope our financial problem will be resolved. I threatened to report him to the Feds if he didn't return the money he stole."

"How did you do that?"

I picked up the papers and placed them back in the brown folder. "Let's just say I showed him some documents that appeared to show proof he stole from us."

"Lovie, what did you do?"

"Well, I sort of created some documents that looked authentic, but really weren't because I'm still waiting on the copies to be sent to me."

"You are your mother's son."

"Glad that you are pleased with my methods."

"What did Royce say?"

"He's not aware of anything...not yet, anyway."

"Don't tell him anything until the money's been deposited. In fact, let's all get together so you can share the news with the entire family tomorrow night."

"Sounds like a plan to me, Mom."

We ended our call. I sat back in my chair, leaned back, and closed my eyes. The tension in my chest eased.

CHAPTER 36

Lexi

Thanks to Lovie, the Joneses would be celebrating tonight. I'd been in the kitchen cooking all evening. I wanted things to be just right for our celebration. I couldn't wait to meet Hope's new boyfriend.

Royce walked in the kitchen and wrapped his arm around me. "I don't know if that's you smelling good or the food."

I playfully hit him. "You know it's me, so stop tripping."

I faced him, and we kissed. The buzzer on the stove went off interrupting our intimate moment. "I better get back to the food. So, you did confirm with the kids, right?" I asked.

"Yes, darling. They should be here any minute."

"Good. I need to have a talk with that daughter of yours. Why am I the last person to know about this new guy?" I turned the buzzer off and removed the roast pan from the oven.

"I just found out about him myself."

"You should have called me the moment you found out," I said, as I opened up the cover and the steam almost hit me in the face.

"You know now. Lighten up on me, baby."

I looked up and saw Royce's smile. It reminded me of why I loved him. No matter how gloomy things got, he had a way of brightening up my life. I loved that man more than life itself. The doorbell rang.

"Keep them out of my kitchen, please," I said as Royce left to answer the door.

I hummed a Whitney Houston tune as I placed the food on serving trays.

Lovie walked in. "It's official. We're in the money," he sang.

I did a victory dance. "Yes. Thank you, baby." I hugged him and we twirled around. "I can't wait for you to tell Royce."

"Me, too. He's been looking so depressed lately," Lovie responded.

"Now, if I can only get him to get Jason out of our lives for good."

"After tonight, I'm sure there will no longer be a problem." Lovie patted his pocket. "I got the papers from the broker. This letter is all the proof I need."

I hugged Lovie again. "You just don't know how happy you've made me."

"Mom, you're squeezing me to death."

I laughed as I released him. "There's the doorbell again. That must be your sisters."

"I'll go find out," Lovie said.

I carried the food to the dining room table. Charity, Royce, and Lovie were standing in the room. "I see Hope is late as usual."

Charity got up to assist me. "She'll probably be extra late since she's bringing a guest."

Lovie said, "This should be interesting."

Royce said, "Please don't give the guy a hard time."

We all looked at him. I said, "This is coming from the man who thinks that no man is good enough for his girls."

"I was right about that Scotty, wasn't I?"

"Yes, but please don't bring up his name to me ever again." Charity followed behind me to the kitchen.

"So what can you tell me about this guy?" I asked, as I handed her the tray with the rolls.

"Nothing. I was supposed to meet him a couple of nights ago, but that didn't work out."

I picked up the roast pan. We walked back to the dining room. Royce got up and assisted me by placing the pan on the silver cooling rack so it wouldn't mess up the gold tablecloth.

The doorbell rang. "I don't know why you all insist on using the doorbell when you have keys," Royce said, as he pushed his chair back.

"Dad, I got it," Lovie said.

Royce remained seated as Lovie went to answer the door.

I sat down and waited for Hope to enter with her mystery man. I exhaled the moment they walked through the door.

"Everybody, I want you to meet my boyfriend. Tyler this is my family. Everybody, this is Tyler."

Tyler smiled and looked around the room. "Nice to meet y'all."

Charity blurted out, "This is who you've been seeing?"

"Charity, don't be rude." I looked at Tyler. "Come, sit next to me."

Hope said, "Yes, so you'll be close to her when she starts bombarding you with questions."

"I can see where Hope gets her beauty from." He picked up my hand and kissed the back of it.

Hope turned to Royce. "Dad, you're not going to say anything?"

"I have a lot to say. I just don't know where to begin." Royce sounded like he had a frog in his throat.

CHAPTER 37

Royce

So Tyler wasn't lying. He'd figured out a way to infiltrate his way into my daughter's life. He was quite the charmer. Lexi laughed at some of his corny jokes. The only two people who didn't seem to be enjoying his company were Charity and me.

"Tyler, what high school did you go to?" Lovie asked him.

"Marshall High," he responded.

Charity said, "I was under the impression you grew up in Shreveport."

Hope interjected, "He was always here, so you might as well say he grew up here."

Lexi placed her drink down. "So, what type of work do you do? It's going to take a man with a big account to keep my daughter happy."

"Mom. You're making me out to be some kind of gold digger."

Lovie started singing, "I ain't saying she's a gold digger."

"Lovie, that's enough," Lexi said.

"Son, didn't you have a big announcement to make?" I asked, looking in Lovie's direction.

"Yes, but…," He looked at Tyler. "I think I'll wait and tell you later."

Tyler said, "Don't mind me. If things go right, you never know, I might become part of the family."

Charity spat out her drink.

"Son, if you're getting that serious with my daughter, you and I need to have a talk." I stood up. "Follow me."

"Dad, be nice," Hope pled.

I led Tyler into the living room. I turned to make sure we were alone. "Have a seat." I went to the bar and poured myself a drink. I didn't bother to ask him if he wanted one.

"You have a beautiful home." Tyler looked around the room. "I didn't expect anything less."

"Tyler, let me get straight to the point. What the hell are you doing with Hope?"

A smug look crossed his face. "Do you really want to know the answer to that?"

I bent down and got in his face. "I'm going to say this once, and please don't have me repeat myself. You need to leave my daughter alone. This fight you claim you have with me is with me. Leave her and my family out of it."

Tyler laughed. "You don't dictate what I do. It's in your best interest to do what I tell you to do or...," Tyler held his hand up and looked around. "You could risk losing all of this."

"Your threats are no good here. I suggest you go back in there, tell Hope you had an emergency or something, and get the hell out of my house."

Tyler stood up. "I have no problem going back in there with your family and exposing you for the liar and cheater that you are."

"What happened between your mother and I was our business, and I will not be blackmailed by her ungrateful son."

"You've never done anything for me. Because of you, I lost my mom."

"You keep saying that, but your mom made her own choices. If you knew your mom as well as you said you did, then you would know didn't nobody control Ruth Ann, but her."

Tyler seemed to be thinking about what I was saying. “It doesn’t matter. You broke her heart and now I’m going to break yours. Do you want to lose your daughter or your wife? I’ll let you decide.”

“I’m losing neither.” I refused to back down, or give in to a blackmailer.

“You’re going to lose something alright. But I’ll decide when and who.” Tyler stood up.

“I need to speak with my family in private. I’ll escort you out and tell Hope you’ll call her.” This was my house, and nobody controlled anything here but me. I went and opened up the front door and escorted him out.

“Don’t think this is over,” Tyler said, as he walked down the driveway toward his car.

I slammed the door shut.

Hope came up behind me. “Dad, did you kick him out?”

“No, he had to leave. He’ll call you later. Follow me back to the dining room so we can hear Lovie’s big announcement.”

Hope paused. “But, he could have at least said good-bye.”

“He’s very rude. I don’t like him.”

“But I do and that’s all that matters.” Hope walked ahead of me and took a seat.

I rubbed the top of my head and took a seat back at the head of the table. I looked at Lovie. “Tyler had an emergency.”

“I’m sure he did,” Charity responded.

I looked in Lovie’s direction. “Son, I understand you had some news you wanted to share with the family.”

Lovie stood up. “Tonight’s a night of celebration. Mom, the champagne.”

Lexi popped open the cork on the champagne and we all poured glasses. Lovie held his glass up. “Tonight, the Joneses’ financial portfolio has been restored.” Lovie looked at me. “Tonight, Dad,

I'm happy to announce that not only is the original amount of money you invested back in your bank out, but you're twenty-five percent richer."

Tears of joy fell down my cheeks. I got up and pulled him into a bear hug. "Son, I don't know what to say. I didn't expect to get this emotional. You have made me so happy. Y'all don't know how many sleepless nights I've had due to this fiasco."

I returned to my seat.

"I can imagine because I've worked day and night to figure out what happened." Lovie looked around the room. "I hope y'all don't mind, but I need to talk to Mom and Dad alone."

Charity stood up. "No, I don't mind. I need to make a quick run somewhere anyway. Hope, if you want, I can drop you off at home."

"Sure, since my ride abandoned me."

Lovie's news meant one thing. My best friend betrayed me.

CHAPTER 38

Charity

It took every ounce I had not to slap the crap out of Tyler when he walked in the dining room with Hope. I glanced at Hope sitting in the passenger seat. She was clueless that her so-called boyfriend was my lover and had been for months. I tuned her out as she whined on and on about him.

I headed to our place to drop her off, but made a quick U-turn. Hope's body shifted to the right hitting the passenger door. "Slow down. You're going to kill us both," she yelled.

"Somebody might die today, but it's not going to be me."

"What's your problem?" Hope looked at me. "You've had an attitude all night. Oh. I know what it is. You're jealous aren't you? Jealous that I'm happy."

I gripped the steering wheel. "Hope, you have no clue, but you're about to find out."

I jumped on the interstate and got off on the exit that would take me straight to Tyler's place.

"Wait, how do you know where Tyler lives?" Hope asked.

I parked the car and exited the door without saying anything else to Hope. She jumped out and rushed behind me.

"Charity, talk to me."

"No. I'm jealous of your happiness, remember."

By now, we'd reached Tyler's door. I knocked on the door. Tyler opened it. I didn't wait to be asked in. I walked right past him. Hope stood in the doorway.

Tyler said, "You might as well come in. This might take a while."

I crossed my arms and tapped my feet. "Tell her."

Hope looked at Tyler. "Yes, Tyler, tell me because this whole scenario is making me feel uneasy."

Tyler walked up to Charity. "Listen, baby, we can talk about this. Alone."

"Baby? Did you just call my sister, *baby?*" Hope ran up to Tyler and started hitting him. "I can't believe you've been cheating on me with my sister!"

Tyler yelled, "Get your sister!"

I didn't move. Tyler deserved every punch, and I dared him to raise up and try to hit her. I grabbed Hope's arm. "That's enough. This joker owes us some answers."

Tyler rubbed his arm. "Feisty, aren't we?"

"Somebody tell me what the hell is going on here." Hope looked at both of us.

I poked Tyler with my finger. "It looks like your man has been playing the both of us. This is the guy I've been having my sexual escapades with."

It broke my heart to see the tears flowing down Hope's face. "Everybody told me not to trust you. This whole time you've been sleeping with Charity."

"How long did you think you would be able to get away with it?" I asked.

"As long as I could." He sounded like he had no remorse.

"Why, Tyler? Why?" I asked.

"If y'all stop badgering me, I'll tell you. You might want to sit down for this."

"I'll stand," I responded.

"Me, too," Hope said.

"Suit yourselves." Tyler sat down and looked up at us.

"I didn't mean for things to get out of hand, but there's something you both should know."

"Just get to the point, because you've already wasted enough of our time." I shifted from side to side.

"Your dad killed my mom."

Hope blurted out, "Liar. My dad's not a murderer."

"He might as well be. He broke her heart."

"Don't tell me you think you're our brother. Aw man, this is some sick psycho type stuff here." My hand flew up to my forehead.

"No, he's not my daddy."

I exhaled. "Whew. You had me scared for a minute."

"Your dad had an affair with my mom."

"I don't believe you," Hope said.

I added, "Our dad loves our mom. He would never do something like that."

Tyler picked up a photo album on a nearby table and handed it to me. "See for yourself."

Hope, with clenched teeth, remained standing in the same spot and stared at Tyler. I turned the pages, and for once it didn't appear Tyler was lying. The evidence stared me straight in the face. The man I'd trusted all of my life was in intimate pictures with Tyler's mom. "How do I know these weren't taken before my parents were married?"

"Back then, dates were imprinted on the photos. Take a look."

I removed several of the photos, and the dates coincided with a time where it was clear my parents were married. Lovie would have been about one or two years old. It was possible that my mom could even have been pregnant with me.

I held the photos out toward Hope. "Seems like this is the only thing Tyler isn't lying about."

Hope looked at the pictures and then threw them at Tyler. "I hate you."

Tyler reached for Hope. Hope jerked away. "Don't you ever touch me again."

"Hope, I'm sorry. But you're just a casualty of your dad's affair. If he hadn't hurt my mom, I never would have hurt you."

"You are a piece of work." I threw the photo album at him. It missed his hand and fell on the floor. I grabbed Hope by the arm. "Come on, Hope, let's go."

"I'll be there in a minute. I need to talk to Tyler."

I released her arm. "Fine, I'll be in the car."

This revelation was a lot to digest. I wondered if my mom knew. My dad had a lot of explaining to do. No wonder he didn't like Tyler. He didn't want him to spill his little secret. Well, the secret was out.

CHAPTER 39

Hope

I stood there and stared at Tyler for a minute. My emotions were all over the place. I closed my fists and held them by my side. I wanted to hit him again. I'd just introduced him to my family as the man I loved. I'd never felt so humiliated.

I could feel the tears about to fall from my eyes, but I willed them to stop. I wouldn't give him the satisfaction of seeing me cry again.

"I hate you. I hate the fact that I let you get in here." I patted myself on the chest near my heart. "You're evil, and as sure as my name is Hope Jones, you will pay for hurting me."

"Hope, now that things are out in the open, it doesn't have to mean the end of us."

"Are you delusional? There's no way in the world I can be with you now."

I turned to walk away. Tyler came up behind me and wrapped his arm around my waist. "Don't leave like this. Come on. We can get through this."

I wiggled my way out of his grip. "There will never be a *we*. In fact, *we* never existed. You've been playing me this entire time." I waved my hand back and forth in front of him. "Silly me, making the mistake of falling in love with your ass."

"Baby, I'm sorry you got caught up in all of this. You're really a nice girl. This here—it was just collateral damage," Tyler said, without blinking an eye.

"Screw you, Tyler. I hate you. Please lose my number because I don't want to talk to you ever again."

I stormed out of the door. Tyler stood in the doorway. "Hope!" he called out several times.

I ignored him. I hopped in the passenger side of Charity's car. Without exchanging words, she drove us home.

When we got home, I went straight to my bedroom. Charity was fast on my heels. She sat on the edge of my bed.

"We need to talk," she said.

"I don't feel like talking," I responded. I picked up one of my fluffy pillows and squeezed it.

"I know you're hurting right now. Truth be told, I am too. Although I'm not in love with Tyler, I did care about him a little. I mean, we've been kicking it these past few months, and I thought at the very least we were friends."

"No, you two were fuck buddies. Get it right."

"He fucked me royally, too."

I looked at Charity. "I don't know if I should be pissed at him, you, or myself."

"I tried to warn you, but I'm not the one to say 'I told you so.'"

"You just did." I hit the pillow to let out some steam.

"At least we both know the truth and we can move on from here."

"Easy for you to say. How does one heal a broken heart?" I fell down on the bed.

"One day at a time." Charity rubbed my back to comfort me.

I couldn't give in to the pity party I wanted to have for myself. I needed to pull it together. I wiped the tears from my face and sat up in the bed. "I can't believe Dad had an affair. There's no telling what Mom is going to do when she finds out," I said, in between sniffles.

"I'm hoping she doesn't find out," Charity responded.

"Somebody has to tell her. If it was me, I would want to know."

"I'm going to talk to Dad and get his side of the story. Tyler's lied to us so much I don't know what to believe."

"But pictures don't lie. You saw them. We both did. They were more than just friends." I couldn't get the image of my dad with this other woman out of my head.

"Well, let's talk to Dad first. Then again, maybe we should just let it go, and pretend like we don't know."

"I don't know if I can do that," I admitted.

Charity pulled out her cell phone and dialed a number. "Lovie don't ever answer his phone when I need him." She placed the phone on the bed.

My phone rang. I didn't have to look at the caller ID because I knew the ringtone. It was Tyler, and he could go to hell as far as I was concerned. When he should have been calling, he wasn't. Now that I don't want to talk to him, he's blowing my phone up.

Charity's phone rang. "It's the devil."

"Yeah. He called me, too."

Charity pulled me into a hug. I lay on her shoulder and cried.

CHAPTER 40

Lovie

It felt good to be able to restore the company's money. The sense of pride I felt from giving my father back what he'd lost was bittersweet. After dinner last night, I showed him the proof he wanted to see. The look of despair in my father's eyes when he came face-to-face with his friend's betrayal made me want to strangle Jason with my bare hands.

I drove around all night before deciding to go home. I'd planned to confront Jason, but at his office. I tried to be patient as I sat in front of the receptionist's desk.

She glanced at me. "He should be through with his phone call in just a moment, and then I'll let him know you're here."

"No problem. I have a little time." I picked up one of the magazines and thumbed through it.

The receptionist called out, "Mr. Jones, he'll see you now."

"Thank you." I placed the magazine on the chair and went inside Jason's office.

My mouth flew open in shock. "Dad, what are you doing here?"

My dad sat in one of the seats across from Jason. "I needed to talk to Jason face-to-face in a neutral zone."

"Great minds think alike." I sat in the chair next to my father.

Jason tapped on his desk. "I see what this is. You trying to double team me. Well, you got your money. What more do you want from me?"

My dad responded, "I want to know why. You're the closest thing to a brother I have. Man, if you were strapped for cash, I would have given it to you."

"Like I wanted a handout from you."

"No, you would rather steal from him." I hit my fist on his desk.

"Look here son, you better watch your tone with me," Jason said.

"You have to earn respect to get respect. The moment I realized you were stealing from us is the day I lost all respect for you."

"Royce, you better keep him under control, because I've had it up to here." Jason held his hand high off the desk.

In a low, calm voice, my dad repeated himself. "Why, Jason? And then we'll both be out of your hair."

"Because I could. You should never give that type of control of your finances to anyone." Jason looked at me. "And that even includes your son." He emphasized the word son.

I could tell my dad hadn't slept. "But me, of all people? We've been through some things. I was there when you lost your folks. You were there when I lost mine. Damn, man, you're my kids' godfather."

"I didn't set out to steal from you, but I did it once and you didn't notice. So, each time, I took a little more and more—"

I interrupted him. "Until you drained us dry."

"Hey, I did leave y'all with something. You weren't completely broke. You still had money to live on." Jason didn't sound like he had any remorse.

My dad jumped out of his chair and over the desk. He grabbed Jason by the collar. I could see the veins popping out from my dad's forehead. "I don't ever want to see you again. If you see me first, walk in the opposite direction."

He pushed Jason a little as he released his collar. Jason fell back and coughed. "I understand you're angry, but that wasn't called for."

"You're lucky that's all I did. The only reason why you're not in jail is because Lovie made a deal with you, and one thing about a Jones, we are men of our word."

"But are you sure he's a Jones?"

"What the hell is that supposed to mean?" My dad looked down at Jason and asked.

"Mama's Baby, Daddy's Maybe."

My dad pushed the items on Jason's desk at him and stormed out.

I stood up. "You heard my dad. Stay away from my family."

Jason laughed. "You'll be back, son. You'll be back."

"I'm not your son, so stop calling me that." I turned and walked away.

Jason sang, "Mama's Baby, Daddy's Maybe." He sang that over and over.

His receptionist wasn't at the desk or I'm sure she would have called Security on us with all of the noise coming out of Jason's office.

I don't know why I didn't recognize my Dad's car when I first arrived, but it was parked near the front entrance. I tapped on the window. He rolled it down. "You okay?" I asked him.

"The truth is, no. I have a funeral to do today, and my heart just isn't in it."

"What all needs to be done? I can do it as long as it doesn't require me to handle the body."

"No, some of the workers will handle that. You just need to make sure everything goes smoothly. Be there to comfort the family. You've seen me do it. You know what to do."

"I got it. I always got your back. You see that now, don't you, Dad?"

He looked up at me with love in his eyes. "Lovie, I know. Sorry

I've given you a hard time. I just wanted to make you tough and able to stand on your own. Not depend on the family so much for your needs like your sisters do."

"I know, and I appreciate that. You better go before I lose some cool points because I'm getting all mushy."

We both laughed. After he'd pulled off, I sat in my car for a few minutes. The realization that I was about to facilitate my first funeral solo set in. What had I gotten myself into?

CHAPTER 41

Lexi

Life for the Joneses was getting back on track. I couldn't wait to get back to my normal routine of shopping and hanging out at the country club. I missed frequenting my favorite boutiques. "Mrs. Jones is back in action," I said out loud, as I eased out of the bed.

A day of shopping required a nice, casual outfit. I stared at the clothes that were color coordinated in my huge walk-in closet and found the perfect outfit. The teal pant outfit still had the tags on it.

Twenty minutes later, I was slipping on the clothes and primping in the mirror. I saw a few gray strands trying to peek out around my edges. I made a mental note to make a hair appointment with my hairdresser Tameka, so she could get rid of them with a bottle of jet-black hair dye.

"My keys, where are my keys?" I dumped the contents of my purse on the bed. Still no keys.

"Are you looking for these?" Royce stood in the doorway dangling my car keys in his hands.

I jumped. "Royce, you scared me."

He handed me the keys. "We need to talk."

"I got a busy day. Can it wait until later?"

"No, it can't."

I didn't like the tone of his voice. "What is it? I thought you would be at work. Is it one of the kids? What's going on?" I asked question after question.

"You can say that. Come with me."

I followed Royce to the living room. He went straight to the bar and poured two glasses of bourbon. He handed one to me.

"I'll pass," I said.

"Suit yourself." Royce carried both glasses with him. He sat one on the coffee table and held the other one while seated in his chair. He looked up at me. "You may want to sit down for this."

"Royce, you're scaring me."

I took a seat on the couch. I rubbed my hand through my hair. He gulped down the first glass of bourbon, placed it on the coffee table, and then picked up the other glass. "I paid a visit to Jason. I came this close..." He held out his fingers as if measuring. "From choking the shit out of him."

"What happened?" Royce rarely cursed, so he had me on edge.

"I grabbed him by the collar and told him what was on my mind. Before I could leave, he dropped a bombshell on me. I tried to ignore it, but I can't get his words out of my head."

"Well...what did he say?" I stuttered.

"'Mama's Baby, Daddy's Maybe.' Do you know what he means by that?"

"What? What?" I immediately got on the defensive. "How am I supposed to know? I can't explain the words of a crazy man."

"You sure you don't have anything to tell me?"

"Royce, you must have had more than those two glasses of bourbon. You're sounding a little drunk to me." I stared at Royce. I attempted to control my eyes from blinking more than usual. I clasped my hands to hide my sweaty palms.

"You wouldn't be lying to me, now would you?"

I couldn't look Royce in the eyes. I didn't want him to see the truth. I jumped off the couch. "You are not going to take out the

situation with Jason out on me. I'm going shopping, and I'm using the bank card. Do you have a problem with that?"

Royce backed down. He slouched down in his seat. "No. After all I've allowed him to put our family through, you deserve a shopping spree. Just don't go overboard."

"I won't." I leaned down and kissed him. "Baby, we got through the money woes, and we'll get through this."

Royce gripped my hand. "You don't know how hard this is. I loved him like a brother. I trusted him with my life."

I kneeled down in front of him. "Baby, you have me. You have the kids. We're going to get through this together."

Shopping could wait. My husband needed me. I went upstairs and used my best aromatherapy bath gel to make Royce a hot, bubble bath. I led him into the bathroom and helped ease him out of his clothes. I didn't bother to take off my designer outfit. I didn't care about it getting wet. I picked up the sponge and gave Royce a sponge bath. He exhaled and released the tension from his body.

Seeing Royce in this vulnerable state tugged at my heart. I wouldn't dare confess to him about the one-night stand with Jason. The idea that Lovie may not be his would devastate him. That's one secret I planned to take to my grave.

CHAPTER 42

Royce

The last few hours were all a blur to me. I remembered coming home. I remembered confronting Lexi about Jason's accusations. I remembered the feel of her hands over my body as she washed the tension away, but I don't remember how my life ended up like this. Where did I go wrong? When did I turn a blind eye to things going on around me?

Part of me knew Lexi wasn't being completely honest with me, but the other part of me wanted to let sleeping dogs lie. Jason had taken enough from me. I wouldn't allow him to take away anything else.

I squeezed Lexi tight as she snuggled her body closer to me. She must really have been concerned about me because even after I encouraged her to go on a shopping spree, she stayed to make sure I was fine. I wasn't about to let anything destroy this bond between me and the woman I loved.

My stomach growled.

Lexi shifted her body. "I guess I better find us something for dinner."

"No. Tonight, I'm treating you. Why don't we both get dressed and go out?"

"I can't recall the last time we've gone out to dinner." Lexi seemed to perk up.

"It's been awhile. Put on something sexy." I patted her on the butt.

"Do that again, and we won't make it out of the bedroom." Lexi smiled at me.

Lexi and I both loved Italian food, so we went to our favorite Italian restaurant. The low lighting added a romantic ambiance. It felt good to be out enjoying each other's company over dinner.

"Don't look, but there's Jackie and her husband," Lexi said.

"Be nice," I responded.

Jackie and Greg Grayson approached our table. I had to admit that Jackie was a beautiful woman. Of course, I wouldn't say it to Lexi. In my opinion, Jackie was a little too young for Greg. Greg kept a tight rein on her while he continued to play the field.

"Good to see you two out. We were beginning to wonder if the rumors were true," Greg said.

"You can't always believe what you hear," I responded.

"True. People talk about me all of the time." Greg looked at me and then at Jackie.

Jackie, in an irritating, high-pitched voice, said, "People are always trying to tell me something about Greg, but I don't believe them. They are just haters. Women will tell you anything to get next to your man." She placed her hand on his chest.

I looked at Lexi. She smiled and tilted her head.

The waiter walked up to the table. "Would you like two more chairs?"

Greg said, "No, we were leaving. I just wanted to come speak to my friend."

The waiter left us alone.

"Greg, it was good seeing you."

Lexi and I watched them walk away. When we were sure they were outside of earshot, we laughed.

Lexi said, "They are so busy worrying about the state of our relationship, they need to be concerned about what's going on in their household."

"You got that right. The Joneses are solid." I smiled. I meant every word I said. "Contrary to what they are showing to the public, they are on a shaky foundation."

Lexi leaned on the table. "Do tell. Hubby, you've been holding out on me."

"Well, I'm not one to gossip, so you didn't hear this from me." I laughed, and continued. "Greg has a baby on the way."

"No!" Lexi seemed surprised. "Please tell me that's not so. Jackie said Greg's been telling her he had a vasectomy and didn't want any more kids."

"Greg told me himself. And no, Jackie is not the baby's mama."

"Oh my goodness." Lexi took a sip of her wine. "I would like to be a fly on the wall when Jackie finds out."

I couldn't help but laugh out loud again. Here I was gossiping about other people with my wife. I had to admit, it felt good to talk about other folk's problems. Lord knows, we'd seen more than our share.

Lexi and I ended the night with a night cap and a night of love-making. She could still make my toes curl and make me howl at the moon like a wolf.

"Baby, you still got it," I said, as I looked up into her eyes.

"You best believe it," she responded, as she straddled me.

CHAPTER 43

Charity

It'd been two days, and I hadn't spoken to either one of my parents. It wasn't because they hadn't tried to reach out to me; it was because I've been avoiding them.

I was torn about what to do, and Hope hadn't been any help. She was too caught up in her emotions. I didn't understand why she couldn't just forget about that no-good Tyler.

My business line rang. "Mahogany's, how may I help you?" I answered.

"It's a shame I have to call you on your business line to talk to you." The sound of my father's voice caught me by surprise.

"Dad, I was just about to call you," I lied.

"Sure you were. What are you doing for lunch? I have a few hours. Maybe you, me, and Hope can get together with your mom."

"Dad, I need to talk to you, but can it just be the two of us?" I asked.

"Sure, Baby Girl. What's wrong?" he asked.

"I'd rather not discuss it over the phone. Why don't you come over? I'll make something."

"I'll be there around one."

We ended our conversation. Hope was gone, and I hoped she remained out for a few more hours. I went through the cabinets, found some spiral pasta, and made a seafood pasta salad and two sandwiches.

I'd just gotten everything fixed when the doorbell rang. I greeted my dad with a hug and kiss.

We chatted about getting our money back, but I could see the pain in his eyes when he brought it up. "Just because we got our money back, it doesn't mean you girls can go back to shopping like crazy. I will let you go on one wild shopping spree but that's it."

"Dad, cool, but you know what? These last six months have taught me to be more grateful and yes, spend less. Now, I'm not turning down the shopping spree because a sister still loves to shop. But, I promise to be more responsible going forward."

"That's my girl." He gave me a high five.

I removed the empty dishes from the kitchen table and placed them in the dishwasher. "Dad, there's something I need to talk to you about."

"I'm all ears," he responded.

"I was talking to Tyler."

"You need to stay away from him."

I crossed my arms and sat back at the table across from him. "You don't have to worry about that. He's the last person I want to see."

A concerned look swept across his face. "Is Hope with Tyler now?"

"Nope. They broke up two nights ago."

"After the dinner?"

"Yep. Right after we went to his place and confronted him about being a two timing jerk."

"Say what?"

I informed him of how Tyler tried to play the both of us. His eyes squinted in anger. His nose flared.

"Dad, and that's not all. He shared with us that you and his mom had an affair."

He looked away in shame.

"So, it's true."

In a low voice, he responded, "Yes."

"How could you?" I was on the brink of crying, but held back the tears.

"Let me explain. It's not what you think."

I hopped from the table and rushed to my room. I acted like a little girl instead of the grown woman that I was. Everything I'd believed my father to be was shattered with his one-word response, "yes."

He followed me. "Please, Charity, listen to me."

"I don't want to hear it." The tears fell. I couldn't stop them.

He placed his arms around me. I beat him on the chest. He held me tighter. "Get it out. That's it baby, get it out."

I pulled myself together. I wiped my face with a tissue and sat on my bed. He pulled up a chair and sat down in front of me.

Sniffling, I said, "If I can't trust you, what man can I trust?"

"Your words cut me here." He pointed to his heart. "I hate you had to find out like this."

"I wish I didn't know at all."

"Tyler's bitter. He feels I took away his mom, so he wants me to lose the three most important women of my life: You, Hope, and Lexi."

"I'm going to be honest with you. All of this has been a lot to digest. I thought you and Mom had a good relationship."

"We do, but things haven't always been like they are now. We've had our issues, but I wouldn't trade your mom in for anyone else. She's my rock."

"If she's your rock, why did you have an affair with this woman?"

"I was young, and wanted it all. No excuse. Lexi and I were having problems. Ruth Ann took me away from those problems."

"How long did this affair go on?" By now, my tears were drying up.

"A few years, until one day I realized that what I was doing wasn't fair to Lexi or Ruth Ann. I cared about Ruth Ann, but I love your mother."

"How did this Ruth Ann feel about your decision?"

"She cussed me out, but then begged me to continue the affair. She said she would do anything just to have me in her life."

Curious, I asked, "You weren't tempted to continue the affair?"

"Of course, but Lexi was getting to be more demanding at home. I had to be a man, and be the man my dad taught me to be."

"Does Mom know about this?" I asked.

"No, she doesn't." He looked at floor.

I caught a glimpse of Hope standing in the doorway. I wasn't sure how long she'd been there. My dad's eyes followed my glaze.

CHAPTER 44

Hope

"Don't stop talking on my account," I said, when I'd gotten busted for eavesdropping.

My dad looked up at me. "I was explaining the situation with Tyler's mom to Charity."

"I heard." I remained standing in the doorway.

"There's no excuse for what I did. There are not too many things I've done in my life that I regret, but I do regret the affair I had with Ruth Ann."

"And you should." I leaned on the wall near the door.

Charity asked, "My question for you now is, how do you plan to make this right?"

"I recommitted myself to Lexi. I spent the last twenty-something years of my life making sure that my family had the best of everything. I'm the man I should have been all along."

I shrugged my shoulders. "But everything's been based on a lie. You were in love with one woman, but married to another."

He turned around in his chair. "I've loved Lexi from the first day I saw her. I wasn't in love with Ruth Ann. I cared for her, but that was just it."

"I don't understand you men. It's just easy for you to use a woman, and then spit her out when you've used her all up." I was really talking more about Tyler than him.

"I made a mistake. Please forgive me." I could see the pain in his eyes.

Charity said, "I'm going to need some time."

"Me, too," I responded.

"If you girls don't forgive me, then he's won. Tyler's main goal was to cause me to lose you."

"You should have thought about that before cheating on mom." I frowned.

He looked at Charity. "Charity, tell me you understand."

Charity looked away.

He looked at me. "Hope, come on. I'm still the same man you both grew up loving."

Charity said, "Dad, I think it's best that you leave."

I moved from in front of the door. "We'll call you, if and when we're ready to talk."

"Please, don't let him win," he pled.

He attempted to hug me, but I moved out of the way. I watched him walk down the hall slouched over.

"Charity, maybe we were too hard on him." I felt guilty.

"What just happened here is nothing compared to what's going to happen if Mom finds out," she responded.

"Should we tell her?" I asked. I sat down in the chair my dad abandoned.

"It's not our place to tell her."

"But, if you knew a man was cheating on me, I would want to know."

"This is different. The affair was over twenty years ago. It's not like he's still messing with the woman."

I thought about it. "True, but still. He shouldn't have done it, and it pisses me off that he did."

"As upset as I am with him right now, I'm not going to tell Mom," Charity said.

"She's been calling me. She says it's time for a girls' day out."

"I've been avoiding her calls," Charity confessed.

"So what do you suggest we do?" I asked.

"Nothing. Let Dad deal with this. This is his problem."

"Then why do I feel guilty for not telling Mom what I know?" I closed my eyes and leaned back.

"It's your choice. I'm choosing to not say anything," Charity responded.

I left Charity alone and went to my bedroom. I pulled out my diary and wrote an entry; something I hadn't done in a while. My hand flew to my stomach. I rushed out of my room, bumping into Charity. "Excuse me." I kept on to my destination, the toilet.

I felt 100 percent better afterward. I washed up and went back to my room. I snatched my diary out of Charity's hand. "This is personal property."

"I didn't know you still kept a diary."

"It's a lot you don't know about me."

Charity looped her arm with mine. "We need to remedy that. We seem to always be in competition with one another. That shouldn't be the way it is."

"I can't help it. I've always had to compete for Mom's and Dad's attention."

"Please. They dote on you. I'm the one who has to do extra just to get attention."

My cell phone beeped. It was a text message from our mom. "Mom wants to go to the spa tomorrow."

"I have to check my schedule. I'm running a business now, so I can't just go off on these unscheduled escapades anymore."

I rolled my eyes. "Oh, yeah, I forgot. You're Ms. Business Woman now."

Charity left my room. I sent my mom a quick text message to confirm.

While texting her, Tyler called. "What do you want?" I yelled.

"I need to see you."

"I think we've said all that needs to be said," I responded.

"Hope, I miss you."

With those few words I felt my heart tug. "Where?"

"Meet me at my place."

Charity came back in my room. "I can't tomorrow. I have a meeting with a new customer."

I stared at the phone, tuning Charity out.

Charity asked, "Hope, are you even listening to me?"

"Sorry. I was thinking about something." I fumbled through my purse for my keys. "Charity, I'll talk to you later. I need to run somewhere real quick."

I knew it wasn't a good idea, but I went to meet Tyler.

CHAPTER 45

Lovie

I sat at the light, minding my own business, when Hope's car pulled up beside me. I blew my horn to get her attention, but she didn't look my way. I dialed her number.

"Look to your left," I said, as soon as she answered.

She glanced in my direction. I rolled down my window and waved. She rolled her window down. "I didn't see you over there."

"I know. You look like a woman on a mission. Where are you headed?"

"To meet a friend."

The light changed, and people behind us blew their horn.

"I'll talk to you later." I rolled up my window, and we pulled away from the light.

Curious, I decided to follow Hope. She drove straight to her boyfriend's apartment. I didn't stop. I kept driving past the apartment complex. It was something about her boyfriend I didn't like. I headed to see Charity.

Charity greeted me at the door. "Come on in. I was in my room printing out brochures."

"How's business?" I asked, while following her to her room.

"It's going good. Business is steady."

"That's a good thing. I'm proud of you."

"Aww, that means a lot coming from you." Charity blushed.

I shifted the vacant chair and took a seat. "You know I'm not one to beat around the bush. What's up with this Tyler guy? I see Hope is spending a lot of time with him."

"Not anymore. Not after we discovered he was two-timing the both of us."

My mouth flew open. "Say what?"

Charity removed the printed brochures from the bin. "I don't know if you noticed my reaction to Tyler. The reason why I was shocked is because we had been seeing each other for months."

"I told her he was no good. I know how we are. His actions showed he didn't care for her."

"We don't have to worry about that anymore. She's no longer seeing him."

"Unless she knows someone else who lives in his apartment complex, that's where she is now."

Charity picked up her phone. "I'm calling her."

I glanced over the brochure while Charity made the phone call.

Charity said, "She's not answering."

"She's stubborn. She knows the deal, so if she gets back involved with him it's on her." I placed the brochure in Charity's hand.

"That's just the half of it." Charity walked toward the door. "You might need a drink for this one."

Less than ten minutes later, we were both seated in the living room. I popped off the top of a bottle of Corona and drank it.

"Dad had an affair," Charity blurted.

I spit out some of my drink. "Say what?"

"Right before you were born, Dad had an affair with Tyler's mom."

I sat the bottle down on the nearby table. "You got to be kidding me."

Charity crossed her legs under her. "I wish I was. Dad confirmed it when we called him out on it."

Both of my hands flew up to my forehead. "This can't be happening." *Should I tell Charity about Mom's affair with Jason? Looks like all of their skeletons were falling out of the closet.*

"I'm so disappointed in Dad. I always thought he and Mom were the perfect couple," Charity said.

"As much as we may not want to admit this, they are people just like we are. They had a life before us kids."

"If you would have seen the pictures, you would be in shock."

"If only you knew." *She had no idea of all of the things I knew.*

Charity attempted to call Hope again without any success. "I can't believe Hope is over there," she said. "Tyler's motives were never pure. He plotted to get next to Hope and me to get back at Dad. His intentions were to take one of us from him, the way he feels Dad took his mom away from him."

"How long did this affair go on?" I picked up the bottle and swished the beer around.

Charity repeated to me what our dad had told her. "Hope knows, so that's why I'm surprised she's over there."

"What's his apartment number?" I asked.

"Twelve sixteen."

"I'm about to put an end to this." I got off the couch and put the empty beer bottle in the trash. "I'm going over there."

"Maybe I should go with you," Charity said.

"No. It's best that you don't. Just in case things get ugly."

"That's why I need to be going with you."

Charity grabbed her keys and followed behind me. "You can ride with me," I said.

I ended up parking right next to Hope's car. I followed Charity to Tyler's apartment.

"Move away from the peephole," I told her.

I rang the doorbell and turned to the side, so he could only see my side profile.

Tyler opened the door. "May I help you?"

I responded with a pop in his face with my fist. He stumbled and fell. "Where's my sister?" I asked.

Charity walked past me and called out, "Hope! Hope!"

Hope came out of the back room wearing nothing but a man's shirt. "What are y'all doing here?" she yelled.

Charity said, "No, why are you here? After everything this man has done."

Tyler rubbed his jaw. "Man, I'm going to give you that. Or maybe I should press charges?"

I rubbed my fist. "Go right ahead. I suggest you don't if you have any outstanding warrants. I won't be the only one going to jail today."

I looked at Hope. "Go put some clothes on so we can get out of here."

"I'm grown. You don't tell me what to do."

I looked at Charity. Charity pushed Hope toward the bedroom. Tyler and I were now alone in the living room.

Tyler said, "She'll be back. She loves me."

I jumped in Tyler's face. "If I ever catch you with my sister again, your jaw won't be the only thing hurting."

He didn't flinch. "Are you threatening me?"

"Take it like you want to. But keep away from my sisters."

Hope followed Charity out of the room, but this time fully dressed.

"Come on, let's get out of here," I said.

"Hope," Tyler called out several times.

Charity pushed Hope out the door. I followed behind them.

CHAPTER 46

Lexi

I thought getting our money back would be the end of our problems. That life for the Joneses would go back to normal. When Royce confronted me about Jason, I thought I was going to die. My mission to cater to Royce's every need, and show him he was the only man I desired appeared to be working. Well, up until a few days ago at least. Royce seemed distracted for some reason.

Royce's fiftieth birthday was coming up soon, so maybe he's going through a midlife crisis. Now that our finances were intact, I planned to throw him a party fit for a king. We've had our share of ups and downs in our relationship just like any other couple. We were just good at hiding it. He's been a great father to my three kids and an exceptional lover. I couldn't have asked for a better husband.

"Baby, what's wrong?" I asked Royce, as I massaged his shoulders while he sat at the kitchen table.

"Nothing I can't handle."

"I know it's been hard finding out your best friend betrayed you."

"It's not just that. I'm thinking about selling RJ's."

I stopped massaging his shoulders. I walked around so I could see his face.

"Where is this coming from?" I asked.

"I've been thinking about selling. That other funeral home is willing to offer a substantial amount. I'm getting older. The kids are all doing their own thing."

"But Royce, Lovie's working with you now. Train him on what he needs to know. This is your family's legacy. You can't just give it up."

"I'm not going to make any rash decisions. It's just something I'm thinking about," Royce assured me.

"Stop considering it." I sat down in the chair and pulled it close to him. "You've been under a lot of stress. Jason was the source of that stress. Now that he's out of your life, you should see your stress level go down. I know mine has."

"Jason's been texting me. Says he wants to talk to me about something. Something that he should have told me a long time ago."

I tapped my foot under the table. "He's trying to weasel his way back into your life. Ignore him."

"That's what I said. I just hate throwing away a forty-year friendship because of money."

"Look at me." Royce looked up. I held his hand. "All we need is each other. Forget everybody else. You've been telling me that for years. So now it's time for you to take your own advice."

Royce smiled. "You're right. I have you and as long do, nothing else matters."

Royce left for work. As soon as I made sure he was gone, I got busy planning his birthday party. First thing in order was the guest list. Who could I invite over to make jealous? I wanted all the busybodies to know that my marriage was stronger than ever, so they could stop trying to put us in divorce court. No other woman was going to be able to get their claws in Royce. They would have to kill me first. I didn't plan on going anywhere.

I needed to hire a planner to help me with this. *Duh, my daughter.* I called Charity and set up a meeting with her. We would discuss business, but I also needed to know why she'd been avoiding me since the dinner party.

It felt good to go back to valet parking. The valet attendant appreciated the tip I gave him as he went to park my car. Charity was already seated at a table in the restaurant. I saw her wave her hand to get my attention.

She stood up and we hugged. "So glad you could meet me. Missed you at the spa the other day, but Hope told me you were busy working."

"I've been meaning to call you back." I could tell Charity was lying.

"That's neither here nor there. We have a party to plan." I pulled out my notebook.

We gave the waiter our lunch order and got back to discussing ideas.

Ruby walked up to our table and interrupted us. "Lexi, I thought that was you."

I looked around. "You're here by yourself?"

"No, my hubby's here." She pointed to a table near the door. He waved. I waved back.

"Ruby, we're planning a party for Royce so expect an invitation in the mail within the next week."

"Will do. I just wanted to come speak. See you at our luncheon."

"Okay, dear." I smiled.

She walked away.

"That outfit she has on is so tacky. With all of the money she has, you would think she would have better taste," Charity said.

"Dear, money can buy a lot of things, but it can't buy class. Either you have it or you don't."

We went back to planning Royce's party.

Charity drew a design on a piece of paper and showed it to me.

"I like that," I said.

"I will let you see the invitation after I design the whole thing."

"We don't have much time."

"It'll go out as soon as you give me your approval," she assured me.

I smiled. "Look at my baby. She got her own business. You make your mama so proud."

Charity blushed. "I learned how to throw a party from the best, right?"

I chuckled. "You got that right. One thing I know how to do is throw a party."

CHAPTER 47

Royce

Days at work seemed to drag on. Even with business better than ever, I couldn't shake this bout of depression that fell over me. Alcohol had become my trusted companion. It was after six, and instead of being at home with my beautiful wife, I was at the bar drowning my sorrows with drink after drink.

Jason took a seat next to me. "I knew I would find you here."

"Needed to unwind. Didn't feel like going home." I tipped the glass to make sure I got every last drop of liquor.

"I'm sure Lexi's worried about you."

"I'll call her when I leave here. But why do you care?" I called for the bartender. "I'll have another bourbon."

Jason said, "Cancel that. I think he's had enough to drink."

"I'm a grown man. I know when I've had enough." I looked at the bartender. "Bring me my drink."

The bartender said, "I think he's right. You've been drinking it like it's water. You should slow it down. At least give it a little time before drinking another."

"Fine. I'll go to another bar where they don't mind taking my money." I reached into my pocket, pulled out my wallet, and threw some money on the counter.

"Come on. I'll drive you," Jason said.

"I'm not ready to go home." My words slurred.

I stepped from off the bar stool. The room felt like it was spinning. Maybe I had drunk too much.

Jason grabbed my arm. "You don't have to go home, but I'm not letting you behind the wheel."

The last thing I remembered was Jason opening his passenger door. By the time I sat down in the seat, I'd passed out.

"Lexi," I called out. My head felt like a tractor-trailer had hit it. The bright lights hurt my eyes.

"Darling, I don't know who Lexi is, but I'm sure I can make you forget about her if you give me the chance." A woman wearing nothing but black lingerie got up on top of the bed.

I blinked a few times. "Who the hell are you?"

"I'm the woman who is about to make your fantasies come true." She crawled closer to me.

I pushed her away. "Where am I? And how did I get here?"

The strange woman laughed. "You were here when I got here. I've been sitting here waiting for you to wake up."

I shifted to sit up in the bed. My head hurt worse the more I moved. I realized that I was nearly naked. I only had on my boxers. I grabbed the bed spread.

"Young lady, I don't know how you got in here, but I think you need to put on your clothes and get out of here."

"But we haven't had sex yet."

"And we're not. I'm a married man."

"Hey, your marital status has nothing to do with me. This is just a business transaction. What you do is your business."

"I'm not paying you anything. I don't even know who you are."

"Now you want to have amnesia. Well, good thing I saw the money on the table waiting for me." She reached into her bra and pulled out a wad of money before placing it back in her bra. "You look sort of familiar. Do I know you?" she asked.

"I doubt it. Now, please leave."

She mumbled a few obscenities. She put on some clothes, and left me wondering how I ended up in this position. I glanced at the telephone. It gave me the hotel name.

Now I had to figure out how I got here. A light bulb went off in my head. I looked for my pants. The sight of myself in the mirror scared me. I didn't like the view of the man staring back at me. My eyes were bloodshot.

I located my pants. I checked to make sure the prostitute hadn't stolen anything else from me. I pulled out my wallet, and my money and credit cards were all intact.

My cell phone beeped. There were several missed calls from Lexi and Lovie. Three o'clock flashed across my phone screen. I called Lovie several times until he answered. He agreed to come get me.

Fifteen minutes later, I eased in the passenger side. "Son, looks like you've been rescuing me a lot lately."

"At least you didn't try to drive home," he stated, as he pulled away.

"Your mom's going to kill me."

"Yes. That she is. I did call her to let her know that I was bringing you home."

"Jason's behind this. He was supposed to take me home. Instead, I ended up here."

"Dad, I don't know why you insist on dealing with Jason. He's a crook. Face it."

"I'm hard-headed, but I've learned my lesson."

Lovie's phone beeped. He glanced it. "Oh, no. Dad, what did you do?" he asked.

"I just told you. I drank too much and ended up at the hotel."

Lovie handed me his cell phone. I looked at the display. "What in the hell?" I blurted.

Lovie asked, "So you're sleeping with prostitutes now?"

"Son, I did not sleep with this woman. You got to believe me."

"How do you know what you did? You were drunk. Even you admitted that."

"That's just it. If I'm drunk and passed out, you best believe I wouldn't be able to perform sexually. I'm the first to admit that."

"Well, you better hope Jason didn't send this picture to mom."

Wait until I get my hand on Jason. I wanted to kill him.

CHAPTER 48

Charity

Hope's been avoiding me since Lovie and I rescued her from Tyler's clutches. She promised me she was through with him for good this time. Did I believe her? Absolutely not.

I'm still upset at Dad for cheating on Mom, but it was over twenty years ago. So I was willing to pretend like I didn't know. Like Lovie said, my parents are just like us. They make mistakes.

Hope promised to go with me to the craft store. There were so many things I needed to do to prepare for our dad's party. I knocked on her door. I didn't get an answer.

"Hope, open up," I said.

Still no answer. I turned the doorknob and looked inside. She was nowhere to be found. I went to her window and looked outside. Her car was gone.

"Oh, well." Looked like I would be going to the craft store by myself.

My eyes caught a glimpse of her diary. I walked to the door. I turned and walked back near the window. I picked up a pen and flipped open the diary. What I was doing was wrong, but in light of Hope's actions I felt justified. I dropped the pen, picked up the diary, and skimmed the pages.

"Oh my God." The words on the pages jumped out at me.

I glanced out the window again. Hope still hadn't made it back. I took her diary to my room and made a copy of some of the pages.

I heard the front door open. I rushed and placed the diary back on the edge of her table.

I bumped into Hope leaving her room. "What are you doing in my room?" she asked.

"Uh...Uh," I stuttered. "I thought you were in there. I didn't know you had left."

Hope held up a bag from a nearby drug store. "I had a headache and we were out of medicine."

"Since your head's hurting, you don't have to worry about going to the store with me," I said.

"Good. I'm not feeling it anyway."

I moved out of Hope's way. She went inside of her room and shut her door. I sighed with relief. I grabbed the copied pages I'd made of her diary and placed them in my purse. I grabbed my keys and left.

I sat in my car and took the time to thoroughly read the pages. I called Lovie. "Where are you?"

"I'm at the funeral home. What's up?"

"Don't go anywhere. I'm on my way over."

I jetted across town. I skidded into a parking spot at the funeral home.

"Hey, Shannon," I said, as I entered.

"What's up, girl?" she asked.

I didn't have time to hold a long conversation with her, so I responded, "Nothing much. Just came by to see Lovie for a minute."

I walked down the hall. My dad's office door was closed, which was fine with me. I went straight to Lovie's office. I shut the door.

He looked up at me and said, "Hi, Sis."

I pulled out the papers and handed it to him. "I'm only here for you to talk me out of killing him."

I paced back and forth while Lovie read Hope's diary entry.

"I'll kill him." Lovie threw the papers on his desk.

I held my stomach. "Every time I think about it, it makes me want to puke."

"Has he ever tried to touch you?" Lovie asked me.

"No, never." I tried to control my breathing.

Lovie got up and helped me to a chair. "This man has caused so much pain to our family."

I looked up at him. "He has to be stopped."

"You're right about that."

"Lovie, I didn't mean for you to do anything. We need to talk to Hope, and find out the details from her."

Lovie picked up the paper and waved it. "This is all I need right here. I don't need to know anything else."

"Lovie, promise me you won't do anything. Let me talk to Hope, and then we can decide on what to do next."

Lovie walked around in circles. "Charity, I feel like I'm losing it. Everything is all screwed up. I don't know if I'm coming or going."

"Lovie, I'm sorry. If I'd known you were dealing with some other stuff, I would have tried to handle this on my own."

"You did the right thing. I got this. If you can't depend on your older brother, then who can you depend on, right?" His attempt at joking failed.

"Lovie, you're scaring me."

Lovie sat back down behind his desk. "I'm sorry. I'm going to be okay. This is a lot to digest."

Someone knocked on Lovie's door. "Come in," Lovie said.

"Shannon told me you were here." My dad walked in.

We hadn't seen each other since I discovered his infidelity. I stood up and hugged him. He seemed to hold on to me longer than he normally did. The anger I'd had against him disappeared.

"Dad, sorry I can't stay. I have some errands to run."

Lovie held up the papers. "You're forgetting this."

"Thanks." I grabbed the papers from Lovie and placed them in my purse.

The only person who had the answers I needed lived in the house with me. She couldn't avoid me forever.

CHAPTER 49

Hope

Patience was never one of my strong points. As soon as I saw Charity's car pull out of the driveway, I went to the bathroom and removed the box I bought out of the bag. I'd lied and told Charity it was medicine, but it wasn't.

I glanced down at the white stick and sighed with relief. "I'm not pregnant. Thank you," I said out loud, as I looked up toward the heavens.

Charity nor Lovie had to worry about me hooking back up with Tyler. I'd promised God if I wasn't pregnant that I would never be with Tyler again. Temptation kept calling me. Tyler would call and send text messages. The more I ignored him, the more calls and texts he would send.

I sat on the edge of my bed and thought about my life. I thought about the bad decisions I'd made. My life had spiraled out of control. If I could just shake Tyler from my system, I would be okay. I don't know how long I sat on the bed rocking back and forth, but the sound of Charity's voice broke me out of my self-induced trance.

"When did Uncle Jason start molesting you?' Charity blurted out.

She caught me off-guard. "I don't want to talk about it."

"Either you do, or I'll go find out what I need to know from him." Charity stood with her arms crossed.

My biggest fear—being exposed—had happened. I couldn't look Charity in the face. "It started when I was eighteen."

Charity sat down on the bed beside me. "What about before then? Had he touched you in any way before then?"

"No. I promise you, he hadn't."

Charity embraced me. "Are you still sleeping with him?"

"No, not since Tyler."

"No wonder you think you're in love with Tyler. Tyler's older. Probably reminds you of Jason. Well, do know this, Lovie knows about this, and he wants to kill Jason for what happened between the two of you."

The years of shame exited my system in the form of tears. I cried on Charity's shoulder. Charity rocked me.

I stopped crying. "I'm okay. I knew it was wrong, but once it started, I couldn't stop."

"I don't blame you. It's him. He's been manipulating you."

"But—" I said.

Charity interrupted me. "No buts. Don't take up for the pervert. He's going to pay for what he's done to you."

She stormed out of my room.

I crawled up on the bed, pulled my legs up, and held on to my knees. My entire world was changing right before me. My phone rang. It was Lovie. I thought about ignoring his call, but decided it would be best to get the interrogation over with.

"Why didn't you come to me?" Lovie sounded hurt.

"I couldn't. I didn't want anyone to know."

"So, are you still sleeping with him?" Lovie asked.

"Of course not. Although, he did threaten to expose me to the family if I didn't."

"Oh, he did, huh? Let me deal with him." Lovie hung up.

I dialed Lovie's number several times, but all my calls were sent straight to voicemail.

I ran to Charity's room. "Lovie just called, and I think he's going to do something to Uncle Jason."

"He's not our uncle so stop calling him that," Charity yelled.

"Lovie won't answer his phone."

"I just got off the phone with Lovie. He's not going to do anything. He's just pissed. Like I am." Charity put on a pair of jeans and fastened them.

"Why are you changing clothes? Are you going somewhere?" I asked.

"Yes, I'm going out. Is that okay with you?"

"Give me a minute, and I can go with you."

"No. I would rather go by myself." She pulled her hair up in a ponytail.

"Fine." I pouted and left the room.

CHAPTER 50

Lovie

"Charity, I want you to stay in the car." I parked my car behind Jason's.

"I'm going in with you," she said, ignoring my plea.

Charity could be just as stubborn as our mom. "Fine, come on," I said as we walked up the walkway to Jason's door.

"Maybe I should do the talking," Charity suggested.

"You do that. While I size him up," I responded.

I rang the doorbell.

Jason opened up the door. "I'm surprised to see you two."

"Are you going to invite us in, or should we talk out here?" I asked.

Jason looked around us. He unlocked the screen door. "Come on. I hope this isn't going to be long."

Charity walked in first. "It's not going to take long at all."

Jason kept his distance from me. I don't blame him. Every time he was in my presence, I wanted to hit him. I kept my hands by my side.

Charity paced the floor before taking a seat. I waited for Jason to sit before sitting next to Charity.

The only sound heard was the television. Jason cleared his throat. "I would offer you something to drink, but I know this is not a social call."

Charity said, "There's something Lovie wanted to talk to you about."

Charity looked at me. What I was about to reveal would shock Charity, but she insisted on coming with me. "Jason, you're good at trying to blackmail people, so let me get down on your level."

"Son, you sure you want to go there with me?"

I held my hand up. "Wait. Let me finish, and then you can say what you want to say."

"I'm listening."

I looked at Charity. "Do you mind giving us a moment? I promise I'll behave."

Charity seemed reluctant at first, but stood up. "I do have to use the bathroom, so I'll be right back."

Since we'd been over Jason's place many times, she didn't have to ask for directions.

I faced Jason. "I need for you to stop harassing my folks."

Jason faked innocence. "I don't know what you're talking about."

"You tried to set up my dad with a prostitute. I found the prostitute, and she confirmed it."

"Can't pay a hoe enough for them to keep their mouth shut."

"But you can pay them enough to talk."

"So what? There's so much you really don't know."

"You can keep it to yourself. Be warned. If you don't stop harassing them, I will be going to the police."

"You promised me if I returned the money, you wouldn't."

"That was about the embezzling, but I have something even more damaging."

"What?" Jason didn't seem too cocky now.

"I'm sure you wouldn't like getting arrested for messing with a minor."

The color disappeared from his face. "I've never slept with a minor, so go right ahead."

I pulled out a copy of Hope's diary entry and handed it to him. He read it. "You can't prove anything."

"Who do you think they will believe? A young naive girl who trusted her uncle, or a con artist?"

He threw the paper at me. "What do you want from me?"

"I told you what I wanted. If I hear from my mom or my dad that you've giving them any type of drama, the police will be the least of your worries."

"Fine. You got what you want. Satisfied?" He extended his hand out to shake mine.

"I'll pass on the handshake. Just be a man of your word for a change."

I stood up. "Charity, are you ready?"

Once we were seated in my car, Charity asked, "Why did you really want me to leave?"

"Some things you don't need to know."

"Look, I'm not Hope. So spill it."

I was bursting with secrets, but didn't want to burden Charity. She was already harboring the knowledge of Dad's affair. She didn't need to know about our mother's. "It's nothing I can't handle. Just know that Jason will no longer be a thorn in the Joneses' side."

CHAPTER 51

Lexie

Six weeks. That's how long I'd been preparing for Royce's big day. The day was finally here. Royce insisted on going to work today. I tried to talk him out of it, but failed.

I'm a control freak. Charity got her organizational skills from me. She'd actually done a good job, but I'm so hands on that I'm sure I got on her nerves during the whole process. I'm hoping when people see how wonderful Royce's party goes, they'll be blowing up her phone with requests.

"Mom, you're in the way," Charity said, as she walked behind me while I stood in the patio doorway.

"Sorry. Just making sure everything is up to par."

"It will be. I promise you that." Charity walked past me and went to supervise the men who were putting up the tents with the tables and chairs.

It was a nice, spring day with no rain in the forecast, so I wanted to have the party outside in our huge backyard. Besides hors d'oeuvres, guests would be served a three-course meal.

Satisfied that Charity had everything under control, I went back inside. "Mrs. Jones, Mr. Jones' tux just arrived. Where should I put it?" Sherrie, one of the ladies Charity hired, asked.

I reached for the garment bag. "I'll take it upstairs with me."

I needed to get dressed for the party anyway. I went upstairs and showered. An hour later, I stood in front of the floor-length mirror in my bedroom.

"Hi, beautiful." Royce walked up to me and kissed me on the lips.

I glanced at the clock. "I was beginning to think the birthday boy was going to be late for his own party."

"Oh, no. And have you kill me? I just turned fifty. I want to see fifty more." Royce laughed.

I went back to putting on my make-up. "Your tux is in the closet. I've laid out your other clothes on the bed. Your shoes are in the box."

"What would I do without you?" he said, as he removed his clothes and walked to the master bathroom.

"Let's hope you'll never have to find out," I responded.

By the time Royce finished his shower, I was fully dressed. I admired myself in the mirror. The violet, strapless, silk chiffon dress accented my curves. I slipped my feet into a pair of white, diamond-studded pumps.

Royce stood fixing his tuxedo jacket. His vest and handkerchief matched my dress.

I picked up the pearls on the dresser. "Can you help me with this?"

Royce fastened the pearl necklace and gently placed a kiss on the nape of my neck. It sent chills down my spine. "Don't start nothing you can't finish," I teased.

"I can finish it," Royce assured me.

We locked lips. The sound of someone knocking on our door interrupted us.

I wiped the lipstick from his lips.

"Saved by the knock." Royce looked back at me and smiled. He opened the door.

Charity walked in. "Happy birthday, Daddy."

"Thanks, baby girl." They hugged.

"Mom, you look gorgeous."

"And so do you," I responded. "I see you've changed clothes."

Charity now had on a dark-purple, knee-length, beaded dress. She wore matching purple, snakeskin pumps. Charity and Hope were the best of both me and Royce.

"I just came upstairs to let you know the guests have arrived. Everybody's waiting on the guests of honor."

Royce held his arm out. "It's time to make our grand entrance."

"Are Hope and Lovie here?" I asked.

"Yes. Hope just arrived a few minutes ago."

"Then I'm ready." I placed my hand on top of Royce's arm.

We followed Charity down the cascading, spiral stairway. She waited for us at the bottom, then walked up and whispered into the ear of a man wearing a tuxedo. He announced, "Ladies and gentlemen, I present to you, Royce and Lexi Jones."

He moved to the side. I plastered a smile on my face and held my head up high. I grasped Royce's arm tightly. The room was filled with some of our friends and frenemies, and all eyes were on us. My smile got bigger since tonight not only signified Royce's fiftieth birthday, but announced to the city that the Joneses were together—stronger than ever.

CHAPTER 52

Royce

I couldn't help but smile with pride. Lexi definitely knew how to throw a party. The funeral business really made a person appreciate seeing another year. Turning fifty was an important milestone in anyone's life. Some days, I felt like I was still in my twenties, yet on others, I felt every bit my age.

I soaked in the birthday greetings. I shook hands and hugged people as we walked through the dining room, en route to the patio.

"Royce, how does it feel to officially be an old man?" my cousin Michael asked.

"I'll let you know in another ten years," I responded.

"Lexi, I must say, you do know how to throw a party. Food is good. Music is good. I can't wait for dinner," Michael stated.

"Michael, you don't have to wait much longer. Follow us, it's time for dinner to be served."

There were place cards at each table, so Lexi and I waited for everyone to locate their seats. Pastor McNeil said grace over the food, and soon everyone was piling food on their plates.

In between bites, I said, "Babe, you outdid yourself. You got all of my favorites. I might have to loosen this bottom button on my jacket."

"I normally wouldn't serve Southern cuisine at a dinner party, but this is your night, and I wanted it to be special."

"It is." I wiped my mouth and then kissed her on the cheek.

"Ooh, I love it," Shannon said, from her side of the table.

"Stay out of grown folks business," Lexi said.

"Mama, be nice," Charity said.

"I'm always nice," Lexi responded.

I cleared my throat. Lexi looked at me and I looked back at her. She said, "I'm just saying."

The waiters went around to each table and poured champagne. Lovie stood up, holding his glass in the air. "We wanted to thank everyone for helping us celebrate Dad's birthday. Dad, do you have anything you want to say?"

Everyone clapped. I stood up and raised my glass. "Thanks, Lovie." I looked down at Lexi. "I want to thank my beautiful wife for being by my side. I love you, baby."

"Oohs" and "Awws" were heard. Lexi's eyes glistened with love. She held her glass up in the air. "I love you, too."

I looked around the table, and my eyes stopped on my kids. "God couldn't have blessed me with better kids. Lovie, Charity, and Hope." I paused for a moment to soak it all in. "You make my days worth living. I love you all."

"We love you, too, Daddy," they responded.

I stared out at my guests. "To my family, friends, and colleagues, thank you for sharing a few hours of your time with me. It means a lot to me to see each one of your faces. As you know, with the kind of work that I do, I normally only see a crowd like this at a funeral. It's good to see you on this side."

Some people laughed. I looked down at Lexi. "Baby, do you have anything you want to add?"

Lexi stood up. "I want to thank everyone for coming. Royce is the best thing that's ever happened to me."

I couldn't resist leaning down to kiss her.

Someone yelled out, "Wait until later."

We giggled. Lexi continued, "Thank you all for coming. The party isn't over. It's just beginning. Enjoy yourselves."

Two men wearing white aprons pushed over a table with a huge birthday cake trimmed in black and gold, and shaped like a huge football. Lexi led me to where they stood. There were two lit candles, the number five and the number zero, on top of the cake.

I soaked in the excitement of hearing everyone sing "Happy Birthday" to me. I blew out the candles. Lexi handed me knife. I cut the first slice of cake, then placed it on a saucer. Lexi cut a piece off with a fork and placed it in my mouth. I kissed her, not caring if the icing messed up her lipstick.

She licked her lips. I kissed the icing off. If there were any doubts to how things were going in the Jones house, it would be put to rest. Things between Lexi and me were going just lovely.

"Eat up, everybody!" I said.

The furniture had been moved out of the living room and den, so it was like a big ballroom. We returned to the house, and music was blasting. Some of my favorite songs were playing.

"Lexi, come on. Dance with me."

Lexi and I got the party started by dancing to an old Johnnie Taylor song. "See y'all don't know anything about that," I said.

The dance floor filled up with other couples dancing. Lexi and I danced, laughed, and enjoyed each other's company.

"Lexi, darling, you don't mind if I borrow your husband for this next dance, do you?" Marisol, an ex-girlfriend of mine, asked.

"I do mind, but since it's his birthday, I'm willing to share him tonight only." Lexi had a smile on her face, but little did Marisol know she didn't like her. She would rather drink snake venom than see me dance with her.

"Marisol, I'm going to sit this one out. I promised Charity the next dance."

"Oh. Well, maybe another time."

"Smart move," Lexi said under her breath.

I planned on ending this night with some birthday sex, and I wasn't stupid enough to let someone, especially Marisol, come in between that. I wasn't giving Lexi a reason to not give me what I've been yearning for this entire night—to feel her in my arms.

CHAPTER 53

Charity

I stood in the doorway and watched the success of my dad's party unfold around me. I smiled watching him laugh and talk with his guests.

"You did a great job. I'm proud of you, baby." My mom hugged me.

"Glad you approve."

"Of course, you know I had to tell everyone you organized the party. Be prepared for your phone to be ringing off the hook."

"If things keep going the way they have, I'm going to need to hire more people."

"Hope isn't doing anything. Have her help."

"I tried that. She's not dependable."

"Let me talk to her."

I looked at her. "Do you really think that's going to help?"

"Once I tell her the news that Royce and I talked and we have decided to cut out your huge allowance, she'll be changing her mind."

"When did y'all decide this?" I asked.

"A few weeks ago. We were just waiting on the right time to talk to you all about it."

"Well, that's fine with me. It's your money, so I'm not going to pout."

"You and Lovie will do fine. But I'm really worried about Hope," my mom confessed.

"She'll be all right. She needs to learn that pretty looks don't always pay the bills."

Hope wouldn't get any sympathy from me. I felt my parents babied her too much and she was a spoiled brat. She was getting older, and needed to learn how to be more responsible.

"Dear, looks like your dad needs rescuing," my mom said, as she left me alone with my thoughts.

I walked outside to get a breather.

"Nice party," Tyler said.

I turned to face the sound of his voice. My mouth dropped open. "What...what are you doing here?"

"I think we have some unfinished business." Tyler eased from out of the darkness and under the bright light.

"Now is not the time." I walked closer to him. I didn't want to risk anyone else seeing him, especially Hope.

Tyler rubbed his hands together. "I was wondering how festive things would be if I crashed Royce's birthday party."

I pulled him by the arm and led him toward the driveway. "There's nothing you and my dad have left to talk about."

Tyler stopped. I almost fell trying to pull him. I continued, "I'm serious. You're not welcome here. I suggest that you leave."

"Not before I do this."

Before I could protest, Tyler kissed me. I slapped his face.

"Ouch." He rubbed his cheek.

Hope yelled, "You're busy telling me to leave him alone, because you want him for yourself."

I faced her. Fortunately, everyone was still inside so there were no nosy bystanders.

"Hope, it's not what you think."

"The hell it isn't." Hope folded her arms.

"Tyler, leave now or I'm calling the police," I said. I retrieved the cell phone from my small purse.

He held up his hand. "No need to do that. I'm going. Tell your dad I said Happy Birthday."

Hope and I watched Tyler walk down the driveway.

"Hope, before you go mouthing off, Tyler kissed me. I didn't kiss him. Since you saw everything, you saw me slap him too."

"You probably just did that because I was there."

"He was trying to be a party crasher. I was trying to get him to leave."

"Sure you were."

"Believe what you want. I don't have time for the drama."

"Whatever." Hope threw her hand up in the air and followed behind Tyler.

"Hope!" I called out her name several times, but she ignored me.

I rushed inside the house and located Lovie. I pulled him to the side. "Hope's outside with Tyler."

Lovie stormed out with me fast on his heels. He walked straight to Tyler's car. Hope didn't see Lovie until he grabbed her by the arm.

"Get back to the house," Lovie said.

"You don't tell me what to do," Hope responded.

A police car flashed its lights and stopped. One of the officers stepped out of the car. "Ma'am, are you alright?" he asked Hope.

I answered for her. "She's fine." *When did policemen started looking this good?* I reminded myself to focus on the problem and not the officer.

"Little lady, I wasn't asking you. I'm asking her." I read his badge. "Officer Underwood, this is my sister and my brother. The man in the car is trespassing, and we need for him to be off our street."

"And you are?" he stared at me.

"I'm Charity Jones."

"Well, Ms. Jones, the only person causing a disturbance is your brother and sister. This dude is on a public street, so there's nothing I can do about it."

"But—"

Tyler smiled. I wanted to smack the evil smile off his face.

Officer Underwood passed me his business card. "If he comes to your house, then you can call me, and I'll do something. In the meantime, I suggest you all hold it down. You do have neighbors, and I would hate to get a call about you all disturbing the peace."

I rolled my eyes. "Fine."

Reluctantly, Hope followed Lovie and me back up the sidewalk. The officer stayed behind and said something to Tyler. A few seconds later, I noticed Tyler pulling away. The officer waved at me. I smiled, turned back around, and continued back into the house.

CHAPTER 54

Hope

"I'm tired of everybody treating me like a helpless child." I addressed Lovie as we walked in one of the bedrooms, with Charity behind us.

Charity shut the door.

Lovie said, "I can't protect you if you keep putting yourself in harm's way."

"Charity, tell Lovie what happened."

"The kiss with Tyler is nothing to tell. He snuck it on me. I slapped him. That's it."

"I feel like you don't want me with him because you want him all to yourself."

Charity threw her hand up in the air. "Are you serious? That's crazy. I don't want Tyler. He's a snake that purposely set out to hurt you, me, and our family. Why would I want to be with a man like that?"

Lovie interjected, "Why would you want to be with a man like that?"

"Because...because I might be pregnant," I responded. My hand flew to my stomach.

"No. Say it ain't so," Charity pulled me into her arms.

I tried my best not to cry. I pulled away. "I have a doctor's appointment to make sure. I took a test, and it came back negative, but I still haven't gotten my period."

Lovie looked at me with fury in his eyes. "How could you be so irresponsible?"

"I'm sorry. When it comes to Tyler, I'm weak."

Lovie held both of my hands. "Look at me."

I did as instructed. "I'm sorry," I said again.

Lovie squeezed my hand. "You are a Jones. You are stronger than this hold this man has on you. You will not talk to him or see him again. Understood?"

I looked away. "I will try."

"No, promise me, you won't," Lovie said.

"But, if I'm pregnant, I will have to," I responded.

Charity said, "If you're pregnant, you have us. We'll help you with the baby. But Tyler is not welcomed here."

The door flew open. My mom walked in. "You all are having a family meeting, and didn't invite me?"

She walked in and closed the door. Guilt swept across my face. Charity and Lovie tried to come to my rescue.

Charity said, "It's time for the gifts." Charity grabbed my mom's hand and led her out of the room.

Lovie said, "Come on."

He pulled me out, and I followed him to the living room. I tried to be happy and laugh appropriately as my dad opened his gifts, but on the inside I felt bad. In fact, my stomach felt queasy. I ran to the nearest bathroom and relieved myself of dinner. I washed my face with a cold, wet towel. I looked in the mirror and didn't like the face staring back at me.

I couldn't keep this up. All of the lies and secrets were taking their toll on me. I pulled out my cell phone. I pulled the toilet seat down and sat on it.

Someone knocked on the door.

"I'll be out in a minute," I yelled.

I dialed a number. "I need your help."

Slim answered. "Anything for LJ's little sister."

"If I wanted to get rid of somebody, how much would it cost me?"

"Whoa. Hold up. I'm going to pretend like I didn't hear you say that. In fact, I don't know what you're talking about."

"But, Slim, I need you."

"I suggest you talk to your brother. Good-bye."

Slim hung up without waiting for me to say another word.

If I was pregnant, there's no way I would share my child with Tyler. I opened up the bathroom door to go out. Lovie rushed me right back in and shut it.

"Hope, have you lost your mind?"

"What?" I hope he still wasn't tripping about Tyler.

"I just got a call from Slim. Don't you ever, I mean *ever*, call him about something like that again."

"He's your friend. I'm sure with everything else he's in to, he could take care of my problem for me."

Lovie scolded me. "Whatever you're thinking about doing, don't. Don't make that request to anyone else. You hear me?"

"Yes." I pouted.

Lovie was all in my face. "I'm serious. You could get someone killed talking like that."

"That's the whole point."

"Let me deal with Tyler. Stay away from him."

I rubbed my stomach. "I can't have him trying to take my baby."

"So, you are pregnant?"

"I'm not sure. But if I am, I just don't need any interference from him."

"I got this. Just chill out. Dad's looking for you."

We left the bathroom. Our dad stood mingling with his guests. I tapped him on the shoulder. He turned around and gave me a hug. I wished I could stay wrapped up in his arms forever and remain his little girl. In his arms, I felt protected.

CHAPTER 55

Lovie

I felt like I was working security. Between the incident with Tyler outside and having to check Hope, my nerves were on edge. I understood why people resorted to drugs and alcohol. I needed something to ease my mind.

I grabbed a glass of champagne from the first tray that came my way. I gulped it down so fast, I ended up grabbing a second one before the waiter got far.

"Slow down, or you're going to need me to drive you home," Charity said.

"Keep an eye on Hope. She's calling around looking for a hit man."

"She's lost it. I'll deal with her when we get home."

"Please do. Slim's my man, but when it comes to his life and freedom, there's no love."

My dad walked up to us and placed his arm around my shoulder. "Son, I can't tell you how proud I am of you. Because of you, I have the money back. Business is booming and things between me and Lexi...," He looked at my mom. "Well, let's just say, your pops is one happy man."

He pulled me into a bear hug.

My mom clapped. "My two favorite men."

Michael said, "So LJ, when are you going to let your old man retire and take over the family business?"

My dad responded, "This old man has no immediate plans on retiring."

Michael was my dad's first cousin, and in my opinion he had always been a little jealous. My grandfather didn't have any other kids, but he did provide for his siblings' kids. Although they didn't have a lot of stake in the funeral home, they had job security and were given small shares. Big Daddy made sure he took care of his family before he died.

Michael was only concerned about his money. As long as RJ's was making money, he was making money.

"No business talk tonight," I jumped in and said. "Tonight's all about celebrating The Man." I grabbed another glass of champagne. I raised it. "To the hero of my life. To my dad."

We clicked our glasses, and I took one big gulp.

A waiter whispered something in my mom's ear. I watched my mom head out the front door. I didn't want to interrupt my dad's conversation with his guest, so I excused myself and followed her.

People were coming in and out. I looked around to see where she went. I caught a glimpse of her standing outside, away from the light. I squinted my eyes. It looked like Jason. My mom moved her hand back and forth. They appeared to be arguing but I couldn't hear what was being said.

I didn't want the situation to blow up and get out of hand, so I walked up to them. "Everything all right here?" I asked.

"No. He needs to leave," my mom responded.

"I'm not going anywhere until I speak to Royce."

I jumped in Jason's face. I held my nose. His breath reeked of alcohol. I backed up a little. "Look. You need to leave."

Jason staggered back. "Lexi, tell him. Tell Royce, I'm sorry."

"Lovie, go back inside. I got this."

"No, Mom. I'm not leaving you out here with this drunk."

"I'll be alright. I don't need Royce to come out here. He's been having a good night. This would ruin it."

I looked at my mom and then at Jason. He was in no position to drive. I could care less what happened to him, but I didn't want to risk him hurting anyone else.

"Come on," I said.

"I told you I'm not going anywhere until I say what I came here to say."

"Tell me. If it's something I feel my dad should know, I'll tell him tomorrow."

"Lexi, you better get this boy."

"Lovie, I told you, I got this." My mom snapped at me, causing me to pause.

"Yes, son. She told you she got this."

I ran back up in his face. "Stay out of this."

"Lexi, you want to do the honors of telling him?" He staggered back a little.

"Go, Lovie. Please," she begged.

My feet were glued. I couldn't move. Jason laughed. "Since you want to play the messenger, tell Royce he's not your dad. I am."

I punched him in the face. My mom grabbed my arm. "Lovie, you shouldn't have."

Jason grabbed his cheek. "Go ahead. Hit me again, if it'll make you feel better."

I pulled my hand back to him again. My mom grabbed my arm. I jerked it away, causing her to stumble. "Mom, is what he said true?"

Her silence was all the confirmation I needed. Every vein in my forehead felt like it would pop.

Jason laughed. "What you got to say now, Son?"

"Stop calling me that," I yelled.

I pushed him when I walked past him. I hopped in my car without saying anything else. I jumped on the interstate and pushed the car to over one hundred miles. I jumped off on the exit that led to the club.

I sat in the parking lot and decided not to get out of the car. I drove and drove, ending up in Dallas, Texas, three hours away. I checked into a hotel. I fell on the bed with all of my clothes on. I closed my eyes and thought back over my life.

Did my dad know he wasn't my biological father? So many questions floated around in my head.

Sleep evaded me. My phone blew up with messages from my mom. She was the last person I wanted to speak with.

CHAPTER 56

Lexie

Getting Jason to leave after Lovie stormed off was no easy task. He finally agreed to leave once I lied and promised to talk to Royce on his behalf. I refused to let anything spoil Royce's night.

After everyone left, Charity stayed behind to take care of the cleanup. I took care of Royce. I made sure his night ended with us making love. Now that my job was done, he was snoring next to me in the bed.

I was concerned about Lovie. I eased off the bed and grabbed my cell phone. I checked to make sure Royce was still sleep and went to the bathroom.

I called Lovie over and over until he answered. "Lovie, are you all right? Where are you?"

"Dallas."

"We need to talk."

"You've had twenty-six years to talk to me."

"Jason was drunk. He doesn't know what he's talking about."

"Why didn't you say that when I asked you?"

"Because." I looked at the door to make sure it was still closed. "Because, although it was only one time, there's always a possibility."

"I can't believe this shit."

"Stop cursing," I said.

"Damn, Mom. What do you want from me? You've put me in a real bad situation. Do you know how it makes me feel to find out that the man who I thought was my father is not my father?"

"That hasn't been confirmed. Royce is your dad as far as I'm concerned."

"Was there ever a DNA test?" Lovie asked.

"No. I don't need a DNA test. You are Royce's son in his heart and in mine."

"I need to know. I need to know who my daddy is."

"Royce is your daddy."

"I don't care how you want to handle this, but in the morning, I'm driving back to Shreveport. I want a DNA test done by the end of the week."

"But, Lovie."

"No buts, Mom. I mean it."

Lovie hung up the phone.

I hugged myself and rocked back and forth. What was I going to do? News like this would devastate Royce. Our relationship was solid, but would it be able to withstand a twenty-seven-year-old secret?

I closed my phone and slid in the bed beside Royce. I wrapped my arms around his waist and tried my best to go to sleep, but couldn't. I held him tight throughout the night.

I don't know when I drifted off to sleep. The light from the sun peeking through the curtains greeted me. My hand was no longer around Royce's waist. His spot in the bed was empty. I stretched and eased from under the covers.

Saturdays were busy days in our business, so it wasn't a surprise that Royce had already left. I dressed and went downstairs. The house was neat and clean. It didn't look like a party had been held here the night before. If Charity wasn't my daughter, she would get a nice tip for taking care of everything. With her taking charge, I was able to concentrate on Royce, and it was very important last night that I did.

The house phone rang.

"Mom, I'm headed over there," Lovie said and hung up.

Instead of making a cup of coffee like I'd originally planned, I drank a glass of vodka and orange juice. I checked the refrigerator and made a plate from some of the leftovers. I didn't really have an appetite, but I needed another drink so I had to put something on my stomach.

"Mom, are you drinking?" Lovie asked, startling me.

I looked up at him. He was still wearing his outfit from last night. He looked as bad as I felt.

"Dear, have a seat."

"This isn't going to take long." Lovie sat down in the seat next to mine.

"I'm sorry about everything," I blurted out.

"I've had time to think. We don't need to do a blood test. I don't want to hurt Dad."

I squeezed Lovie's hand. "Thank you," I whispered.

"In my heart, Royce Jones is my dad."

I silently thanked God for answering my prayers. "He is your father. You look like him. You two act alike. Jason is just trying to wreak havoc in our lives."

"Mom, I don't want you to worry about Jason anymore. I'm going to take care of him."

"No, you need to stay clear of Jason. For him to come over here like he did last night means he's losing control. It's best that you stay away."

"What if Dad had seen him? He's done enough to this family. I refuse to let him do anything else."

Lovie jumped up out of the chair and stormed off.

"Lovie!" I called out. Lovie didn't stop. I heard the front door slam.

"Lord, please don't let him do something he'll regret later."

CHAPTER 57

Royce

"Happy belated birthday, Mr. Jones," Frank, one of my workers, said as we were preparing to head out to a funeral.

"Thank you. I missed you last night."

"I had to stay at home with my mom. You know she has dementia, and my wife had to work last night."

"Sorry to hear that."

Frank said, "I heard about it. Glad you had a good time."

"It was fun. My wife and daughter did a great job."

We chit-chatted all the way to the church. We were supposed to meet another one of my workers at another church in two hours. I'd spent all day going from one funeral to another. I sent Lexi text messages in between locations. She normally would have messaged me back or called, but she was probably exhausted. She deserved a day of rest to herself.

"Frank, I'll lock up. See you on Tuesday," I said, as I grabbed my jacket off the coat rack.

I heard a noise. "Frank, did you forget something?" I asked out loud.

"This isn't Frank." Tyler walked to my doorway, revealing himself.

"Oh, it's you. What are you doing here?" He stood in the doorway, and I stood in the center of the room.

"We need to talk."

"When I tried to talk to you, you didn't want to. So at this point, we have nothing to talk about." I dangled my car keys. "Now, I'm headed out, so you need to leave."

"I don't think either one of us is going anywhere." Tyler didn't move. He raised his hand.

My eyes focused on the silver, shiny gun in his right hand pointed directly at me. I eased back a little. The back of my leg hit the chair, causing me to stumble a little. I caught myself from falling.

I held my hand out. "Wait a minute now."

Tyler pointed the gun down. "Sit. We have a lot to talk about."

Not wanting to set him off, I did as instructed. The jacket in my hand fell to the floor.

"Get your wife on the phone," he insisted.

"Leave Lexi out of this. This is between me and you."

He pointed the gun and fired toward the wall near my shoulder. The sound resonated through the room.

"Tell her you need her to get down here."

I looked up at Tyler's cold, black eyes. "You can do what you want, but I'm not calling Lexi to come down here."

Tyler gripped the gun. "You're not running this show. I said get her on the phone."

"I will do whatever you want, but I'm not asking her to come here."

"Fine. You can do it over the phone."

Reasoning with Tyler didn't seem to be an option. I would do anything at this point. "What do you need me to do?" I asked.

"I want to hear you tell her about my mom."

I picked up the phone and dialed Lexi's number. The call went to voicemail. I exhaled. "She's not answering."

"Try it again."

This time instead of calling Lexi, I dialed Charity's number. "Lexi, dear, I'm glad I got you."

"Dad, it's me," Charity responded.

"I know, Lexi. I've been so busy today that I didn't get a chance to call you. But I'm calling you now."

"Stop with the small talk and tell her," Tyler yelled.

"I'm trying. This is hard for me," I looked up and said to Tyler.

He waved the gun. "Do it now, or I swear I'll shoot you."

"Oh my God, Daddy, where are you?" Charity yelled.

"Lexi, I'm still at work, but that's not what I called you about."

I could hear Charity talking to the 9-1-1 operator on her other phone.

"Lexi, I have a confession to make. I cheated on you."

"Tell her with whom," Tyler directed.

"Lexi, I cheated with Ruth Ann. We were together for a couple of years."

"You loved her. Admit it."

"I loved Ruth Ann," I lied.

Tyler walked to the desk, snatched the phone out of my hand, and hung it up. His arm had to be getting tired, but he continued to hold the gun up.

"Now what, Tyler?" I asked.

"Give me a minute." He eased the gun down just a little.

"Hand me the gun. I'll pretend like this never happened." I eased my chair back and stood up.

"Sit. I'm warning you."

"No. You've done enough damage. This has to end now," I said, as I walked closer to Tyler.

"Royce, I don't want to shoot you, but if you don't stop, you will give me no choice."

By now, I was up on Tyler. We wrestled for the gun. The gun went off.

"Oh no!" I yelled.

CHAPTER 58

Charity

My heart stopped beating briefly when I realized my dad was with Tyler. He must have had a gun on him. When my dad called me and kept calling out my mom's name, I knew something was wrong. With him on my cell phone, I called the police from my business line.

I jumped in my car and drove straight to the funeral home. I called Lovie while en route. The police were already there when I pulled up.

Officer Underwood saw me and pulled me to the side. "Ms. Jones, I need to talk to you for a minute."

"My dad's inside. I need to get to him."

"Don't panic. Someone's been shot. We're waiting on the paramedics."

"Is it my dad?" I asked.

Officer Underwood responded, "At this point, I have no information."

"But, you just told me someone was shot."

"That's all I know."

"You're supposed to be the police. Find out!"

Lovie's car pulled his car beside mine. He jumped out of his car and ran up to me. "Where's Dad?" he asked.

In between tears, I responded, "I don't know. Somebody's been shot. They won't let me inside. I don't know if it was him or Tyler."

"I'll be right back." Lovie left to try to gain entrance to the inside of the funeral home, to no avail. I noticed the officer turning him around.

"Did you call Mom?" Lovie asked.

"Not yet. I wanted to see what was going on first."

"I better call her before someone else does," Lovie said.

"Too late," I said, when I heard my mom's car screeching into the parking lot.

She jumped out of the car and ran through the crowd that had formed.

"Royce!" she yelled out.

Lovie grabbed her. "Mom, calm down. We don't know anything right now. The police are handling the situation."

News media and bystanders were filling up the parking lot.

I explained to my mom and Lovie what happened. I left out the confession that my dad was forced to make over the phone.

"I was on the patio. I'd left my phone on the kitchen counter," my mom explained about not being available for his call.

"That's okay, mom. He got me, and I called the police."

We hung on to each other. The waiting was killing us. It'd been thirty minutes, but no one was telling us anything.

"Where's Hope?" my mom asked me.

"I don't know. I've been trying to reach her, but I haven't been able to get an answer."

We were talking about Hope when Officer Underwood walked out. The paramedics followed him, rolling a bed with a body bag.

My mom fainted. Lovie caught her right before she hit the concrete sidewalk.

My heart skipped a beat. I exhaled when my dad walked out of the funeral home, bloodied but alive. I pushed past everyone, and to Officer Underwood's dismay, into my father's arms.

I'd forgotten about the lies, deceit, and betrayal. The only thing that mattered was the fact that he was alive. He squeezed me tight. "I love you," he repeated over and over.

"I love you, too." He rocked me back and forth.

Officer Underwood said, "I hate to break up this reunion, but we need to get your father down to the station so we can question him some more about what happened."

"You're not going to put him in your police car, are you?"

Officer Underwood looked at me and then at my father. "No, but he's in no condition to drive himself."

"I'll drive him. We'll meet you there," I responded.

Cameras were flashing and news reporters were asking questions. Lovie had revived my mom. My mom and dad's reunion was caught by the cameras for the world to see. She cried tears of relief as they clung to each other.

"I'll drive," Lovie said.

We all piled up into his SUV. I sat in the passenger side, while my mom and dad sat in the back seat.

So many questions were running around in my head, but none would come out. I found myself looking behind me to make sure my dad was not a mirage—that he was actually real and alive.

"I'm so glad it was Tyler and not you in that body bag," I said.

"Me, too, baby girl," my dad responded.

"What happened?" my mom asked.

"We can talk about details later," my dad said, as I looked back and watched him hold on to my mom.

There were news reporters waiting outside of the police station. Officer Underwood escorted us inside.

"As long as your dad cooperates, he should be going home tonight," he assured me.

I squeezed my mom's hand. We sat and waited in the lobby as the police interrogated my dad about the shooting.

CHAPTER 59

Hope

I was lying on Tyler's bed with my hands tied behind my back and my ankles tied. I couldn't move. It'd been hours since he'd tied me up. My phone rang. It was in my purse, which was on the nightstand. I heard the ringtone I had setup for Charity play several times.

Since I'd been here, I realized Charity and Lovie were right. I should have left Tyler alone. I thought telling him about the possibility of me being pregnant would draw us closer together, but instead, it upset him.

Would anyone think to look for me here? My life flashed through my mind. I'd made so many bad choices; most of them concerned men. I thought about the relationship with Jason. I shouldn't have allowed it to continue as long as it had.

I tried to justify my actions of being promiscuous as a teenager with the fact that my parents didn't show me enough love. In reality, that's a lie. My parents showered me with love and anything my heart desired. Charity and I seemed to be in competition with one another because of our own selfish actions. There was no reason to compete.

Where did things go wrong for me? At least Charity had the drive to do something with her life. As for me, guess my time was almost up, so there was no need for me to try to figure out what I wanted.

How could Tyler do this to the mother of his child? He should have been overjoyed with the prospect of being a father, but instead he accused me of trying to trap him and called me all sorts of names.

I coughed. My mouth felt dry from lack of fluid. The sound of the door opening startled me. I closed my eyes in fear. I tried to control my breathing as I waited for Tyler to enter the room.

I heard several voices, but none sounded like Tyler.

"We got someone tied up." The voice was closer.

I opened up my eyes and cried when I saw the policemen.

"Ma'am, I'm Detective Franklin. We're going to get you out of here."

Someone took a picture of me. One of the officers took out a knife, and I felt the rope loosen around my wrists. I brought my hands to the front and rubbed them. I winced in pain. The same officer cut the ropes around my ankles. I eased up on the bed.

"Tyler Williams is responsible for this," I blurted.

"Ma'am, what's your name?"

"I'm Hope Jones. Can someone call my dad, Royce Jones, or my mom, Lexi?"

The officers looked at each other. "Ms. Jones, we called the paramedics—as soon as they check you out, I'll have one of the officers take you home."

"Can someone hand me my phone over there? I need to talk to my parents."

The officers looked at each other again. "Is there anyone else you can call?" the officer asked.

"Yes, my sister."

"What's her number? I'll call her for you," the officer responded.

A few minutes later, I was on the officer's phone talking to Charity. "Why are you at the police station?"

Charity gave me a condensed version of what had occurred. "I'll be there," I responded.

I tried to stand up, but fell back on the bed. One of the officers tried to assist me. "The paramedics just pulled up."

A man and woman rushed in and took my vital signs. The female paramedic asked, "We can take you to the hospital for further testing. That's up to you."

"No, I just need someone to take me to the police station."

The officer who first saw me said, "Your father's been released. Your family should be at home by now, so I'll drop you off there if you like."

"Yes, please do."

I grabbed my phone off the nightstand and followed the officer through the apartment. There were police going through Tyler's things. I saw the photo album sitting on the table.

"That's mine. Can I have it?" I asked.

"It's part of our evidence," one of the officers said.

"Has it been tagged yet?" the officer who was taking me to my parents' home asked.

"No."

He picked up the photo album and handed it to me. "She's been through enough trauma for one day."

The officer tried to lift my spirits as he drove. When the front door opened, I flew into Lovie's arms. "Where's Dad?" I asked.

"He's in the living room."

I turned and faced the officer. "Thank you for rescuing me."

"Ms. Jones, we are sorry for your tragedy. If you all need anything, call me."

I took his card and slipped it inside the photo album.

"What's that?" Lovie asked, as we walked toward the living room.

I shoved it in his hands. "It's the photo album that was at Tyler's. Get rid of it."

Lovie looked at me curiously. "Don't ask me any questions, Lovie. Just do it."

Lovie took the photo album and headed toward the den. I walked in the living room by myself. "Daddy!" I cried out.

My mom sat on the edge of the sofa holding my dad's hand. I bent down and hugged him.

My mom reached for me. "Baby, are you alright? One of the officers told us what happened."

I coughed. "I'm fine. Just thirsty."

"Charity, get your sister some water."

Charity obeyed and returned with a bottle of water.

I sat on the floor beside my dad and gave them a recap of what happened. I'd never been so scared in my life. Thankfully, I was now safe and secure with my parents.

•

CHAPTER 60

Lovie

It'd been awhile since I spent the night in my old bedroom. In light of all that happened, I thought it would be best. My dad was in no shape to field questions from the media and my mom, well…the less she stayed out of it, the better. Being the oldest, I felt it was my duty to be the family spokesman.

The phone started ringing as early as seven o'clock. I spent most of the day filtering calls from reporters.

"I think the people need to see your dad on TV, to know that he's okay," my mom said, as we all sat around the dining room table.

My dad, who had been quiet most of the day, said, "Lexi's right. Let the reporters know we'll do a quick news conference right outside in front."

Two hours later, our family stood outside in front of the house surrounded by local media.

My dad read a statement my mom helped him to write. "We want to thank the community for their outpouring of support. I thank God that He spared my life, but we are saddened that during the ordeal, a young man lost his life. Pray for his family. Pray for the Joneses."

One of the reporters asked, "Why was he there?"

I stepped in front of the microphone. "My father won't be answering any questions at this time. We do thank you for coming and please, keep the Joneses in your prayers."

With our hands locked with each other's, the entire family walked back inside of the house. The reporters were disappointed that their questions weren't answered but the less my dad said, the better.

"Dad, I think it's time you got your attorney involved."

"Lovie, I haven't done anything wrong. Tyler came after me."

"While you two discuss this, I'm going to whip up something for dinner," my mom said. "Girls, follow me."

Charity and Hope followed her. This was the first opportunity my dad and I had time to talk alone. We walked into the den. I glanced at the doorway to make sure we were still alone.

"Dad, what happened yesterday?"

I bit my tongue, trying my best not to interrupt, as he gave me full details.

"I should have handled Tyler when I had the chance."

"And you would be behind bars. I'm glad you didn't do anything to jeopardize your freedom."

"I would do anything to protect the family."

His face fell into his hands. "My sins have caused this family problems. I'm paying for what I did."

"Dad, if you've asked God to forgive you, then He has."

"But your mom is in the dark. I need to confess everything, but I don't think she'll be able to forgive me." He bowed his head in shame.

I patted him on the shoulder. "Your secret's safe with me."

He placed his hand on top of mine, but didn't look up. "I can't do this. I can't let another day go by without telling Lexi the truth about why Tyler was in my office."

"Dad, are you sure? Maybe let things cool down a little. Right now, you're emotional."

I heard my dad sob. "I've failed. I've failed you kids. Your mom."

"We're okay. Shooting Tyler was an accident. It's not like you shot him on purpose."

"But I wanted him dead. If he was, I wouldn't have to worry about him exposing what I'd done to Lexi."

I couldn't argue with him there. "Looks like he solved the problem."

"It appears that way."

I wiped the sweat off my forehead. "So, no more talks of telling mom anything."

"Fine." He shrugged his shoulders.

I looked at my dad's bowed head, then up at the ceiling. *When did I become the bearer of secrets?*

CHAPTER 61

Lexi

I didn't want my family out of my sight. I knew the kids had to go home, but I didn't want them to leave. I hugged them and stood in the doorway with Royce as we watched them walk to Lovie's SUV.

"Dear, it's just the two of us." Royce closed the door.

"Yes, it is."

We walked hand in hand up the stairs. Royce sat on the bed. I stood in front of him. I ran my hand over his head. "I don't know what I would have done if I'd lost you."

He kissed my hand. "I hope we never have to find out."

"I'll go run you some bath water."

While Royce was taking a bath, I decided to go downstairs to make sure all the doors were locked. The books on the shelf in the hallway seemed out of place. I moved the books around. I picked up the short one.

"What in the world?" I said out loud. It wasn't a book. It was a photo album, and it was a photo album filled with pictures of Royce and some woman—a woman I didn't recognize.

Just like that, my life had changed. The pictures appeared to be old, but how old was the question? And how did they end up on my shelf?

I held on to the photo album and went back upstairs. I sat on the bed going through the pictures. Many questions floated in my mind, but one question didn't. Royce sported his wedding band on his finger in the pictures, so I knew beyond a shadow of a doubt that we were married when some of the pictures were taken.

My heart broke into pieces when I removed the pictures and saw the dates on them to confirm. We had only been married for two years. How could he do this to me?

Everything was coming back to me. It all made sense now. During that period of time, Royce took overnight trips almost every weekend. Young and naive, I believed he was working for his dad. I used to cry myself to sleep at night sometimes because I missed him.

Tears streamed down my face as I stared at the pictures.

"Baby, what's wrong?" Royce asked.

I looked up at Royce, and it was as if I was looking at a stranger. Were the last twenty-eight years of my life a facade? Until now, I was proud to be a Jones. But at this very moment, I felt numb.

I threw the photo album at him. Some of the pages fell to the floor. He bent down and picked them up. His face showed shock, and then recognition. He sat down on the side of the bed. "Lexi, I can explain."

He placed his arm around me. I pushed his arm away. "Don't touch me."

"It happened years ago."

"I don't care if it happened yesterday. The fact that it happened at all is what disturbs me." I moved to the other side of the bed and crossed my arms.

"I wanted to tell you, but didn't know how."

"That little boy in that picture looks awfully familiar," I said between clenched teeth.

"That was Tyler. Ruth Ann's son."

I could barely breathe. My hand flew to my chest. "You killed your own son? Oh my God!"

"Tyler wasn't my son," Royce attempted to assure me.

"He was your lover's son. How do you know?" I asked.

"He was already born when I met Ruth Ann."

"I guess I should be relieved, but still. How could you do this to me? To us?"

"I was young. Stupid. We were having problems."

I held my fist up. "So, every time we had problems, you ran into the arms of another woman?"

"No, baby. That was the only time I stepped out on you. I promise you that."

"Now it all makes sense. He threatened to expose your affair, so that's when you killed him."

Royce got up and sat next to me. "I promise you on a stack of Bibles, that it was an accident. Everything happened the way I told you, except the fact he wanted me to tell you about Ruth Ann."

"Tell me this. Were you ever going to tell me about your little fling?"

Royce looked away. "Not if I didn't have to."

"I need you to leave. Leave right now."

"Lexi, you're upset. I understand that, but I'm not going anywhere."

"Fine. But you are leaving this room."

Royce sat there. I said, "Royce, I'm serious. You don't have to leave the house, but you need to get away from me or else I'm going to make sure you're ready to fit in one of those caskets."

This time Royce got up. The anger I felt showed on my face, and he could tell I meant business. I exhaled when I heard the door shut. I fell back on the bed and clung to the pillow.

CHAPTER 62

Royce

Leaving Lexi alone was the last thing I wanted to do, but I felt as if I had no choice. She normally would have gotten up, hit me, or threw something at me, but she did none of those things. That's what scared me. Under the circumstances, she was calm. In fact, too calm. So, when she threatened to put me in a casket, I believed her.

I went down the stairs and opened up a new bottle of bourbon. I poured myself a glass. I sat the glass on the table and took a drink directly from the bottle.

The phone rang. Neither Lexi nor answered. My attempts to drown out my sorrows with alcohol failed. With a heavy heart and a headache, I stumbled into one of the guest bedrooms downstairs. I fell on top of the covers and slept until the next morning.

I woke up hoping that I'd had a nightmare, but reality set in. This was my life. I went up the stairs. With each step, I wondered if Lexi would be able to find it in her heart to forgive me.

I turned the doorknob of our bedroom. It wouldn't open. I knocked on the door. "Lexi, let me in."

"Go away, Royce."

"I need to get some clothes. What am I supposed to do? Wear pajamas all day?"

"I don't care what you do," she responded.

"Please. We don't have to talk unless you want to."

I leaned on the door. I heard a clicking noise. I moved. Lexi opened the door. "Get some clothes, and get the hell out."

"I was hoping we could have a peaceful conversation this morning."

"Well, people in hell want ice water, too, so we don't always get what we want."

I refused to argue with her. I'd caused her enough pain. I went to my closet and got a suit. I went to the dresser and I got a clean pair of boxers, a t-shirt, and socks.

"Will you hurry it up?" She patted her foot.

"Lexi, I'm moving as fast as I can." I lied.

"I'm going to take a shower. Please be gone when I return." Lexi left me alone in the bedroom.

I noticed the photo album on the bed; she must have been looking at it before I came in. I picked it up and threw it in the trash. Lexi could avoid me for now, but she wouldn't be able to avoid me forever. We needed to talk, but I would give her the space she needed.

I dressed and went into work.

"Royce, what are you doing here?" Shannon asked. "I thought you were taking some time off."

"Where did you get that idea from?" I asked, as I walked past the receptionist's area and to my office.

The yellow crime tape was still across the door. I kept walking and went into one of the other rooms.

Lovie rushed in. "Shannon told me you were here. You should be at home. I got things covered here."

"Lovie, you're an accountant, not a mortician. There are things I need to do. People are depending on me to handle their loved ones with care."

"I've been thinking. I should take more interest on that side of the family business, so I want to study mortuary science."

"Son, you don't have to do that on my account."

"It's not. With everything that's been happening, I think I'm finally ready to really learn more about the family business."

I smiled. "You don't know how happy I am to hear that. After the night I've had, I needed some good news." I dropped my head. "She knows."

Lovie walked into the room where I was. "You shouldn't have told her."

I scratched my head. "She found a photo album. I'm still trying to figure out where it was, and how it ended up in my house."

"Please don't get mad. Hope got it from Tyler's apartment. She gave it to me, and I didn't know what else to do with it. So, I put it on the bookshelf. I'd planned to get it and take it with me, but the opportunity never presented itself."

"It's not your fault. It's probably best that everything is out in the open now."

"I guess I should go check on Mom."

"She'd love to see you."

Lovie left to go check on Lexi. Tyler was dead, but yet, he still succeeded in his quest to cause problems in my marriage. I wondered how things would be if I had been on the other end of the bullet instead of him.

I shook the bad thought away.

CHAPTER 63

Charity

My business phone rang constantly. Some of my mom's friends claimed to be calling because they wanted to book me for their next event, but truth be told, they were calling me to be nosy. What happened in the Jones household stayed in the Jones household. They could get their information from the media. If my mom wanted her friends to know more, she would tell them herself.

My best friend, Lisa, sat across from me at the kitchen table. She placed the phone down on the table. "An Officer Underwood says he's coming over. It's something he wants to talk to you about. He sounds sexy."

"I wonder what that's about."

"Girl, is he sexy?" Lisa asked.

"Don't even go there. You know what happened the last time I listened to you."

"It's not my fault Tyler ended up being a two-timing jerk."

"He almost killed my dad."

"Who told you to listen to me anyway?" Lisa ranted.

"You don't have to worry about that...ever again."

The doorbell rang. I got up.

Lisa said, "You might want to smooth your bangs down in the front in case it's that officer with the sexy voice."

"I'm not listening to you," I said, as I used my right hand to move the hair out of my face.

I looked through the peephole, and the eyes of Officer Underwood stared back at me.

I opened the door.

"Ms. Jones, did I catch you at a bad time?" he asked.

"No, come right on in."

I moved to the side so he could come in. I don't know what kind of cologne he wore, but it smelled good. It filled up my nostrils as I led him into the living room.

"I hate to bother you. Is your sister here too? I just had a few questions to ask you both."

"Sure. I'll be right back."

Less than five minutes later, I'd returned with Hope following behind me. They greeted each other. Hope and I sat on the sofa.

"Ms. Jones, how are you doing?" Officer Underwood asked Hope.

"Still a little shook up, but fine."

"How well did you know Tyler?"

"Apparently, not well enough. He kidnapped my sister, and tried to kill my daddy," I responded.

"Calm down, Ms. Jones. These are just routine questions."

"I understand that, Officer Underwood, but I think my family has been interrogated enough these last few days."

"I'm sorry you feel like I'm interrogating you. We're just trying to understand the motive behind his doing what he did."

Hope responded, "He was crazy."

"Exactly. Simple as that." I frowned.

"I didn't mean to upset either one of you. If there's anything else you want to share, please do so."

I looked at Hope. Hope looked at me. Neither of us had anything to add. Officer Underwood stood up. "Ladies, you have my card. If you need me, you know how to reach me."

"Omar, is that you?" Lisa walked in the room and said.

"Lisa, it's been a long time," Officer Underwood responded.

"It sure has." Lisa hugged him. "Charity, this is my cousin's ex-boyfriend."

"Ladies, have a good day." Officer Underwood looked in my direction when he talked.

"I'll walk you out so we can get caught up," Lisa said. "I'll call you later, Charity."

"Dang, who doesn't she know?" Hope asked.

"Tyler. That should have been my sign to ignore him," I responded.

Lisa knew quite a few people around town, and it should have been a red flag when she couldn't find out anything on Tyler, good or bad.

"Well, I'm about to go to my doctor's appointment. Do you want to tag along?" Hope asked.

"Sure." I grabbed my purse and iPad and jumped in the passenger seat of Hope's car.

I couldn't get Officer Underwood out of my mind. I loved his tenacity. Too bad we didn't meet under better circumstances.

CHAPTER 64

Hope

Never thought I would be this young having a child and raising one by myself, but life happens. Many had done it before me.

The doctor walked in the waiting room with his clipboard.

I squeezed Charity's hand.

"Ms. Jones, I regret to tell you—."

"Wait. I don't know if I'm ready for this," I interrupted him.

"Let the doctor finish. He has other patients to see. And stop squeezing my hand." Charity removed my fingers from her hand and shook it.

"As I was saying, Ms. Jones, you're not pregnant, but you are anemic, so I'm going to put you on some iron pills."

Charity looked up at me. "Hope. He said you weren't pregnant."

That's what I thought he said." I sighed with relief. "I'm not pregnant."

"No, ma'am, you're not." He handed me a prescription. "Take these once a day. Try to take them with food, or it may cause some nausea."

"Thank you, Doctor Mack."

The doctor left the room. "I'm not pregnant," I repeated over and over.

"This should be a wake-up call to you. I've warned you about sleeping with guys without condoms. You're lucky being anemic is your only problem."

Any other time, I wouldn't want to hear Charity lecturing me, but today, I didn't care. I wasn't carrying Tyler's baby.

"We need to go celebrate," I said to Charity as soon as we got in the car.

"Go by the house. Lovie said Mom needs us."

"Mama always has drama going on."

"You are one to talk," Charity responded.

"Fine. We'll go by there, but I'm going out to celebrate later."

I pulled up behind Lovie's SUV. He had the door open before we could reach it.

"She's upstairs, and she's not doing too good," Lovie said.

"What's wrong with her?" I asked.

"She found out about Dad's other woman."

"He shouldn't have told her," I said.

"He didn't. She found the photo album."

"Y'all losing me," Charity said.

"I'll tell you about it later," I responded, as we followed Lovie up the stairs.

Lovie opened up our parent's bedroom door. My mom was in bed with puffy, red eyes. I don't recall seeing her look this bad before. Her eyes looked sad. She wasn't wearing designer anything. She still had her robe on.

She sat up. "Lovie called in the cavalry I see. Well, you kids didn't have to come check on me. I'll be all right."

Charity sat on the corner of the bed. "We're here. We're not going to let you go through this alone."

Lovie said, "That's what I've been trying to tell her. She's not in this by herself."

"I'm not trying to get you kids involved in Royce's and my mess. It's something we need to deal with."

"But what happens with y'all affects us. You've been together too long to end up in divorce court," I blurted.

"Dear, Royce couldn't get rid of me that easy. In fact, I would stay married to him just to give him hell. Ain't no other woman going to enjoy my hard work."

There it was. The fire I was used to seeing in her eyes. There was hope for their relationship.

"Lovie, I need to talk to the girls alone, if you don't mind."

"Sure. I'll call and check on you later." Lovie kissed my mom on the cheek and left.

I sat on the other side of her.

She looked back and forth between me and Charity. "I'm not sure what either one of you knows, but the reason why Royce and I are in this situation is because I found out he cheated on me. Although it happened years ago, it still hurts."

"It would hurt me, too." I recalled how I felt when I found out Tyler cheated on me with Charity.

"Mom, we love the both of you. We're not taking up for Dad, but it was a long time ago," Charity said.

"I'm going to eventually make up with your dad, but for right now, I need my space. He needs to give it to me."

"Everybody's been calling and asking about what happened," Charity said.

"I'm sure they all pretended to be the concerned friend. I hope you didn't tell them anything."

"Of course not."

"Good. Let them keep wondering. One thing I learned from your grandfather is that whatever happened in the Jones household needed—"

Charity and I joined in, "To remain in the Jones household."

We'd learned that mantra growing up. We weren't to gossip about our business. It was okay to gossip about others, but never about what went on in our household.

CHAPTER 65

Lovie

My dad was in the same spot I left him. He could have stayed at home, since he wasn't working. He was staring out into open space.

"Is your mom okay?" he asked, acknowledging he knew I was in the room.

"She's going to be all right. Just give her a little time."

"Thank God. I thought she was going to leave me," he admitted.

"She might not leave you, but you might leave her. She's definitely not going to make life easy for you."

"I'm not expecting anything less. If it takes two lifetimes, I plan on making it up to her."

"Dad, just chill out. Seriously."

"I've sent her flowers. Did she get them?"

"Yes. She threw them in the trash."

"I guess I need to swing by the jewelers."

"Negative. You're not listening to a thing I'm telling you. Do nothing. Let this ride out."

Shannon rushed in. "There's a reporter in the lobby who wants to talk to you, Royce. He claims he's learned some new information about Tyler and wanted to get your response."

"Dad, I got this. Shannon, tell him someone will be out in a minute."

My dad stood up. "I can do this."

"Sit, I got this."

I checked my appearance in the hallway mirror. I greeted the female reporter and the cameraman in the lobby.

"My dad's busy working, but I understand you had a few questions. I'll be happy to answer them for you."

I recognized the local reporter. "I'm Debra Curtin, and it'll only take a few minutes."

I looked at the cameraman. "Let's do this," I responded.

"This is Debra Curtin reporting live from RJ Jones Funeral Home. As you know, two days ago, Tyler Williams attempted to kill the owner, Royce Jones. I'm here with his son, Lovie Jones. Can you tell us how your family is doing after this tragedy?"

I looked into the camera. "Debra, my family is grateful that my dad is still alive. It could have easily been him dead. We want to thank you, and other members of the media, for respecting our privacy. We'd also like to thank your audience for the outpouring of well wishes and support."

"Lovie, a source informed us that Tyler came to town with the sole purpose of harming your family. Do you know if that's true?"

"Yes, that's true; but by the grace of God, he was unable to pull off his plan."

"Does anyone know why he targeted your family?" Debra asked me.

"The only person who knew the answer to that question is dead."

"Thank you, Lovie. We hope that this tragic event will be a distant memory for you all. Debra Curtin, reporting live. Now back to the studio."

The cameraman turned off the light. Debra shook my hand. "Thank you. I appreciate you taking the time to talk to me." She slipped a business card in my hand. "If you want to share anything else, please feel free to call me."

"I will."

"And I do mean anything." Debra winked her eye at me and followed her cameraman outside.

"Was she flirting with you?" Shannon startled me.

I cleared my throat. "Mind your business."

"Uh-huh. She probably had this all planned. She ain't sneaky."

"Don't hate." I popped my collar. "I do look good, if I do say so myself."

"Boy, please. Just because you in a suit, don't mean you look good."

My dad came out interrupting our playful banter. "You did good, Son."

"Thanks, Dad. See, told you, I got this."

"That reporter did seem to lean in a little too much. Guess she was trying to show you her cleavage," my dad said.

"I just have that effect on women. You know every woman wants to be with a Jones man."

"Let's hope your mama still wants to be with this Jones man."

Shannon looked back and forth at us. "What's going on?"

"Nothing, Nosy. Get back to work," I said.

"You're not the boss of me," she said, as she walked away.

CHAPTER 66

Lexi

Some people would probably say I'm a hypocrite since my slate wasn't completely clean. No, I haven't forgotten about my one indiscretion. What Royce did and what I did were two different things. One night does not compare to a full-blown affair. Royce lied to me to be with that woman.

Royce threw the pictures in the trash, but I took them out and looked at each one of them. The woman in the photo wasn't prettier than me. She sure as hell wasn't finer than me. Back in the day, I was a brick house. Still am. The woman in the picture didn't hold a candle to me, so I couldn't figure out the attraction. I was puzzled. Why did Royce feel the need to creep?

Yes, we had our share of problems back then, but what triggered him to betray me? Over the years, I'd had plenty of sleepless nights due to the guilt I carried from sleeping with Jason.

It's probably best that I'm just finding out about this affair. If I would have found out back then, I would have divorced him. I could still divorce him. Who was I kidding? I loved that man too much to leave him and again, I'm not completely innocent myself.

I sat at the kitchen table eating my dinner.

Royce walked in. "Hi, baby," he said. He attempted to kiss me. I turned my head.

"Something smells good," he said.

I continued to remain quiet.

"Hmm. Nothing for me, I see," he responded.

"There's plenty of leftovers in the fridge. You know where the microwave is," I responded.

Royce left out of the room. I'm sure he was disappointed I'd cooked something for myself, and not him. I actually timed it so he could see me eat a fresh meal.

"What in the world is going on here?" he walked back in the room.

He must have seen the clothes I'd piled on top of the bed in the guest room.

"I decided to bring some of your things downstairs. You can put them in the closet yourself."

"Lexi, come on now."

I looked up at Royce. "Right now, you have no say-so. Either sleep in the guest room, or I'll go to a hotel."

"Fine," he responded, as he stormed out of the room.

I hated to do him like this, but he needed to learn there were consequences for cheating on me. I didn't want to make it easy just in case he was tempted to cheat on me again.

I heard him moving stuff around. I finished eating, stood in the hallway, and watched. He complained the entire time.

"You could help me," he said.

"I could, but this is more fun." I took a sip of my soda.

"This isn't fair," Royce said.

"Life isn't fair. We have to roll with the punches," I responded.

I went to the living room and sat in Royce's favorite chair. I leaned the recliner back and turned on the news.

I yelled, "Why didn't you tell me you were going to be on the news?" I yelled.

"You're not talking to me, remember," he yelled back.

"Oh, yeah. You're right. Carry on."

The clip from the funeral home played directly after the commercial played. The picture of one big, happy family displayed, and then the reporter interviewed Lovie.

I reached in my pocket for my cell phone. It wasn't there. I didn't feel like looking for it. I picked up the cordless phone and called Lovie. I got his voicemail, so I left him a message. "You did good in your interview. Call me."

I turned the volume back up on the television as loud as it would go.

Even with the television being up loud, I could hear Royce calling out my name.

I hit the mute button. "What?" I rolled my eyes and shifted in my seat so I could see him.

"Have you been looking for this?" Royce waved my cell phone back and forth.

"Nope. I don't feel like talking to anyone."

"Why is Jason texting you?"

"I don't know. Ask him." I bit my lip and turned back in my seat.

CHAPTER 67

Royce

"Here." I practically shoved the phone in Lexi's hand.

She took it and went back to ignoring me and watching television.

Jason had no business texting my woman. She didn't have to tell me. I would find out on my own, after I found something to eat. I hadn't eaten all day, and my stomach was letting me know it.

Two hours later, I knocked on the door belonging to my ex-best friend. Jason opened the door. "Royce, I'm surprised to see you here."

"Me, too."

He shifted to the side. "Come on in. You want a brew?"

"No, I'm good."

We each took a seat. "Jason, we were boys. What happened?"

Jason wouldn't look up at me; instead he stared at a spot on the floor. "I got greedy. Bills started coming in. Everything got out of hand."

"You're an accountant. You know how to budget."

"Every time I turned around you were getting a new car for you, for Lexi, for one of the kids."

"That's the problem. Everybody want to be like the Joneses, but don't know what's going on. Most of the cars we got were leased. I was able to switch cars out every two years because of that. Otherwise, we wouldn't have been switching cars that often."

"Oh, I didn't know."

"No, you didn't, and you didn't bother to ask."

"Sorry, man. Can you forgive me?"

"Before this weekend, I would have said no, but maybe."

"That's all I've wanted. I want to get my friend back."

"What you did was foul."

"I regret it. Believe me."

"You can stop harassing Lexi now."

"Lexi hasn't talked to you?" Jason looked up at me. This time he looked me directly in the eyes.

"Right now, we are not on talking terms."

"In order for us to get our friendship back on track, I don't want any more secrets between us," Jason said.

"I agree."

"Remember when you were running back and forth to Marshall to be with that woman? What was her name?"

"Ruth Ann," I responded.

"Remember how you encouraged me to spend time with Lexi so she wouldn't be by herself worried about you?"

I didn't like the way our conversation was going. "Man, get straight to the point. I don't have time for a trip down memory lane."

"To make a long story short, Lexi and I slept together and—"

Before Jason could get his full sentence out, I had jumped out of my seat and hit him in the face. I punched him several times. Blood splattered everywhere. He didn't even try to defend himself. When I got tired of hitting him, he fell back in his chair.

He looked up at me and said, "I deserved that."

I held my hand up. I was about to wrap them around his neck, but instead, I rushed out of his house and jumped in my car. I sped home. I called out, "Lexi!" as soon as I walked through the door.

I didn't get any response. I walked up the stairs, taking them two at a time. The bedroom door was closed. I didn't knock. I burst in.

"Royce, have you lost your mind?" Lexi's eyes landed on my bloodied shirt.

"How long has this thing with you and Jason been going on?"

"What?" She acted like she didn't know what I was talking about.

"Don't play dumb with me. Jason told me everything. He confessed to your affair. To think I felt bad about what happened with Ruth Ann, when you've been busy screwing my best friend behind my back."

Lexi hopped up off the bed. "Royce, it's not what you think. It only happened one time."

She grabbed my arm. I moved. She fell back on the bed. Rage filled my eyes. "And that's supposed to make it all right?"

"I'm sorry. It's not like what you did. We didn't have an affair."

"When Lexi? When did it happen?"

She looked away. I went and got in her face. I grabbed her chin and tilted it up. "Look at me. When did it happen?"

Lexi responded, "About a year before Lovie was born. During the time you were sleeping with Ruth Ann." Lexi stretched the word "Ann."

"I've been the biggest fool. I guess you and Jason had plenty of laughs about how stupid I was."

"I've never liked Jason. I told you that. I told you he was jealous of you, but you wouldn't listen."

Lexi was talking, but I wasn't hearing her. All I could see was red. I held my head and rocked back and forth. Lexi reached for my arm again.

"Don't touch me," I said with clenched teeth.

Lexi started explaining herself. I didn't want to listen, but I did.

"It happened on one of those weekends you were out of town. I sort of suspected there was another woman. But instead of confronting you about it, I cried on Jason's shoulder. He took advantage of my vulnerable state and kissed me. The kiss led to us having sex on the couch. When I came to my senses, I kicked him out. I tried to warn you about him, but you wouldn't listen."

"I'm married to you, not Jason. You shouldn't have been so easily persuaded. Lexi, he was my best friend."

"And you were my husband. And you weren't there for me. You were there for her." Lexi picked up a picture of Ruth Ann and threw it at me.

Lexi stormed out of the room. I picked up the picture and tore it to pieces. I felt like punching something, but instead I wept for my marriage.

CHAPTER 68

Charity

Our family went from one crisis to another. I just got off the phone with my mom. She wanted us to come to the house to talk about something else.

Since I had more gas in my car than Hope, I drove. "I hope they're not getting a divorce," Hope said.

"If they do, it's not going to make me love either one less," I responded.

Lovie's SUV was already parked. I used my key and entered. My mom and Lovie were seated in the living room.

"Where's Dad?" I asked.

"He's upstairs. I wanted to talk to you all in person. There's something I need to share with you. I want you to hear it from me, and nobody else."

"Please, don't tell me you're divorcing," Hope blurted out.

"No, we're not divorcing." We all turned toward the sound of my dad's voice.

"Royce." My mom whispered his name.

"Continue on," he said, as he took a seat far away from us.

My mom looked at my dad and then back at each one of us. "I'm ashamed to say your dad isn't the only one who's cheated."

My mouth flew open.

My eyes were glued on my mom. "I didn't have an affair, but I did have a weak moment once, and cheated on your father."

Lovie didn't say anything. Hope and I stared at her. I was the first to speak. "So neither of you believe in being faithful. What kind of role models are you guys?"

"The only reason I'm telling you all is because we don't need any more secrets between us."

"Since you're telling the story, tell them with whom," my dad said.

"Royce, maybe we shouldn't."

Lovie blurted out, "It was with Jason."

All eyes were now on Lovie.

I looked at Lovie and then at my mom. "Is that true? You and Uncle Jason?"

"I'm afraid so."

I ran out of the room. My dad ran behind me. He grabbed me into a tight hug. I cried on his shoulder. "Let it out. That's it, Baby Girl."

"Our family is falling apart." I wailed on and on.

"It's going to be okay. This is just a speed bump. We've made it through other hard times." He did his best to assure me, but at that moment I didn't believe him.

My mom walked up. "Royce, let me."

I felt his arm dropping from around me. My mom replaced his arms with hers. I wanted to pull away, but I didn't. She said, "I'm sorry. What I did hurt you...it hurt your father. I'm not trying to make any excuses, but that was a different time. I was a different woman. Immature. I didn't understand the trials and tribulations of a marriage, especially to a man like your father."

"But with Uncle Jason? That was supposed to be his best friend."

"Exactly. Now you understand why I've never really liked him. He's been a thorn in my side ever since it happened."

"If you were doing the same thing Dad was doing, then you shouldn't have been upset when you found out about Tyler's mom."

"Baby Girl, Royce's affair with that woman is what caused me to seek comfort in the arms of another man in the first place."

She walked and looked out the window. "Back then, we were in a smaller house. Royce left me by myself almost every weekend. The house felt huge and empty without him there."

I walked up near her. "So Uncle Jason's always been a snake in the grass?"

"Why do say that? I thought you girls adored him at one time."

"I did until I found out what he did."

"If it was up to me, he would never have handled the accounts for the business, but your dad made the decision, so I left it alone."

I contemplated whether to expose Jason and Hope's affair. Even though Hope was legally eighteen when it started, something just didn't seem right about it. It was borderline incest to me.

"Mom, I think you should talk to Hope."

"I am. I wanted to make sure you were okay first."

"I'm not okay with any of this." I threw my hand up in the air and went back in the living room.

Lovie was standing in the corner talking on his phone. My dad was changing stations on the television, but the volume was low so there was no sound.

Hope was flipping through a magazine.

My mom walked back in the room. "Hope, Charity thinks I should talk to you. Why don't you follow me to the kitchen?"

Hope looked at me and mouthed the words, "Did you tell her?"

I shook my head.

She mouthed the words. "I'm going to get you."

I sucked on my bottom lip.

CHAPTER 69

Hope

I wanted to kill Charity. It was not her place to tell Mom about Jason. Our family was dealing with enough stuff. My mom didn't need to know what Jason and I had been doing. She poured two glasses of juice and sat at the table. She placed one glass in front of me.

"I'm sorry for all of this," my mom said.

I sipped on the orange juice. I didn't have much to say.

"Charity said you had something you needed to get off your chest."

"Charity has a big mouth."

"Look, dear. We've had too many secrets in this family. If there's something you need to say, just say it. It's not going to make me feel any different about you. I love you. You're my baby."

The tenderness I saw in my mom's eyes softened my heart toward her. I closed my eyes. "Jason and I have been sleeping together since I was eighteen."

I exhaled and opened up my eyes. My mom grabbed her heart. "I'm going to kill him."

She ran toward the closet and started fumbling through it.

"Mom, what are you doing?"

"I'm looking for the gun. I can't believe he did this to my baby."

I grabbed her arm.

"Baby, move out of the way." She went back to looking through the closet.

She ran toward the living room. I ran behind her. She shouted, "Royce, where did you move the gun that was downstairs?"

"It's put up," he responded.

"I need it."

Lovie and Charity looked at me. "Mom, no you don't. He's not worth it."

Lovie ran up to my mom and tried to calm her down. "Mom, sit. We can talk about this."

My mom looked at me. "Why didn't you tell me?" Tears flowed down her cheeks.

"I didn't know. I swear I didn't know."

My dad, who normally didn't get hysterical like my mom, yelled, "Somebody tell me what's going on, now!"

My mom said, "That friend of yours molested my baby. I'm going to kill him."

My dad looked at me. "Is that true?"

"I was eighteen when it first happened."

"Lexi, you won't have to kill him. I'm going to kill him. He's harmed my family enough." He got up and ran upstairs.

"Mom, you got to stop him. He's not worth it. I promise you he isn't."

She ignored me. She looked at Lovie. "Make sure your sisters are okay. I'm going with your dad."

"Mom, let me handle this," Lovie said.

"No. I should have removed him from our lives the night he took advantage of me. He will no longer do any harm to this family."

My dad came down the stairs holding a gun. I ran up to him. "Dad, please don't. Hasn't enough blood been shed?"

"Lovie, get your sister." was his only response. He pushed me out of the way.

"Please," I pled, as my mom and dad jumped into my father's car.

I looked at Charity. "This is all your fault. You shouldn't have insisted that I tell."

Lovie paced back and forth. "Look. No sense in playing the blame game. Somebody has to stop Dad before he does something he'll regret doing later. I'm out."

"But, you're supposed to stay with us," I said.

"Charity, take care of Hope. I got to beat them there."

Lovie pulled out his cell phone and made a phone call while rushing to his SUV.

"We can't just stand here and do nothing. Come on." Charity grabbed her purse and keys and led me to the car.

We sped out of the driveway and almost hit one of the neighbors.

"Slow down," the neighbor yelled out their window.

"Buckle up," Charity said.

I buckled my seatbelt. Charity ignored traffic laws. She slowed down at stop signs instead of coming to a complete stop. The food I'd eaten earlier threatened to find its way out as I held on to the dashboard. She whipped the car left and right until we made it to the interstate. I said a silent prayer.

CHAPTER 70

Lovie

The night skies were on our side. That meant fewer people would be around. I drove through Jason's neighborhood. I slowed down and passed by Jason's house. My parents hadn't made it yet.

I drove around through the alley and parked my car. I put on my black leather gloves and placed the Glock in my pocket. I surveyed my surroundings.

I tiptoed around the side of the house. I opened the screen door to knock. I looked behind me. The door squeaked and fell open. I pulled out my gun and walked in. I called out, "Jason, it's me."

No response. I eased inside further into the house. I quietly entered the living room. There were no signs of Jason. His car was outside, so he had to be here.

I called out his name again. "Jason."

Still. No response. I went to the living room and there was Jason, lying in a pool of blood.

"Who did this?" was the first question that ran through my mind. I knew it wasn't my dad because he hadn't had time to get here yet.

I had to think of something, and quick. This was now a crime scene.

Before I could do anything, I heard my mom say, "Oh my God!"

My parents were now standing beside me looking at the same scene.

My dad's hand shook as he held the gun. "Son, did you do this?"

"No. I swear he was like this when I got here."

"We need to call the police," my mom said.

Both my dad and I looked at her.

He said, "Are you crazy? Look at us."

She looked at me holding my Glock. She looked at my dad holding his .38 special. "Y'all need to put those things away. We can't just leave him here like this."

"Did you forget he molested our daughter?" My dad pointed the gun. "I should put another bullet in him for good measure."

I placed my hand on his arm. "Don't do that. Y'all need to get out of here. Let me take care of this."

"I'm not leaving you to take the fall for this," my dad said.

"Why don't we all leave? I'm sure when he doesn't show up at work someone will call," my mom said.

I could hug her. "Yes, let's get out of here before anyone notices we were here."

They walked out first. I closed the door behind me.

"Where's your car?" my dad asked.

"I'm parked in the back."

Before we could leave, Charity pulled up. I ran to their car, before either could get out. Hope's window rolled down. I put my head inside. "You need to leave now. Meet us back at the house. Pronto."

"But—" Charity said.

"No buts. Don't have time to argue."

Charity continued down the road. My father sped off. I wished he hadn't done that. I noticed a neighbor turn their light on. I slipped back in the night and went to my car. I drove slowly down the alley and onto the main street.

We all made it back to my parents around the same time. "What just happened?" Charity asked.

The only good thing about this whole situation was my parents were no longer upset at each other. They were seated next to each other holding hands, each trying to comfort the other.

I hate it took something drastic to do so, but regardless of what happened after this, I was grateful.

"Is anyone listening to me?" Charity yelled.

I spoke out first. "Jason's dead."

"Dad, did you kill him?" Hope asked.

"No, he didn't kill him. He was dead when we got there," I responded.

"Where were the police?" Charity asked.

"Dear, we didn't call the police," my mom responded.

"So y'all just left him there to die?" Hope blurted.

I grabbed Hope by the shoulders to make her look at me. "He was already dead. There was nothing we could have done for him."

Hope sniffled inbetween tears. "This is all my fault. I should have kept quiet."

My dad said, "It's not your fault. I wished you would have said something to us earlier and believe me, he would have dead earlier."

"Royce, don't say that," my mom said.

"Well, the truth is the truth."

The truth for me was the fact that I went over there with every intention of killing him, so that my parents wouldn't have to do it. The question now was who beat us all to it?

CHAPTER 71

Lexi

I got up from beside Royce and went to the bar. I poured myself a drink and took a big gulp. I turned back, and four sets of eyes were looking in my direction.

I looked at Hope. "Stop crying. This is not your fault. You're the victim here."

Charity placed her arm around Hope to comfort her.

I poured myself another glass. I poured a glass for Royce and handed it to him. He looked confused and unsure of what to do.

I sat down next to him.

"Like Lovie said, Jason was dead. There wasn't anything we could do for him," I said.

"Someone should have called the police," Charity said.

"No, we need to stay out of it. You hear me?" I looked at Charity, daring her to disagree.

"Fine," she responded.

Lovie said, "I can have my boy Slim go clean the place up."

Royce responded, "Don't have your thuggish friends do a thing. We don't want to be beholden to nobody. You do that, and Slim and his goonies will think you owe them for life."

Lovie put his phone back in his pocket. "I guess you're right."

"Yes, Royce is right. I grew up with men like Slim. They will do you a favor, but it will cost you your life for the rest of your life."

"Okay, Mom. I get the point," Lovie responded.

"I just want to make it clear, so you won't go doing anything behind our back." I looked at Hope and Charity. "Girls, I'm glad you didn't come inside. The image we saw will forever be embedded in my mind."

Royce said, "I hate to say this, but I feel relieved—relieved that he's dead and I wasn't the one who had to take his life."

I squeezed his hand. I felt the same way. I just didn't voice it. "Everybody look at me."

When it was clear that I had everyone's attention, I said, "Your father and I talked on the way home. It's in each of our best interests to pretend like we don't know a thing. If the police ask questions, act surprised."

"But that's lying," Hope blurted.

"I'm not trying to be funny, but you've done a lot of that, so this shouldn't be a hard thing for you to do," Charity said.

"Dear, be nice. Your sister's been through something traumatic."

Charity rolled her eyes.

"I'm serious. No one is to say a thing to the police. We must keep a united front."

Royce added, "If you slip and say anything out of the ordinary, it could throw suspicions on any of us. Be natural in your responses."

Lovie added, "Don't give many details. Most guilty people try to give details when they are trying to get away with something."

"Exactly. So, the less you say, the better. Are we all on the same page?" I asked.

Royce squeezed my hand. Lovie shook his head. Hope shook her head.

"Charity?" I asked.

"Yes, Mom. I promise to keep my mouth shut."

"Good. It's been a long night, so y'all go home and try to get some rest."

A few minutes later, I was hugging each one of them. I stood in the doorway and watched them leave. Royce was still in the living room. I went upstairs and took a long hot bath.

When I returned to the bedroom, Royce was lying on his side of the bed.

I opened up my mouth to protest, but stopped myself. Instead of saying anything, I slipped under the covers. He got in behind me and wrapped his arms around me. I didn't reject him. I held on to his hands. Exhausted from earlier, I closed my eyes and slept. Visions of Jason's dead body flashed through my mind in nightmares.

"Tell him." I could hear Jason's voice as clear as day.

My eyes flew open.

All I could see was the moonlight seeping through the curtains. We were still in the room alone. Scared, I snuggled up closer to Royce. This time, it took a while for me to fall asleep.

CHAPTER 72

Royce

Lexi had gotten up early to cook breakfast, but I didn't have an appetite.

I nursed the cup of coffee in front of me until it was time for me to go to work. Lexi helped me put my jacket on. She brushed some lint off the front. "Remember, go in to work. Act natural. Act like nothing has happened."

"There's still yellow tape blocking me from entering my office, so that's going to be hard to do."

"You know what I mean," Lexi said.

I looked down into Lexi's eyes. "Baby, how did we get here?"

"Not trusting one another with the truth."

"You know I love you, right?" I brushed my hand gently on her face.

"Yes, and I love you."

"Then let's promise each other that from this day forward, no more secrets."

Lexi blinked a few times before responding. "No more secrets."

"Now give me a kiss, so I can get out of here and get my day started."

Lexi tilted her head backward. I placed my lips on top of hers. Our lips locked. There was no tongue action, but we didn't need it. The feel of each other's lips was enough.

I left for RJ's with a smile on my face. Regardless of what came my way today, I would be able to handle it since Lexi and I had made up. I hadn't forgotten about what she did, and I knew she didn't forget about what I did, but that was our past. This was now, and now was all that mattered. I loved her with all of my heart, and couldn't anything ever break that bond. Tyler and Jason had tried, but both had failed.

I was still smiling when I walked through the doors of RJ's. Shannon shouted, "Royce, did you hear?"

"Hear what?" I stopped in front of her desk.

"Your friend Jason was found dead in his home. Apparently, there was an early morning fire or something."

I scratched my forehead. "Oh, no." I faked concern.

"It was on the morning news. They're going to show it again in a few minutes."

"I'll watch it in the conference room." I rushed to one of the conference rooms and turned on the television. I called Lexi. "Turn on the news."

I hung up with her and sat down. I tapped my hand on the table. "Hi, Dad," Lovie said, as he passed by the room.

"Son, come here."

Lovie came back and entered the room. "What's up?"

"Have a seat. Shannon told me some disturbing news a while ago."

"She told me you would probably want to talk to me."

"Hold that thought." I turned up the volume.

Without moving my lips, I said under my breath, "Shannon's coming."

Lovie said, "Don't nobody deserve to die like that."

Shannon walked into the room. "Are you guys going to be okay? Royce, I know you and him were close."

I held my head down and rubbed my forehead. "This is hard."

Shannon patted me on the back. "If there's anything you need, I'm here."

"Yes. Please filter my calls today. I just want to be left alone."

"Will do. Lovie, you need anything?"

"Yes, a drink." Lovie forced a smile.

"We have coffee, water, and soda. Your pick."

"I was thinking of something stiffer."

"That, Cuz, you'll have to get on your own." Shannon patted Lovie on the back and left us alone.

I stood up. "Let's go to your office."

Once we were inside of Lovie's office, I closed the door. "Son, you didn't have anything to do with that fire, did you?"

"Of course not. When I left the house, I went straight home. I called over a girlfriend, and didn't hear anything about it until just now."

"Just trying to make sure. I'm glad you got the girlfriend to come over because you may need an alibi."

"I don't need an alibi. I didn't do it."

"I believe you."

I didn't mean to frustrate Lovie, but this whole situation had us all stressing.

CHAPTER 73

Charity

Lisa kept going on and on about Jason in my ear. I held the phone away, and I could still hear her talking. I wanted to tell her I didn't want to hear anymore. I took a drama class in school, so instead, I put my acting skills to use. I pretended to be upset about his death.

"If you need me, I'm here," Lisa assured me.

"I'm going to be okay."

"You're one strong lady. If all of this had happened to me within a week's time, I don't know what I would do."

"Lisa, I just need some time alone."

"I can take off work. I got some comp time."

"No. Don't do that." The last thing I needed was for Lisa to come over. She liked to ask a million and one questions and I wasn't in the mood.

I checked on Hope. She was laid across the bed, still asleep. I didn't want to disturb her. We had sat up talking late into the night. She felt guilty about Jason's death. I assured her that Jason's actions caused his demise.

I listened to what my parents and Lovie said last night, and wasn't totally convinced they didn't have anything to do with it. But did I really want to know if they did? No. So, I would accept their statements as truth.

I didn't have an appetite, but was thirsty. I opened up the refrigerator, and the only thing in there was a stick of butter and a couple of cans of soda. I wanted some juice.

I'd been neglecting doing some household duties. I got dressed and drove a couple blocks over to the grocery store. When I returned home, Lovie's car was sitting in the driveway.

He got out when he saw me park.

"Perfect timing. You can help me take these bags inside."

"I take it you've heard," he said.

"Yes, Lisa called and told me about the fire."

We talked about the situation, as he helped me take the bags into the kitchen.

"According to the news, the police haven't determined if any foul play was involved."

"We both know that there was," I said.

"Exactly. I just wanted to come over to talk to you in person. Some conversations shouldn't be had over the phone."

"Lovie, how's Dad taking all of this?"

"He's bugging. He keeps telling me to remain calm, but he's the one tripping."

"Calm down. You seem a little hyped over this yourself."

"I'm thinking whoever killed Jason is the same person who set the fire."

"Who do you think did it?"

"I have my suspicions, but I'm not stupid enough to ask around about it."

"Really? Who?"

"Jason's stolen from other people, so it could be any of them."

"As long as it wasn't one of us, I'm fine with it." I continued to put up groceries.

"Get this. Jason's sister wants us to handle his funeral."

"Is Dad going to do it?" I asked.

"He has no choice. She's waiting on them to release the body. The coroner's doing an autopsy first."

"I bet you Mom is stressing out."

"Maybe one of you can go check on her. I'm going back to the funeral home. I just wanted to stop by and tell you what was going on."

I hugged Lovie. "Before I forget, Lisa asked about you."

"Tell your girl I said hello. If she hadn't upped and married that joker, she would have been my wifey."

"Whatever. Lisa don't want you."

"She's always had a crush on me. I just never acted on it."

"She's happily married now, so too late."

"My loss." Lovie teased.

I locked the front door after Lovie left.

I was halfway back toward the kitchen when the doorbell rang. Lovie must have forgotten something. I opened the door and there stood Officer Underwood.

"Ms. Jones, it's not safe to open the door without finding out who's on the other side."

"Officer Underwood, what are you doing here?"

"I was in the neighborhood. Decided to drop by to see how you were doing."

"Do you always make house calls?"

"When I have questions, I do."

"I thought I answered all of your questions."

"Can we continue this conversation inside?"

I allowed him in.

"We can talk right here, if you like."

"No. I was about to make a sandwich. Do you want one?" I asked.

"I am kind of hungry."

"Follow me."

I don't know what got into me. I swayed my hips more than usual. Officer Underwood followed me into the kitchen. He took a seat at the table. I fixed two sandwiches and then sat across from him.

In between bites, he said, "This is good. I've never had a sandwich this good."

"Flattery doesn't work on me, Mister Officer."

"Please call me Omar."

"Omar, I'm surprised to see you not in your uniform."

"That's because I'm off duty. I shouldn't be here, but I couldn't get you off my mind."

His comment caught me a little off guard. I didn't expect him to be so forward. "I am unforgettable."

"That you are. How are your mom and dad doing?" he asked, shifting the conversation away.

Was this a trick of his? I would have to tread lightly. Just because he was a police officer, it didn't mean he could be trusted.

"They're doing fine under the circumstances."

"Odd you would say that. I heard about your uncle."

"He's not really my uncle," I responded.

"But still, I'm sure that you're hurting."

I stood up and turned my back toward Omar. I blinked my eyes several times. I squeezed them real tight. There, finally, a tear. I sniffed a few times. My voice quivered. "I'm trying to hold it together."

A few seconds later, I felt Omar's arms around me. "I'm here if you need me."

I leaned my head on his chest and sobbed. These tears weren't fake. These were not tears of grief for Jason. They were tears of relief—the relief from knowing that Jason couldn't hurt Hope, my mom, or my dad ever again.

CHAPTER 74

Hope

What had I walked in on? Who was this man with his arm wrapped around Charity?

I cleared my throat. Charity and the man turned around. I recognized him as Officer Underwood.

Charity said, "Hope, this is Omar."

"I remember him."

He walked up to me and extended his hand out. "I just stopped by to see how you ladies were doing."

"Looks like you two have gotten to know each other a lot better."

Charity grabbed my hand. "Omar, we'll be right back. Have a seat."

Charity led me out into the hallway.

"What are you doing with him?" I whispered.

"He was comforting me."

"I can see that. But you know we don't need him asking a lot of questions."

"Let me deal with Omar. You just act normal."

We returned to the kitchen. He was drinking a glass of orange juice. "I hope you don't mind. I was thirsty."

"No. Help yourself," Charity responded.

I left Charity and Omar in the kitchen. She may have been all right with having him here, but I wasn't. It just dawned on me that he wasn't wearing his uniform. I hoped Charity knew what she was doing.

I stayed in my room until I heard his car pull off. I stood in the doorway and waited for Charity to walk down the hall. I leaned on the wall with my arms crossed.

Charity walked right past me. I followed her to her room. "Oh, no. You're not getting off so easy. What's with you and Omar?"

"Nothing. He's a concerned officer."

"When I walked in the kitchen earlier, his arms were around you, and you were all on his broad chest."

"He is fine, isn't he?" Charity sat behind her desk. She turned on her laptop.

"I've sworn off men."

"So you're swinging the other way now?" Charity looked at me with a raised eyebrow.

"No, Sis. I'm still strictly dickly, but I'm taking a vacation from all men. I think it's about time that I find out what I want to do with the rest of my life."

"Besides being a spoiled brat."

I rolled my neck. "Takes one to know one."

Charity chuckled. "You got that right. We are spoiled."

I shook my head in agreement. "The job you offered me. Can I still have it?"

"What? This is a new day." She hummed the Alicia Keys' song, "It's a New Day."

"Stop playing. I'm serious."

"I'll email you a list of things I need done."

"How much are you going to pay me?"

"Umm." Charity reached for her desk calculator and started typing in figures. I saw the machine move. "I can either pay you a percentage per job, or ten dollars an hour with you committing to at least twenty hours a week."

I extended my hand. "Deal."

We shook hands. It was official. This time I would take working with Charity seriously.

"Lovie dropped by earlier. Someone tried to burn up Jason's house."

"It's always something," I responded.

Charity repeated the things Lovie shared with her. I thought about what she said as I headed to the bathroom to run a bath. I eased my body in the hot water filled with bubbles. Every muscle in my body screamed with joy.

I leaned back on the tub and closed my eyes.

"You'll always be mine," I heard Tyler say.

I jerked my head. I'd dozed off. Spooked a little, I hurried up and got out of the tub.

I dressed and started a new journey in my life. Who would have thought that my first real job would be as an assistant to my sister?

I would be her best-dressed employee, and Charity didn't know this, but soon she would be moving me into another role. I would take the assistant position for now, but a girl couldn't afford to wear designer wear on ten dollars an hour. If I was going to be Ms. Independent, I needed a higher salary.

CHAPTER 75

Lovie

I stopped by the Bottoms Up club. It was where I got all of my news about what was happening on the streets. I greeted the regular patrons. Slim sat in his usual spot. He held his hand up to get my attention. I waved at him. He motioned for me to come over.

I hugged some of the young ladies surrounding him. He used his hands to shoo them away. They moved along, leaving us at the table by ourselves.

"What's up, fam?" Slim asked.

We gave each other a fist pound.

"Just trying to maintain," I responded.

"Too bad what happened to your unc."

"Life is short," I responded.

"I got you on the first round," Slim said.

"No, man, I'm good. I just came through to holla at my boys. I'm about to head out."

"If you need something, I got your back."

"I know I can always count on you."

Slim leaned forward. "I'm serious. I always got your back."

Our eyes locked. No other words needed to be said. I patted him on the shoulder and left the table.

I reached the front door and turned. Slim's eyes were still on me. He held his drink up and tilted it in my direction. I nodded my head and continued out the door.

I turned the volume up on my radio and drove home. I was in my zone and didn't realize the police were behind me until I heard the sirens.

I checked my speedometer. I hit the steering wheel. I was speeding. I slowed down and pulled over to the side of the road. I reached for my license and registration.

I rolled my window down and looked in my rearview mirror. The officer walked beside my car with his weapon drawn.

"I need you to exit the car with your hands up in the air."

I did as instructed.

Another police car pulled up behind his. The officer got out.

"What you got here, Bill?"

"He was going twenty miles over."

"Name?" the officer who pulled me over asked.

"Lovie. Lovie Jones. My wallet is on the front seat."

The other officer went to my car. He shined his flashlight on my wallet. He got on his walkie talkie and gave my driver's license information to the dispatcher.

"Where were you going in such a hurry?" one of them asked.

"Home. I was listening to music. Not paying any attention."

"You been drinking?"

"No," I responded.

The officer went to his car and came back with a breathalyzer machine. I took the test and passed.

One officer whispered to the other. I couldn't hear what they were saying. Another car pulled up. A plain-clothes officer jumped out of the car with a German Shepherd.

I tried to remain calm. I sat down on the ground while they searched my car for drugs. My cell phone rang, but I didn't dare reach for it because I didn't want to give them any reason to shoot me.

"You look familiar," one of the officers said.

"You probably saw me on TV. My father owns RJ Jones Funeral Home."

"Why didn't you say something? You got us out here wasting time."

The officer went up to his comrades. "Man, we can end this. He's clean."

The officer who stopped me handed me a ticket. "Sir, you've been cleared to leave. I suggest you slow it down."

No apology. Nothing. I didn't argue. I put the ticket in my pocket and hopped in my car. I checked my rearview mirror and eased back onto the highway. I sighed with relief. I normally rode around with my Glock, but I'd left it in my bedroom nightstand and forgotten to take it with me.

I called my dad and told him what had just occurred. "They didn't harm you, did they?" he asked.

"No, Pops. Soon as they realized I was your son, they let me go."

The cops had me spooked. I pulled up in my driveway. I looked over my shoulder and down the street to make sure I hadn't been followed.

[illegible] the [illegible].

The [illegible] I [illegible] down the [illegible] back [illegible].

CHAPTER 76

Lexi

I viewed my reflection in the mirror. The big, brimmed, black and white hat fit perfectly on the top of my freshly done hair. It matched the black and white dress I wore.

"Are you ready?" Royce walked down the stairs and asked me.

"I'm ready to put on the performance of my life."

I got in the back of the limousine with Royce. We held each other's hands but didn't say anything as the driver drove us to the church where Jason's funeral was being held.

"We don't have to do this," I told Royce.

"Jason's sister is counting on us to be there."

I was able to avoid Jason's wake the night before. I didn't want to go to his funeral, but we had to keep up appearances. No one could know that none of the Joneses could stand Jason. I put on my big, black shades to cover my eyes.

"You look like Joan Collins with those big shades on," Royce said.

"Can you see my eyes?"

"Nope."

"Perfect."

The limousine driver opened the door. Royce exited first. I got out next. The church parking lot was filled with people coming to pay their last respects. I spoke to everyone as we made our way into the church.

Royce whispered, "The casket is closed, but we should walk by as if we're saying good-bye."

"Royce...Lexi. We want you to walk in with the family." Sheryl, Jason's older sister, walked up to us. She was thin and pale. She looked like she hadn't eaten anything in days.

I looked at Royce. He said, "Sheryl, maybe we shouldn't."

"I insist." Sheryl reached for my hand.

As much as I hated Jason, my heart ached for his sister. I could tell she'd been crying. I embraced her.

"We'll do it," I responded.

"Where are the kids?" Sheryl asked.

"They're probably already inside," I assured her.

It was their choice whether to come or not. As long as Royce and I were here to represent the family, it wouldn't cause any suspicion.

The usher opened the door to the sanctuary. The minister walked in front holding his Bible and started reciting scriptures. The congregation stood up.

I held on to Royce's hand as we walked up the aisle behind Jason's family. I could see familiar faces in the audience as we walked by.

We walked up to the casket, paused, and went to take our seats.

The minister got up and said a few words. After the Old and New Testament scriptures were read, someone sang a solo. Several people got up shouting.

The homegoing service for Jason was spiritual. If they'd only known the man we knew, the service would have been shorter. He was heartless, selfish, and a thief. Several people got up to express what they would miss about Jason. It seemed Jason was good at camouflaging his true self.

Sheryl turned around. "Royce, it's okay if you get up and say something."

I squeezed Royce's hand. He shifted in his seat. I whispered, "You don't have to if you don't want to."

"I think it's best."

I disagreed, but let go of his hand as he walked up front to the podium. I clenched the program. Someone coughed out loud. I looked in the direction and locked eyes with Charity.

I looked back up front at Royce. He cleared his throat. "I'm here this morning to express a few words about the man of the hour, Jason Milton. For some, Jason was a good brother."

Sheryl shook her head in agreement.

"For some, Jason was a good uncle and good provider."

Some of Jason's nieces and nephews mumbled a few things.

"For some, he was a good boss."

"Yes, he was," I heard Jason's secretary yell out.

"For some, like me, Jason had been a good friend."

Royce paused. "I'm sorry. I can't do this." Royce got choked up.

He walked back to his seat. I removed the handkerchief from his jacket pocket and handed it to him. I wrapped my arm around him and comforted him.

The funeral continued. As much pain as Jason had caused us, the fact remained Jason had been Royce's best friend for over thirty years. Having to come to grips with the betrayal and the pain he'd caused us couldn't have been easy on him; it wasn't easy on me.

Royce squeezed my hand as we listened to the rest of the service. It seemed like the pastor preached longer than necessary. I'm sure I wasn't the only one who was ready for the services to be over. He should have shortened it at least out of respect for the family. I couldn't even imagine what they were going through.

One of Jason's ex-wives got up, and sang a solo. Then, it was time to leave.

The kids joined us in the processional as we walked out of the sanctuary.

Whether our grief was sincere or not, we had all been crying for one reason or another.

CHAPTER 77

Royce

I wasn't just going through the motions. I truly was in mourning. I'd lost my friend long before we found him laid out in the pool of blood. The day I found out he stole from me hurt. The pain resulting from betrayal hurt even more. Finding out he'd slept with my wife and daughter, felt like a dagger being dug into my heart.

No matter how much I drank, the pain wouldn't go away. The only time I felt at peace was when I was sleeping. I was doing a lot of that lately. After the funeral and the burial, I left my workers in charge, came home, and went straight to bed.

Lexi's been trying to get me to get out of bed. The kids were here. They wanted to see me. I didn't want to disappoint them. I'd disappointed them enough. I was supposed to protect them, but instead I brought the monster into our house.

"Baby, it's getting late. The kids will be leaving shortly. Don't you want to come down and spend a little time with them," Lexi said from the doorway.

"Tell them I'll be down in a minute."

It took everything within me to drag myself out of bed. I went to the bathroom and washed my face. I went to the closet and found some jeans and a New Orleans Saints t-shirt.

When I made it downstairs, they were all seated in the living room. They too had changed into comfortable, casual clothes.

Charity and Hope greeted me with a hug and kiss on the cheek. Hope held my hand. "Thought we were going have to come crash in your room for a minute."

"I was just tired."

I sat down in my favorite recliner.

Lexi walked in the room carrying a plate and a drink. "You haven't eaten anything all day. Someone from the church brought us a whole bunch of food."

Lovie wiped his mouth with a napkin. "Whoever baked this pound cake, put their foot in it."

Lexi said, "That was Lula. She can make some of the best pound cakes around here."

I agreed. "Forget the rest of the food. Just bring me a slice of cake."

The doorbell rang. Lexi said, "I'll get it. Eat up."

A few minutes later, she walked in, followed by Officer Underwood. "I hate to disturb you. Especially today, but Mr. Jones we need to ask you a few questions."

The smile on my face disappeared. The hair on the back of my neck stood up. I placed the plate on the table. I stood up and greeted him. "Whatever you have to ask, you can ask in front of my family."

"Sure, sir."

I motioned for him to sit down. Charity moved over. He sat next to her. He pulled out his notepad and a pen.

"It's come to our attention that Jason Milton wasn't killed in the fire. He'd received a fatal gunshot wound prior to the fire."

Hope yelled out, "Are you serious?"

She needed to bring it down a notch. If she overreacted, it would look suspicious.

"So, it wasn't an accident?" I asked.

"No, I'm afraid not. You were his best friend. Do you know any reason why anyone would have wanted to see him dead?"

Everyone looked at me. I paused before responding, "No. None. Everyone liked Jason."

"Apparently not, Mr. Jones. Someone didn't like him because they killed him." Officer Underwood wrote in his notepad.

Had I said too much? I wiped my hands.

Lexi stood beside me. "Officer Underwood, can this wait another time? He just buried his best friend."

I squeezed Lexi's hand. "Dear, he's only doing his job."

"One of the neighbors thinks they saw your car the night before the murder," Officer Underwood said.

"Jason and I spent a lot of time together, so that's nothing unusual," I responded.

"Can you confirm the time?"

Before I could respond, Lexi said, "That night, he and I both stopped by. It was about nine-something, wasn't it, dear?"

I squeezed Lexi's hand hard. She knew why. She should have kept her mouth shut. Let the police think I was a suspect, but she shouldn't have put herself in the picture. I looked at her and then back at the officer. "Yes, Lexi's correct."

"Did you see anyone suspicious as you were leaving?" he asked.

"No. Nothing out of the ordinary," I responded.

"Well, according to the coroner, the time of death was between ten and midnight. It's probably a good thing you left when you did because you two could have become victims too."

Charity said, "I couldn't bear losing either one of you."

Officer Underwood grabbed Charity's hand. "They're going to be fine."

He released her hand and looked at me. "If you like, I can make sure there's extra surveillance in the area. Whoever killed Jason Milton may think you saw something and come after you too."

"Officer, I appreciate it, but I don't think that will be necessary."

He stood up. "If you change your mind, you have my card."

"Yes. It's in my wallet, as a matter of fact."

"Charity, can you walk me out?" Officer Underwood asked.

Lexi said, "We'll both walk you out. Would you like a plate or something to drink? We have plenty of food."

"No, ma'am. I'm still on duty."

"Come on. If you don't tell, I won't tell."

"Well, it wouldn't hurt," he responded.

Lexi turned around and winked her eye at me.

I mouthed the words, "Get him out of here."

She gave me the thumbs up signal.

"Dad, you did good," Lovie said, as he took a seat near me.

"Just telling the truth, Son."

Hope, Lovie, and I didn't say anything else. I sat hoping and praying that Officer Underwood would leave sooner than later.

I heard the front door close.

Lexi walked in the room and said, "He's gone."

"That was close," Lovie said.

"Too close." I sighed with relief.

CHAPTER 78

Charity

It had been a few weeks since Jason's funeral, but the whole family was still walking on eggshells. Omar had been finding every excuse to call me.

"Dear, that young man seems to be interested in you. You should talk to him. See where his head is," my mom said to me one day over lunch.

Which translated into, talk to him and see what he knows about Jason's case.

I began having second thoughts about accepting his dinner invitation. It was too late, however, because he was walking around to open my door.

The door opened. Omar extended his hand out. I reached for it and exited out his sports car. He gave the valet his keys and we walked inside of the casino and straight to the restaurant.

"There's one thing I've been trying to figure out," Omar said, while we waited on our food.

"What?"

"You're pretty. You're smart. Why don't you have a man?"

I felt a sigh of relief. That was an easy question. As long as it had nothing to do with Jason, I could answer. "Because I don't. Next question."

He licked his big, juicy lips. "Will you accept my application? I'm a hard worker. I come on time and I'll do anything—and I mean anything—to make sure you're happy."

He emphasized the words "hard" and "come". He had me squirming in my seat. Although I regret sleeping with Tyler, I didn't regret allowing myself some sexual freedom.

"Officer."

He interrupted. "Call me Omar."

"Omar, who said I was taking any applications?"

He reached over the table for my hand. "Well, if you are taking applications, I want to put mine in, and I'm willing to interview on the spot."

"I'm a hard person to work with. Slackers need not apply."

"That's not me."

"Cheaters. This is not the place for you."

"So far, I'm none of those."

"Liars can keep it moving."

"I might get this job," he said, with confidence.

"There's a ninety-day probationary period."

"Ninety days. That's nothing." He blew on his fingers.

"I call the shots."

"Charity rules. I follow directions well."

"Then Omar, your application has been accepted."

"When can I start my first day on the job?" he asked.

"You might be required to put in some overtime."

Omar made a muscle. "I'm built for that."

Our playful banter continued throughout dinner. It'd been awhile since I'd had fun, out on a real date. He walked me to the door. He assisted me with putting the keys in the lock.

I stopped and blocked him from coming in. "I would invite you in, but I'm sure you have to get up early in the morning."

"I traded shifts with a co-worker. I don't have to be to work until three p.m."

I threw caution to the wind. I pulled him inside. Our lips locked. I heard him moan. I moaned. I led him down the hallway and to my bedroom. I'd never brought a man to my bedroom. He was the first.

We tore each other's clothes off. We were now only in our underwear. Omar picked me up. I wrapped my legs around his waist. He carried me to my bed. I fell back on the bed, and he fell back on top of me. His lips never left mine. His hands roamed my body. He unfastened my bra with his hands. He cradled one nipple with one hand, and his mouth left my lips and wrapped around my other nipple.

My panties were soaked with desire for Omar. He eased them off with his available hand, and brought me to an orgasm using his fingers. He replaced his fingers with his lips. I rocked back and forth on the bed.

He removed a condom from his wallet and placed it on his long and stiff manhood. It felt like the Fourth of July. I saw sparks the moment our bodies united. I had lost all control and so had he.

Omar cradled me in his arms and we fell asleep as if we'd known each other forever.

CHAPTER 79

Hope

I'd promised myself that I wouldn't sleep in all day, so I got up around nine instead of noon.

"Charity, what's on the agenda for today?" I burst through her door. "Oops."

Omar and Charity were naked in her bed. The sheet covered them, but still. I knew they were naked because I could see his brown, muscular chest. Yes, I was definitely checking him out.

I'd vowed off men for awhile, but big Sis hadn't. I eased the door shut and went back to my room.

A few minutes later, Hope entered. She held on to the belt of her robe. "I'm sorry you had to see that."

"And I thought I moved fast. I ain't got nothing on you." I reached my hand up for a high-five. "Oh, you leaving me hanging."

"Please, don't tell anyone about this."

I twisted my fingers in front of my closed mouth. "My lips are sealed. Charity got a new boyfriend."

She picked up my pillow and threw it at me. "He's not my boyfriend."

"I'll cook us breakfast," I yelled.

Charity did most of the cooking, but I had skills in the kitchen too. By the time they were dressed, I had bacon, eggs, and grits cooked and on plates on the kitchen table.

"Hope, good to see you again, under better circumstances," Omar said.

"Yes, it is." My face held a huge smile.

Charity kicked me under the table. I kicked her back. She winced in pain. I continued to smile. "So, what are your intentions with my sister?" I asked.

Charity spit out her juice. "Hope, that's none of your business."

Omar said, "Charity, I don't mind answering her question. I intend on her being my lady. Right now, she has me on a ninety-day probation."

He looked at her. They seemed to share some private joke.

"Looks like so far, so good," I said.

"I don't know. Let me ask her. Am I doing okay so far?" Omar looked at Charity.

"Stop it. I'm not going to get double teamed by y'all. It's too early in the morning."

He looked at me. "She may not want to admit it, but I think I'm passing."

"It looks that way." I ate my food and then left them alone at the kitchen table.

I know I promised Charity I wouldn't say anything, but Lovie called me and before I knew it I'd told.

"She has no business hanging out with that cop," Lovie said.

"He's one of the good guys. Better him than someone like Tyler."

"Still, I don't like this. I'm coming over."

"If you come over, it'll look suspicious. She'll know I told you something."

"You're right. Keep your eyes and ears open."

I left Charity alone with her company and did the tasks she assigned me. It kept me busy for most of the day.

Charity walked in my room. "He's gone."

I looked up. "I made a few phone calls. Check your planner. We're now booked up until September."

She gave me a high-five this time. "Now, I need you to coordinate with some of the vendors I use to make sure they are available for the events. I'll take one month and you take the next."

I scratched my head. "Sounds like I'm more of a coordinator slash planner than just an assistant."

"Okay. Whatever you want to call yourself."

"I'm glad you said that." I passed her a card I'd printed out. "Event coordinator sounded better than assistant so I made a few cards to pass out to people. I gave them the business number."

Charity didn't say anything. She simply stared at me.

"What?" I asked.

"Has the real Hope been abducted by aliens, and replaced with a clone? This can't be my sister. You are really taking this job seriously. I'm so proud of you."

Charity hugged me.

"So, I take it you're okay with me calling myself that."

"Call yourself whatever you want, as long as you get the job done."

"Great." I have some ideas for the website too. My excitement about her business made me forget all about asking her questions about Omar.

CHAPTER 80

Lovie

I'd asked around about Officer Omar Underwood. He seemed to be on the up and up, but I still didn't like the fact he was dating my sister. I paced back and forth in front of the fireplace in my parents' living room.

"Do you know Charity has been spending a lot of time with the police?" I asked.

My dad eased back in his recliner. "Your mom told me about her and Omar."

I threw my hand up. "Am I the only one who sees a problem with this? All of this has happened so fast. He's probably working undercover, and I do mean undercover."

"Lovie, don't talk about your sister when she's not here to defend herself," my mom said.

"Somebody has to be the voice of reason. It seems like you all have lost your mind."

"I think you're just being paranoid. Ever since those cops stopped you, you've been acting a little different," my dad said.

"You right about that. That could have been the end of my freedom. I'm not going to jail for anyone. You and Mom might not think anything is wrong with Charity spending time with this guy, but I do. He's a cop and if he sniffs around her long, she may let something slip."

"Lovie, let it be. Your sister's old enough to handle her own affairs."

"Do I have to remind you of what happened with Tyler?" The room was silent. "So, give me another valid reason I shouldn't be concerned."

My mom replied, "Because Charity is more like your mama than you think. She won't slip and reveal anything to the officer. In fact, they are coming to dinner, so Lovie, please be on your best behavior."

"Why didn't you tell me he was coming? I should leave."

"You're not going anywhere. This is a family dinner, and I want all of my kids here," my mom said.

"And what Lexi wants, she gets. You should know that by now, Son."

I looked at them both. Less than thirty minutes later, we were all seated around the dinner table. My entire family seemed to be smitten with Omar. Since everyone else seemed to be afraid to approach the subject, it was left up to me to bring it up.

We were eating dessert when I asked, "Omar, have y'all caught Uncle Jason's killer yet?"

"No, but we're this close to."

Charity said, "Oh, really?"

Omar looked around the room. "What I'm about to tell you can't leave this room."

"Agreed," I responded.

"I don't want to tarnish his reputation with you all, but Jason Milton had a few enemies. We found a business card that led us to one of his customers. They didn't have an alibi and, let's just say, I think we have our man. I'm not the main one working on the case, but that's the last I heard."

"Can you tell us who?"

"Not until we tie up some loose ends. I'll be sure to let y'all know so your minds can be at rest."

I guess Charity sleeping with the officer paid off. He felt comfortable giving us the inside scoop.

My dad said, "Son, thank you for this great news. We appreciate the hard work you and your comrades have done to bring Jason's killer to justice."

"I just got a promotion, too. I'm no longer officer. My title is officially Detective Underwood."

My mom held up her glass of wine. "Here's to your promotion."

We held up our glasses and clicked them in his honor. "Congratulations."

Although Omar seemed cool, I still had my reservations about him.

Charity walked Omar out to his car.

I stood at the window and watched them.

My dad patted me on the back. "See, Lovie, told you we didn't have anything to worry about."

I would drop the issue for now, but I still had my eye on Omar.

CHAPTER 81

Lexi

Lovie paced the floor. I jumped in front of him, and he stopped. "Lovie, stop stressing. Your sister's going to be okay."

In my opinion, Omar was a good man. I didn't feel we had anything to worry about.

Charity returned to the living room with a huge smile on her face. "Isn't he the greatest?"

Hope looked up from her seat. "I like him. He's cool."

Royce said, "He seems to be okay. Time will tell."

Lovie remained quiet and took a seat.

I glanced at the faces of each one of them. I thought about the trials we'd gone through this past year. But through it all, we made it.

I sat on the arm of Royce's chair. I gently rubbed his arm. I looked down at him and smiled.

Royce placed his hand on my leg. "Your mother and I have decided to renew our vows on our thirtieth anniversary."

I looked at Charity. "So that means we have about a year to plan it. Charity, I'm going to trust you to handle it for us."

"And me," Hope said.

Charity said, "Yes, Hope's my new event coordinator."

"Congrats, baby." I winked my eye at Hope.

"I'll walk you down the aisle," Lovie said.

"Of course, dear. I wouldn't have it any other way."

"The colors can be purple and gold," Charity said out loud.

"Or red and white," Hope added.

The doorbell rang. I looked at Royce. "Were you expecting someone?"

He responded, "No. I'll go see who it is."

Royce went to the front door. Curious, I followed behind him, but remained in the hallway.

I heard a voice say, "Are you Royce Jones?"

I walked closer to the doorway and saw two police officers standing in front of Royce.

"Yes," Royce responded.

The officer pulled out a pair of handcuffs. "Royce Jones, you are under the arrest for the murder of Jason Milton."

"No, don't put those on my husband," I screamed out. I ran up to Royce.

The kids rushed out of the living room.

Royce looked at Lovie. "Get your mom."

Royce held his hands out, and I put my hands on top of his.

One of the officers said, "Ma'am, we need you to move."

Royce looked down at me. "Baby, it's okay."

No, it wasn't okay. "They can't do this. You're innocent."

Lovie grabbed me and pulled me out of the way.

The officer read Royce his Miranda rights as he handcuffed him. "You have the right to remain silent. Anything you say can and will be used against you..."

I cried out, "You've made a mistake. Royce didn't kill anyone."

Royce looked at me. "Call our attorney."

I stood there feeling hopeless as the officers escorted Royce out to their police car.

"Daddy," Hope shouted.

"I told you Omar couldn't be trusted," Lovie said.

"Omar had nothing to do with this," Charity responded.

Lovie and Charity went back and forth. I did my best to tune them out as we stood in front of the house, and I watched the love of my life driven away in the back of a police car.

Now was not the time for me to fall apart. I had to pull myself together. Royce needed me. My kids needed me. I wiped my tear-stained face with the back of my hand.

I retrieved the cell phone from my pocket. "Mitch, Royce's been arrested. They are charging him with Jason's murder, but he didn't do it."

Mitch, our attorney, said from the other end of the phone, "I'm on my way to the station now."

"I'll meet you there."

By now we're all walking back inside of the house.

"No. You stay put. I'll call you when I know something."

I ended my call with Mitch.

Charity stared at me with fear in her eyes. "Mom, what are we going to do? Dad could go to jail for a long time."

"If I have to spend every dime we have, Royce will not go to prison for a crime he did not commit." I said it with conviction and meant it.

I started walking down the hallway, but stopped. I turned around and faced Lovie, Charity, and Hope. "Kids. There's no need to look sad. We're the Joneses. Together, we can and will get through this."

ABOUT THE AUTHOR

Shelia M. Goss is a national bestselling author and a screenwriter *The Joneses* is her seventeenth book in print. She writes in multiple genres. *USA Today* says, "Goss has an easy, flowing style with her prose…" She's received many accolades in her career, including being a finalist in the mystery category for the 2013 AA Literary Award Show and a 2012 Emma Award Finalist. Her books have been on several best sellers lists, such as: *Essence* magazine, *Dallas Morning News* and Black Expressions Book Club. Shelia loves to hear from readers so feel free to contact her via her website: www.sheliagoss.com or follow her on Facebook at www.facebook.com/sheliagoss or Twitter: www.twitter.com/sheliamgoss.